An Impossible Distance to Fall

MIRIAM McNAMARA

Sky Pony Press
New York

Sky Pony Press books may be purchased in bulk at special discounts for sales promotion, corporate gifts, fund-raising, or educational purposes. Special editions can also be created to specifications. For details, contact the Special Sales Department, Sky Pony Press, 307 West 36th Street, 11th Floor, New York, NY 10018 or info@skyhorsepublishing.com.

Sky Pony® is a registered trademark of Skyhorse Publishing, Inc.®, a Delaware corporation.

www.skyponypress.com

10 9 8 7 6 5 4 3 2 1

Library of Congress Cataloging-in-Publication Data is available on file.

Cover design by Kate Gartner
Cover image credit iStockphoto

Print ISBN: 978-1-5107-3545-3
E-book ISBN: 978-1-5107-3546-0

Printed in the United States of America

To the band of misfits who help me soar
and catch me every time I fall

CHAPTER ONE

MOM SAID DAD WAS DEAD, THAT HE'D FLOWN HIS BIPLANE JENNY OUT over the water and kept going until he ran out of gas—but Birdie refused to accept it, and now she had proof. She smiled ferociously at the paper clenched tightly in her hands. It wasn't the words on the flyer that had brought Birdie here, to the boardwalk of Coney Island on a sunny June afternoon. It was the grainy black-and-white photograph printed beneath those words.

Dad's Jenny biplane.

She had recognized it instantly, when she saw the flyer pasted up at the grocery back home in Glen Cove. That was Dad's plane, his Curtiss JN-4D, its name painted in loopy cursive on the side: *Pretty Bird*. She didn't need to see it in color—her mind painted the image canary yellow and bright blue.

Birdie stuffed the flyer into her pocket and shook her hair back—or tried to. She was beginning to sweat, and her long hair was sticking to her neck. A boy about Birdie's age, smoking a cigarette with a couple of pals, caught her eye and winked. She gave him a quick grin but spun away, before he might think her available. Even if she hadn't seen David in a few weeks they were as good as engaged, and she knew he'd come around once the bank uproar died down. By the time she saw him next, he'd be dying to kiss and make up.

Birdie pushed her way to the front of the boardwalk and peered over the railing. Though it was still early June the beach was teeming with bodies, most of them in bathing suits. Couples sat with screaming children, boys in groups furtively sipped from flasks, and girls with glaringly white skin packed onto towels. Farther down she spotted an empty patch of beach cordoned off, and a few planes lined up close to the low tide line where the sand was dark with moisture. Birdie bounced on her toes as she caught a flash of canary. She knew it! One of the planes was bright, bright yellow.

It was so like Dad to pull something like this. If one venture didn't pan out he would be on to the next, so fast that failure couldn't catch him. She was furious with him, of course, for taking off without a word to her. But maybe he'd thought she wouldn't want to come. Maybe he'd thought she'd prefer to stay while their whole life crumbled around her.

He'd better beg very convincingly for forgiveness when she found him.

She pushed her way down the boardwalk. The crowd thickened the closer she got to the planes, people jammed in elbow to elbow. After a block or so she shoved her way back to the railing and squinted down, and any lingering doubt vanished.

It always made her body feel light when she saw it. Her limbs anticipated liftoff, her lungs opening up to take in the rush of wind. Birdie loved Dad's Jenny as much as he did, maybe more. He'd flown her in it a thousand times. She loved the feel of the plane shuddering as the engine revved. She loved how her heart picked up when it accelerated. She loved how her stomach dropped when it soared. She loved damp air fogging her goggles, she loved the sun baking the top of her cap, she loved being so far above the roads and people and trees and buildings. She loved Dad roaring at her, "For the love of God, Birdie, sit the hell down!" and having the wind whip away the force of his words as she stood in the front cockpit, soaring, arms outstretched, just out of reach.

Two planes sat on either side of Dad's Jenny, one black with yellow stripes, the other red and silver. A few people milled around the planes, gesturing and smoking cigarettes. None of them was Dad, but no matter. Where *Pretty Bird* was, he would be close by.

"It's twenty-five cents to see the show."

Birdie started at the voice behind her. She turned, and something about the dark, challenging eyes that met hers, one thick arched brow lifted, reminded her of Izzy. But this girl had tight curls piled messily on top of her head, not Izzy's sleek dark bob— and this girl was covered in tattoos. A sequined, dark-red costume with one shoulder strap and a short flounced skirt exposed arms and legs covered in images. Strange birds, twisting vines, sinister figures, palm trees, the devil, angels, the moon, the sun— the whole world, practically—marked her skin, all the way down her arms to her knuckles, down her legs to her soft-looking slippers, and all the way up to the strand of pearls wound three times around her neck.

Birdie couldn't imagine what Dad and Mom would do if she got even one tiny tattoo. Well, Mom would disown her. Dad, though—she couldn't remember Dad ever disapproving of her, but a tattoo might do it.

The girl cocked her eyebrow higher and shook the box in her hands, coins rattling inside. She was taller than Birdie by a head, but Birdie was used to that—most people were, and she refused to be intimidated. She drew herself up on her kitten heels and turned back toward the beach, lavender silk skirt swishing beneath the hem of her unbuttoned yellow-and-blue tartan coat. "That's my dad's plane," she said, pointing.

The girl looked her up and down. "Twenty-five cents to see the show," she repeated, enunciating as if Birdie hadn't understood her.

Birdie heard the same thing echoed to her left: "It's twenty-five cents to see the show." A big, clean-shaven man in suspenders was rattling his own box at a couple of men, his dark skin standing out in the overwhelmingly white crowd.

"There's no way I'm paying a quarter to stand on this boardwalk," one of the men said, lip curled. "This here's public property."

Birdie looked the other way—a skinny fellow with shiny black hair in need of cutting, wearing knickers and striped socks, was holding a box out as well, smiling gently as a young girl shyly dropped four quarters in for her family.

Birdie had a little over forty dollars with her; she'd broken the crisp fifty Dad had slipped her for her sixteenth birthday to pay her way to Coney Island. She fished a quarter out of her pocket and held it up. "Robert Williams," she said brightly, "the owner of the yellow-and-blue Curtiss Jenny just over there. Where is he?"

The girl tilted her head. She looked over at the planes. She looked back. She held out her box again, and shook it just a little.

Birdie resisted the urge to flick tattoo-girl in the forehead. She kept her teeth clenched in a smile and slipped her coin in, gentle and sweet.

The girl turned to go.

"Hey!" Birdie grabbed her wrist. The girl fumbled her box, a few coins clattering on the boardwalk. She huffed and crouched down to scrape them up. "Sorry," said Birdie unconvincingly. "I just have to find my dad. I know that's his plane, and I *gave* you a quarter."

The girl shook her head, lips tight as ever as she put her hands under the box and stood.

"Please," Birdie added, and was horrified to hear her voice catch.

The girl studied her another moment, her face unreadable. "Go down another block," she said at last. "Get up close to the beach, where Nathan's Famous is. You'll be able to see everything from there." Then she turned. "Twenty-five cents to see the show," she said, over the shoulder of the next person leaning over the railing.

Birdie took a deep breath and exhaled. She tilted her face up to the warm sun and closed her eyes, listening to the distant tinkling music coming from the Ferris wheel a few blocks over until the tightness in her throat eased.

She was so close to finding Dad. One surly, grubby girl couldn't shake her up.

CHAPTER TWO

"WELCOME, WELCOME!" A VOICE THUNDERED OVER A MEGAPHONE. Birdie stuffed the last bite of her second hot dog into her mouth, wiped the mustard from her fingers with a paper napkin, and leaned over the railing as she finished chewing. The air was heavy with fried dough, popcorn, cigar smoke, and grilled meat. Two Jennys, one of them *Pretty Bird*, rattled to life as a couple of boys hauled on the propellers. The tattooed girl had been right—this was the spot. She'd be able to spot Dad clear as day from here.

Birdie was sweating in her coat in earnest now, mouth sour with mustard. Her stomach fluttered as the black plane, painted like a bumblebee in yellow stripes, taxied away from the other. The flying caps made the pilots look like bugs with smooth leather heads, straps dangling like antennae, their goggles bulging like reflective eyes. The pilot had a mustache like Dad's, but he was noticeably thinner. He could have lost weight since she saw him. Birdie could see the man grin as he yelled something to the fellows holding on to the wings of his plane. They let go, and the plane lurched forward.

"I'm Merriwether," boomed the voice behind the megaphone, "and I'd like to personally welcome you to my MYSTERY CIRCUS OF THE AIR!"

Birdie couldn't tell if a man or woman held the megaphone. The person wore a flying suit in a sensible shade of navy, and had a solid frame and wide stance. Cropped hair whipped wildly around a smooth but strong jaw, but that didn't mean anything these days. Plenty of women had short hair.

"There goes one of our AIR DEVILS now!" The plane bumped along the sand, picking up speed. A stretch of beach the length of three city blocks had been cordoned off. People standing at the end of the makeshift runway ducked and covered their faces as the Jenny lifted off, just clearing their heads. The pilot looped around, waving his cap at the crowd. Then he soared upward, the roar of his engine dulling to a whine as he climbed.

"But what's this?" Merriwether gasped into the megaphone. "This—this is highly unusual—"

Birdie shaded her eyes and looked up. The plane listed to one side, dipping down—then it arched back up—there was black smoke trailing behind the plane! Birdie gasped as the crowd inhaled sharply with one collective breath.

"There must be some sort of malfunction—ladies and gentlemen, I apologize for what you may be about to witness—"

The plane careened down, then up—then looped, smoke still billowing behind—someone screamed and Birdie's heart jumped to her throat—

The man next to her shouted, pointing, "Wait a minute—it's spelling something!" His words were echoed down the boardwalk.

Sure enough, W-E-L-C-O—

"Ladies and gentlemen!" Merriwether roared. "'Air Devil' Charlie HIMSELF would like to personally WELCOME you to the show! Our last show's tomorrow, tell your friends and family to come on down!"

Birdie's thrill at Charlie's daring trick was cut with disappointment. Charlie. Not Mr. Williams, like customers called Dad. Not Robert, like men in suits called him. Not Bobby, like Mom did.

He could have taken an alias, like a gangster might. It wasn't like Dad had done anything so bad as those criminals, of course, but the way David and Izzy and everyone was treating her back home—and she hadn't even done one thing wrong!—she could see how Dad might want to become someone else.

"After tomorrow we're headed to Chicago!" Merriwether continued. "Come in the morning for your last chance at a ride over Brooklyn! Only five dollars! See your home from a whole new perspective!"

Charlie executed some impressive stunts, rolling and diving. With every swoop and roll, Birdie became more sure. Dad was a first-class pilot, but she'd never seen him fly like that. When the pilot landed and pushed his goggles up as he bowed to the crowd, her stomach flopped.

Not Dad's broad smile, not his crinkly eyes, not his confident wave.

She breathed into the knot in her belly. That was only the first act; there was still a whole show to go.

Pretty Bird was next to lurch down the beach. A pilot in the back cockpit of the Jenny—clean-shaven, but broad-shouldered—again, she couldn't tell for sure—her stomach roiled, and she wished she had something fizzy to settle it.

Dad's plane looped around and dipped low, practically grazing the sand. Then it zoomed up, and Birdie ducked with the crowd as the bright-yellow plane zipped close and peeled up right over their heads, so close she could see the rivets in its underbelly. The plane rolled over, again and again, skimming the air just above the boardwalk.

Another leather-helmeted and goggled person stood up in the front cockpit, flashed a lipsticked smile, and waved coyly at the audience, the hem of a short skirt visible—a *girl* was going up in the Curtiss Jenny. Birdie hadn't even noticed a second person in the plane. The announcer blared over the megaphone, and Birdie gaped as she caught the girl's name—*the Death-Defying Darlena!*

"That's something else, isn't it!" the man beside her whooped. The girl leaned over as the plane buzzed above their heads, beaming and waving down, like she was a beauty queen in the back of a brand-new Studebaker in the Christmas parade.

The plane tucked around and did a pass right in front of the boardwalk. Birdie squinted and saw—now the girl was standing on the wing. Speeding through the air, no safety net between the girl and the hard earth—Birdie gripped the railing, wishing it was Izzy's hand, that Izzy was here to squeal with her and squeeze her hand back. Birdie had heard of people like this—wingwalkers. She'd pretended she was one once, dancing a goofy pas de deux with Izzy on the wing of Dad's plane while it sat in the hangar— but she'd never actually seen anything like this.

"Wouldn't you know it," said Merriwether, a rueful note coming through the megaphone. "This beauty's gone and gotten herself engaged to a Brooklyn boy. Congratulations, Coney Island— you get to keep Darlena for yourselves when we leave tomorrow! We'll surely miss her, ladies and gentlemen. We surely will."

Long, long legs soared out of the shortest skirt Birdie had ever seen, fringe tossing in the wind—but Darlena didn't look cold at all, color bright in her cheeks, eyes flashing. She looked warm and bold. The girl swung around the bars between the wings and kicked her heels up coyly. She laughed and held out her hand so that the whole crowd could admire her engagement ring, and everyone clapped and whooped as she sped by. She didn't look the least bit scared or unsure.

Birdie imagined herself up there, with that smile that said everything was fine. Someone else might be frightened, if they were in her position, but Darlena was better than fine—she was flying.

Birdie watched the girl swirl up and up, until she was a speck against the cold clouds. Even when she flew against the sun— Birdie didn't blink.

After Darlena, another plane—not a Jenny, but similar, painted a bright cardinal red with silver wings and tail—took off with a person in each cockpit. Birdie hadn't expected that the show would thrill her like this, distracting her so she hadn't noticed who flew the red plane.

The plane nosed up, and up—straight up—until it was a tiny, buzzing insect, and Birdie couldn't make out its red color against the sky. As her eyes trailed its shape, a speck detached itself. Merriwether was roaring over the megaphone, but Birdie focused all her attention on the speck. It fell closer, and Birdie saw it was a person tumbling through the air. This time she wasn't nervous. She could tell the crowd felt the same—yelling and laughter swelled around her, instead of gasps and shrieks.

A parachute popped open above the falling person, slowing their descent far above the sand. Helmet and goggles. Another man that could be Dad.

The smooth white petal of his parachute rippled. It wrinkled along one edge as the other side sagged upward.

And then it collapsed.

The crowd screamed with Birdie as the man's body plummeted. Everyone surged toward the railing and Birdie was squeezed against the splintered wood, her throat closing as the man's legs windmilled frantically through empty space. He was almost eye level with the boardwalk, hands fumbling against his chest—

A second parachute bloomed above him, so close to the ground, but far enough away that it sucked the speed out of his fall and he hit the sand at a run, stumbling slightly, but remaining upright.

Birdie struggled to catch her breath as he paraded in front of the crowd, beaming and pumping his fist. Everyone was cheering and fanning themselves, incredulous looks on their faces.

It wasn't Dad, of course—it was "Air Devil" Charlie again— but for that moment, she was so happy to see he was alive that it may as well have been her father.

CHAPTER THREE

BIRDIE HAD SEEN A GIRL DANCE IN THE SKY. SHE'D SEEN PLANES FLYING upside down. She'd seen loop-de-loops and barrel rolls and that incredible parachute jump. She'd seen the two Jennys engaged in a mock-dogfight—"The Bird and the Bee!" She'd seen a fascinating fire show performed by the tattooed girl and the young man with the striped socks and floppy black hair, smoking whips and hoops and swords of fire undulating around their bodies and disappearing into their mouths in mesmerizing rhythms.

But she had not seen Dad.

The sky was starting to pink as the sun approached the horizon. She wouldn't be home in time for rehearsal. Mikhail would have kittens; not only did she have a solo in the recital two weeks from tomorrow, Birdie danced a big role in several of the group numbers. At least school was out, so she hadn't worried about missing class today.

Izzy would notice she was missing from rehearsal, and wonder where she was.

Birdie folded her arms on the railing and rested her chin, staring into nothing. The crowd on the boardwalk had thinned, but people still bumped her as they walked past. A boy skimmed her leg with his paper airplane as he zoomed by. She didn't move. The rush of the show was fading. She felt sick, the air quickly turning cold.

She should be headed home, but she could hardly stand the thought. It wasn't just that her beau, her best friend, and everyone else in town was shunning her. She'd caught Mom that morning packing suitcases, and when Birdie had demanded to know what was going on Mom told her that a new bank was taking over the assets from Dad's bank, including their house mortgage—and that they were foreclosing on it. Birdie wasn't sure what "foreclosing" meant, and Mom told her the house didn't belong to them anymore. They had nowhere to live. "But I've got a plan for us." Mom pulled another dress off a hanger, not meeting Birdie's eyes. The table next to her was beginning to dull with dust, lint collecting around its legs on the oriental rug since the maid had been let go soon after Dad disappeared. "Annie's in Dover, and she didn't waste her money like I did. She says she'd be happy to have us."

When Mom's parents died, Dad had used her inheritance to buy their house, open the bank, and buy his Jenny. Aunt Annie was an old maid who could do as she pleased, and of all things, she'd moved with her piles of books and her two West Highland terriers halfway round the world, to the gloomy British countryside.

Birdie sank into the green velvet settee. "I'm not going to *England*," she choked out. "Dad could be back any moment. He could walk through that door right now!"

"I thought you might be resistant," her mom said. "If it's your preference, Bobby's parents said they'd be happy to have you for as long as you want. They haven't heard anything from him, but they're still holding out hope like you. Once you're tired of that, of course, me and Annie can send for you."

Birdie had never been to Granny and Grandpa Williams's house. From what she'd gathered from Dad and Mom's jokes, they lived a decidedly unglamorous, middle-class life near the Catskills. Dad gave them money when they came to visit for Christmas. They were small, gray people that seemed bewildered that their strapping, smooth-talking son had done so well for himself. "I'm not going anywhere," said Birdie, fists curling. "Izzy's here, and David, and Dad knows this is where we'll be—" She stopped short and stared at Mom's hand. Her wedding ring was gone. Dad's ring.

Birdie looked up, venom in her mouth. "You're going to give up on him, just like that?" she spat.

Mom's jaw tightened as she folded another dress over her arm, then set it in a pink-and-white-striped valise. "He's dead, Birdie. He's been gone for almost two months now, and he isn't coming back."

Mom had been like this, blank and flat and not meeting her eyes, ever since the bank failed, and it made Birdie want to scream. "Dad isn't dead," she hissed. "You know he isn't."

"Birdie, *please*," Mom said. "So what if he isn't? Then he ran off and left us with *nothing*. Worse than nothing."

"If you loved Dad, you wouldn't do this." Birdie's voice was rising.

"If your father loved me, he wouldn't have left!" Mom banged a fist into the wardrobe door, a bobby-pinned curl shaking loose.

It was very quiet. Birdie felt like she would explode, her whole skin humming. She knew Dad loved them, it was just that everything had gone wrong so suddenly, and he'd panicked. She was mad at him, too, but she couldn't give up on him until she found him and—

Found him. She'd almost forgotten!

"Oh!" Birdie fumbled in her pocket and pulled out the flyer she'd found earlier that day. She unfolded it, flattening it against her thighs. "Look what I found!" She'd run all the way home to show it to her mother, but since Mom was being so dreadful it had almost slipped her mind.

Mom stared at the picture, her face softening a little. She looked at Birdie with tenderness—or pity. "Oh, Birdie. There's a thousand planes like his, you know that. They made a million of them, and sold them cheap after the war."

Birdie knew Mom would say exactly that. "It's Dad's. It has the same name, Mom." She stabbed it with her finger. "It's the *exact same*. You must not want to believe it. You must *want* him to be gone."

"*Birdie*." A warning.

"You're *glad* he's gone. You're happy to go live with Aunt Annie, and I have to go live in the awful Catskills because it's the only way Dad will find me and I'll be trapped there for God knows how long!" Birdie pushed off from the settee and stood.

Mom turned abruptly and their faces came close. Mom's eyes were sky-blue clear for what felt like the first time since the bank failed. "Bobby left me. He left *us*." She cupped Birdie's cheek, her palm cool. "If he's dead, he's never coming back, and there's no use fussing over it. If he's alive, and he just left us like this— he doesn't deserve for you to wait around for him, hoping he'll appear one day."

"How can you say that?" Birdie flung Mom's hand away. "You know how terrible it's been, how everyone hates him since the bank failed!"

"It's been terrible for *us*, Birdie," Mom said, her voice rising. "How can you not see it? How can you not blame him for what he's done to us?"

Birdie snatched the flyer off the table and clutched it to her chest. "You're not even giving him a chance." She whirled and stomped out of the room.

"I've given him *plenty* of chances!" Mom yelled after her.

Birdie slammed the door shut as she left the house. She'd as good as lost Izzy, David, school at Finch's in the fall, her pretty things, her adoring friends, her glamorous future.

There was no way she was giving up on Dad without a fight.

But all she'd found was his stupid plane.

She'd go back home with no clues as to where he had gone. Coming here hadn't changed anything and she couldn't bear it.

Her eyes went to Dad's Jenny again, and something sparked inside her. There might be a clue she couldn't see from here, some note from Dad, some secret code. She didn't want to ask any of the circus people, after tattoo-girl had been so unhelpful. There might be something she could say that would convince them to let her poke around, but right now she couldn't think of what it was.

A flight of steps led down to the beach to her left. Birdie straightened up and studied the distance between her and the Jenny.

Circus people stood in a ring in the sand at the bottom of the stairs, smoking and gesturing. Tattoo-girl sulked on the bottom steps, a cigarette dangling from her fingers—Birdie would have to get by her first. The boy in the striped socks chatted with the girl, twirling the now-unlit chains he had spun in the show. The big man in the suspenders absentmindedly shuffled a deck of cards, hands undulating near his waist. Merriwether puffed on a pipe, as tall as the men (although Birdie was sure she was a woman now), talking intensely with "Air Devil" Charlie.

Close by, a sandy-haired fellow waved his cigarette and pointed at the sky, talking to two identical-looking younger boys. He nudged one of the boys with his shoulder and laughed, and got shoved back. He lunged for the boy's middle, his abandoned cigarette rolling in the sand, the other boy heckling them as they wrestled. The lot of them didn't seem like they would pay her any mind. After she was past them, she had a clear shot at the Jenny, which was on the far side of the other planes. She could snoop around without being noticed.

The wingwalking girl, Darlena, was nowhere to be seen.

As Birdie approached the top of the steps she saw another person sitting cross-legged in the sand facing the bottom step, holding a small white paper. The person dipped her fingers into a pouch that rested on the bottom step and pinched a small amount of mossy tobacco, dropping it carefully onto the center of the paper. A long bob brushed her shoulders unevenly, like she'd chopped her hair off at the chin and then let it grow back. Her hair was dark and straight, and a dun-colored flight suit showed off a lean, tall figure. Birdie remembered now—she was the pilot who had flown Charlie up for his parachute drop.

Birdie had known women could fly planes—Amelia Earhart, after all, and Louise Thaden. She'd even heard of a Negro woman pilot, who had had to go to France to learn how to fly because no one in America would teach her. There had been a whole air race for women last year, officially called the Women's National Air Derby, although some guy on the radio had nicknamed it the Powder Puff Derby and that name had stuck. Birdie had listened to him narrate the race in an indulgent tone and pictured women in puffy pink dresses daintily flying planes painted like cupcakes and teacups. She'd never actually seen a woman fly a plane.

Powder puff definitely did not describe this girl or the way she'd flown her plane.

Birdie took a step down. She watched the girl pilot massage the paper and tobacco, then bring the cigarette to her mouth and run the paper along her tongue. Birdie took another step down. She watched the girl pilot pull the cigarette away, pick a piece of stray tobacco from her tongue, and flick it into the sand.

As she got closer to tattoo-girl, who sat on the steps just above the girl pilot, Birdie heard snatches of their conversation. "—could have come with us till we were through with the tryout, at least!" Tattoo-girl sucked on her cigarette, the cherry glowing an angry red. She mumbled something Birdie couldn't catch.

The boy in the striped socks swirled the chains in a fig-ure-eight pattern. "Love makes you do crazy things." He had creamy brown skin, and when he paused to push his hair back Birdie glimpsed dark eyes, arresting lashes, and heavy brows.

The lanky girl pilot snorted. "Maybe it's love, maybe not. There's plenty of people telling girls they've gotta settle down before it's too late, and you know what—" She tipped up on one hip and pulled a book of matches out of her pocket. Birdie couldn't hear what she said next, as she put the cigarette between her teeth to strike a match. She took another step.

"I just knew that cake-eater was gonna propose. I just *knew* he was gonna pull something like this," muttered Merriwether. "She's worth ten of him, and I've a mind to tell her."

"The tryout's still a go, right?" suspenders-man asked Merriwether, left hand stacking cards into his right.

"Of course we're still doing it!" snapped Merriwether. "We've still got a hell of a show. We'll figure it out."

"Here, Bennie," said tattoo-girl. "Give me a card. I'll tell us what we should do."

Bennie's calloused hands stilled, and he plucked a card from the deck and handed it to the girl. She studied it for a moment, brow furrowed. She frowned and passed it back.

It says you should all go away, thought Birdie, trying telepathy, *and clear the way for me.*

"What did it tell you?" asked striped-socks boy.

Tattoo-girl swiveled and looked up the steps. Birdie fixed her gaze on a swirl of gulls flying past, dark silhouettes against the sky. Tattoo-girl would probably charge Birdie twenty-five cents again if she caught her watching them, so Birdie ambled down the steps, admiring the horizon and the birds as they turned to specks against the sea. She avoided eye contact, too busy being nonchalant to listen to their conversation anymore.

She couldn't help glancing down as she passed the girl pilot—and their eyes met. The girl had tan, smooth skin, but the skin around her eyes was startlingly pale. Dad's skin did the same thing after he wore flight goggles for hours on a sunny day, although his face always turned lobster red first. The girl smiled at Birdie with dark eyes. "Hey there," she drawled. Her accent smacked of something Deep South, like Georgia or Alabama—as

Southern as it got. The tips of her hair grazed the shoulders of her khaki duster.

Birdie smiled back too eagerly, her pulse pounding though she wasn't doing anything suspicious. But the pilot's eyes skimmed past her as Merriwether asked her something, and she turned away to answer.

And then Birdie was past them, and then the wrestling boys, and Dad's Jenny sat before Birdie on the beach, unguarded.

CHAPTER FOUR

THE GIRL PILOT'S DIRECT ADDRESS HAD UNNERVED HER. BIRDIE MEAN-
dered down to the water's edge before she circled back to the
Jenny from the far side, but her heart rate refused to slow. A hurried glance backward proved that she was hidden, the red-and-
silver plane blocking the line of sight to the circus folks.

The Jenny roosted as serenely on the open beach as it had
in its cozy hangar back home. Wheels and tail skid rested in the
sand, the upper wing a curved awning above her head. Birdie
put her hand to the painted canvas and traced the swirling black
Pretty Bird with her fingers. Even without the name she'd know
it was his. She wouldn't feel so hopeless and so happy when she
looked at it, if it wasn't. She recognized the scuff marks here and
there, little creases in the fabric where canvas showed through
the paint. The stink of oil and grease. The stiff black leather seats
in the cockpits, the same stick and gauges.

Birdie grabbed a strut and pulled herself up on the wing. The
canvas was rough beneath her heels—something, maybe gravel
or sand, had been painted into the wing of the plane since she'd
last seen it. It had texture, not the smoothness she was used to.
She was short enough that she could just stand up straight, her
hair brushing the upper wing. She touched her fingers to it. The
bars between the wings were straight, the wires taut.

Careful to step over the wires and onto the ribby supports, she crossed the wing and climbed into the rear cockpit. This cockpit was her favorite. Although she'd always been a passenger up front when they flew, it was the rear cockpit she hid in to read, to study, to dream, to imagine she was flying away. She settled into the seat and put her hands on the stick, ran a finger over the tachometer. She pretended she was pushing the throttle in, about to take off. She knew exactly what the plane felt like lifting off and setting down. She knew it like an inhale and exhale of breath.

Where would she be now if she'd been the one who'd flown away from home and left it in the care of strangers? She closed her eyes.

Immediately her mind went to the flask of bootleg gin Dad kept under the seat. She reached beneath her, and her fingers brushed what felt like the round metal lid. She curled and looked between her legs, but it was hard to see through the shadows. She reached again, as far back as she could go, and her fingers closed around flat curves. As she withdrew her hand, something paper fluttered to the floor between her feet.

It was his flask, sterling silver. Dad sometimes allowed her a burning nip; he always got a kick out of her disgusted expression, which always happened no matter how she tried to steel herself. The flask often poked out of his back pocket as he ambled out to the hangar to tinker with the engine, or rested on top of the mess on the desk in his study.

The flask, the plane—these things belonged to him so much that they were almost part of him. *So where was he?*

All the air left her in a *whoosh,* and suddenly she was shaking. She pressed her forehead into her hands, swallowing back tears. Was she really going to have to go upstate and just *wait?* She didn't think she could do it, but it was just as unbearable to imagine getting on that steamer and heading across the ocean, giving up on him completely like Mom already had.

Her gaze fell upon the thing that had slid out with the flask, and she squinted into the dimness. It was a photograph, dirty and creased.

Birdie snatched it up. The way the light hit the crinkled bit of glossy paper made it hard to make out. She flattened the image against her thigh, smoothing it with her palms, and her pulse accelerated.

The face was instantly recognizable. Birdie's mind colored her curved, seductively pouting lips a bright, slick vermilion, her puppy eyes dark brown, the thick lashes and tumbled curls a warm chestnut gloss. Gilda Deveaux, the Chicago jazz singer that Dad had hired to sing at Birdie's sixteenth birthday party. Dad sure loved the way she sang, her clear voice carrying just a hint of throaty accent. He loved the way she looked at him, lips painted into a perfect bow, as she sang "Ain't Misbehavin'." Birdie had loved it, and Izzy, too. They'd run around the house, up and down the stairs, screaming the lyrics after the guests had left.

Mom hadn't loved their shrieking at all. Birdie had never heard her shout so loud.

She shoved her hand under the seat again and fumbled around desperately, sure there must be something else there, something of her or Mom, something that said he'd be coming back for them—but she came up with nothing but dust.

The burn of tears left her eyes. She felt empty, thin skin stretched over fragile supports. From the right angle the setting sunlight would shine right through her.

Birdie pulled herself up slowly, stuffing the picture and the flask into her coat pocket. She levered herself out of the cockpit and onto the wing. She grasped the top of one of the bars and leaned away. Slowly, she let her weight swing her around the bar, ducking under one wire while stepping over the next. She caught the next strut and swung around that. Swooping one way, then the other. It was like waltzing, three little steps between each bar. Nothing calmed her like dancing. Nothing else made all the hard stuff fade away. Movement filled every pore of her body and corner of her mind and she could slip into that perfect joy when there was nothing else but that moment. For the past two months, dancing had been the only time she'd felt like herself. As she closed her eyes and imagined she was up in the air, just like Darlena, her sadness dropped away like she'd just lifted off. Dad was on the boardwalk below, applauding her pluck and charm. The struts were partners passing her back and forth. One-two-three, one-two-three—

But Dad would prefer a song that Gilda-from-Chicago might sing, something fun and snappy, to a boring old waltz. Eyes still closed, Birdie changed the tune in her head to a Charleston beat. She did a couple of Jay-Bird steps, flipping her hands back and forth. She could feel the edge of the wing under her toes, but she kept her eyelids screwed shut. She tossed her hair like Darlena had done, imagining she was daring death way up in a bright sky.

"DUN dun-da-dun, DUN dun-da-dun—" said a strange voice, singing a Charleston riff.

Birdie opened her eyes with a gasp, her hand grasping for empty air as her toe caught a wire and she pitched off the wing. She landed heavily, sand stinging her palms and knees.

The man—tattoo-girl had called him Bennie—grinned down at her. "Good thing the plane's grounded, huh?" he said, offering her a hand.

Birdie scrambled to her feet without taking it. "Good thing," she said shortly, wiping her burning palms against her coat.

Behind him, the dark-haired girl pilot was smiling. "I was just picturing what that woulda looked like a hundred feet up. Before the spill—pretty dang good, I'd imagine."

Birdie couldn't tell if the girl was complimenting or mocking her, but the empty space inside her filled up with embarrassment.

"Keep your eyes open next time," the man advised. "Should solve the issue."

Her hands and knees hurt. There was no way she could ask them anything without crying, her eyes watering just thinking about it. And that *would not* do. With everything that had happened the past three months she had never let on how much it hurt—but right now, in front of these strangers she cared nothing about, she couldn't seem to compose herself.

"You okay?" the girl asked, head tilting as she studied Birdie's face. "You hurt yourself or something?"

"I'm fine," Birdie managed, turning away.

"Hey, listen—" said the man, but Birdie shoved her scraped-up hands into her coat pockets and practically ran so they wouldn't see her dashing the tears from her cheeks.

CHAPTER FIVE

BIRDIE ALMOST GOT ON THE VERY LAST EVENING TRAIN THAT WOULD take her back to Long Island. But when it pulled away from the platform, she was still sitting on a wrought-iron bench in the middle of Flatbush Avenue Station.

The big clock in the center of the station said almost midnight when a man in a uniform with a tired look on his face asked if she was all right.

"I'm taking an early train," she said confidently, her brave face back on. He gave up and went away. Janitors came and swept and emptied trash cans. Their movements and intermittent conversation echoed in the empty hall. They dimmed the lamps before they left.

Birdie felt like she was the only one in the world. When she was a little kid she used to be terrified when she woke up in the middle of the night and everything was this still. She'd always loved the murmur of grown-up voices swirling downstairs—nothing comforted her more than the reminder that people were right there if she needed them, whether it was just Mom and Dad, or a whole cocktail party. But if she woke and it was dark and quiet she would cry until Dad stumbled in to comfort her, his head nodding above her as he petted her shoulder. Only then could she close her eyes and fall asleep again, trusting she was safe.

She could cry all she wanted now, but he wasn't coming back.

Birdie touched the metal flask in her pocket. It was warm and solid. She did not touch the photograph of Gilda, but she could feel it smoldering there.

She'd put the memory of Dad with Gilda at her sixteenth birthday party out of her mind, which hadn't been hard—she'd been pretty tipsy when it happened. She and Izzy had snuck out to the hangar with a bottle of champagne while the party swirled inside. Izzy stood in the rear cockpit while Birdie straddled the front of the plane, sitting backwards to face her.

"Ugh, I can't *wait* to go to Finch's with you in the fall," said Birdie, passing Izzy the bottle. They had it all planned out, how they were going to the same prestigious finishing school together.

Izzy squealed uncharacteristically. "Me too!"

"And David and Monty will be practically right around the corner, at Columbia," Birdie said. "We'll visit them every weekend."

"They'll fall more in love with us each time they set eyes on us," said Izzy, continuing the litany they knew by heart.

"We'll get perfect marks."

"Then we graduate."

"And they ask us to marry them," said Birdie, grabbing Izzy's shoulders and shaking them.

"And we'll move to the city!" Izzy crowed, falling against her.

Birdie squeezed her in a hug. "And we'll go dancing every weekend together!"

'And we'll have perfect babies, and summer homes in the Hamptons!" Izzy collapsed into the seat laughing, one hand extended with the bottle.

Birdie grasped for it, giggling, but missed and fell forward, catching herself on the edge of the cockpit. Babies, marriage, all of that would sound terribly boring if it wasn't for Izzy. She had a way of making everything glamorous and exciting, ten times more fun. Izzy grinned up at Birdie from the seat, picture-perfect. The bottom of the cockpit was a pool of darkness that Izzy's pale skin glowed against. Big, dark-brown eyes, slim limbs, stick-straight shiny hair—Birdie had to look away. The champagne was making her goofy.

The corrugated metal of the hangar door rattled, startlingly loud. Birdie gasped, scrambling for cover. Her only hiding spot was the back cockpit, and she dropped down into it. She heard Izzy giggle, then stifle it.

That someone at the hangar door was cursing, laughing, and coming in—

Dad.

Birdie exhaled quietly and listened. Dad's voice sounded jovial. He'd been unfailingly cheerful all winter, despite all the dreadful news coming in since early fall. Black Monday. Black Tuesday. Bankers like Dad throwing themselves out of twenty-story windows, or shooting themselves in their offices when they got the news. But all of that was far away in Manhattan. Out here on Long Island everything seemed to be going on as it always did.

"There she is, my Curtiss Jenny. Pretty, ain't she?" Dad loved to show off his plane when he drank. Birdie could hear the scotch husking his voice.

Birdie heard the murmur of a woman's voice, exclaiming, "You flew that in the war, sir?" then dipping, saying something low.

Gilda Deveaux. The jazz singer he had hired for the party. She had thin, highly arched, penciled brows, hair mussed and curling around her face. Birdie pictured her red mouth, her red curves in an unfashionably tight dress. Her mouth open wide to sing. The look of almost-pain she had, like ecstasy and hurt mixed together. She sang better than Mom, all her emotion on the outside. Mom's mouth had been a tight line as Gilda crooned. Mom looked at Birdie and Dad like that, when she wasn't happy with them.

"I flew it damn well, too—that's why it's in mint condition. The Germans didn't have a chance," Dad was saying. Liar. He only flew it in training—he never made it to the front lines in Europe—but he liked to stretch the truth to make the story better.

It was stifling, hunched down in the tiny space. Birdie remembered she was still holding the champagne, and tipped the bottle back. She gulped. Burning down her throat, fizzing in her stomach. There was more in the bottle than she thought, but what the heck. She finished it off.

Birdie listened to Dad's voice, murmuring low, Gilda laughing in response. They'd leave soon, back to Birdie's big birthday bash inside the house. Suddenly she was very ready to go back to the party. Back to David and Monty, and the rest of her friends and family. Why were they taking so long? *Leave*, she thought.

She wondered what Izzy was thinking, listening to Dad sweet-talk the jazz singer out here, when he thought they were all alone.

Dad's voice had gone quiet, and Gilda's, too. Birdie imagined them standing next to each other with nothing to say. Or maybe they had left, so quietly that Birdie hadn't heard them.

Or maybe they were kissing.

Birdie heard, breathless: "Mr. Williams, please, I really don't think—" And a rattle as someone bumped into the metal wall of the hangar.

Birdie jerked to standing. The champagne bottle in her hand caught the edge of the open cockpit—she lost her grip on it, though she fumbled after it—

The bottle slammed into the concrete floor, shattering spectacularly into little twinkling shards. Gilda screamed.

"Oh!" said Birdie. She and Gilda clapped their hands over their mouths with mirrored expressions of surprise and horror.

"Pretty bird!" Dad said, instantly jovial. "Ah, I was just taking Miss Gilda out here, to give her a look at my Jenny."

Izzy cursed, then slowly stood up next to Birdie. Birdie couldn't stand that Izzy was seeing Dad act like such a fool.

"The boys are probably wondering where I am," Gilda said, giving Dad an accusing look. "We'll be starting that next set here in *un moment . . . excuse moi*, Mr. Williams . . ." Gilda nodded curtly and walked toward the door, hands smoothing her skirt. The seductive demeanor she'd exuded on stage had evaporated, her shoulders tense.

Dad's gaze trailed after Gilda as she slipped out the door. He swirled the scotch in his glass and turned back, eyeing the broken bottle. "Does your mother know you girls finished that off, just the two of you?" he asked Birdie.

Mom would definitely disapprove of Dad taking Gilda out here to see the plane, but she wouldn't like Birdie and Izzy drinking, either. "Aww, come on, Dad," Birdie said, pouting. "You never care if I sneak wine! And it's my *birthday*."

Izzy looked bored, which was how she always looked when she was anxious. She didn't say anything.

"You both should know better," said Dad.

"You won't tell Mom," Birdie said. She was drunk, she could feel it now. Her head was so light, it was hard to think. "Pretty please?"

Dad finally smiled. With his tall stature and broad shoulders, it was easy to believe he had been a war hero. With his friendly smile, it was easy to trust him. "It's all right, pretty bird. None of us has to mention anything about this. It'll be our little secret, what do you say?"

Birdie nodded. Really, she hadn't seen anything from her hiding spot in the Jenny. She knew Dad hadn't been guiltless—but she had no evidence that he had been doing something wrong.

And now she'd found a picture of Gilda, the beautiful jazz singer from Chicago, in Dad's cockpit, but no hint of anything that should have mattered to him.

One of the circus folks must have met Dad, to buy the plane from him. Birdie had run off too quickly. If she got on a train back to Long Island without finding out if they knew anything first, she'd never get a chance to ask them again.

A woman in sensible shoes came and turned up the lamps and opened the ticket window. Birdie did not buy a ticket.

CHAPTER SIX

BIRDIE SHIVERED, THE EARLY MORNING AIR CHILLY AND DAMP ON HER face. She shaded her eyes against the sun and watched the circus folk as they shuffled around the planes, smoking and holding steaming cups. She'd stopped for coffee and a pastry, but she was too anxious to eat and the coffee had burned her tongue. She took a deep breath, trying to calm her jitters. The man who had offered her a hand last night was closest to her, wearing striped overalls and tinkering behind the propeller of the cardinal-red plane. She fixed a smile on her face and strode toward him.

The man glanced up. "Figured you'd be back." He smiled as he wiped his hands on a grease-streaked rag. "Seemed like you had some unfinished business."

Birdie crumbled the pastry in her fingers, buttery dough flaking into the sand. "It's Bennie, right?" She was pleased that her voice sounded confident. "I've got a couple of questions for you."

"Ask away." His eyes crinkled at the corners, grease fingerprints streaking his overalls as he stuffed the rag into his back pocket.

"I'm Birdie Williams, Bobby Williams's daughter. The man who used to own that Jenny, there." She pointed with as steady a hand as she could manage.

"I remember that guy," he said, nodding. "Sounded like he'd hit a rough patch of luck. Responded quick to our ad, thank the Lord. Oscar, the dang idiot, left his Jenny too far down on the beach and

31

the tide pulled it into the water. It was totally wrecked. We needed a replacement in a real hurry, and your daddy gave us a great deal."

Birdie's heart was pounding. "Did he say anything to you? Anything about why he was selling it?"

Bennie shrugged. "He said the bank was coming for his stuff, so he had to sell it cheap and quick. Common enough, these days. Let me see . . . oh! He mentioned Chicago."

Chicago. Birdie's fist tightened in her pocket, and Gilda's picture crumpled in her palm.

The man continued. "I remember that 'cuz we're headed that way for this audition we have. Offered him a ride, actually, but he was in a hurry, and we were here for another while yet." A line creased the man's forehead. "This guy—he's your pop, you said?"

Birdie nodded distractedly. "*You're* going that way? You mean to Chicago?" She vaguely remembered Merriwether announcing that over the megaphone during the show yesterday.

"You!" someone exclaimed behind her. Birdie turned to see the girl pilot running up, her dark hair whipping in the morning breeze. "I can't believe it! We were just talking about you!"

"This is June," Bennie said. "June, Birdie."

"You were talking about—" Birdie's cheeks heated, remembering how ridiculous she must have looked last night. Dancing around like a child. Falling flat on her face.

June flushed, too. Her eyes had looked very dark yesterday evening, but the morning light turned them more of a mossy green color. "About how you looked real nice up there dancing," she said. "With the sun setting, and all."

Birdie's face just got hotter. "Oh, well. Thank you." This girl was so flattering, and Bennie seemed so kind, and they were part of a barnstorming circus that was traveling to *Chicago*—not gray England, not boring upstate New York. She bet every day in their troupe was as exciting and glamorous as living in Manhattan and going to Finch's with Izzy. Maybe even more so.

And Dad had gone to Chicago.

June tucked her hair behind her ear. Her lashes were dark and straight and slanted down. "I'm serious."

Yesterday had been very discouraging, but today things were different.

"I'd like to join your show," Birdie blurted. "I really am a good dancer. A principal dancer, in fact, at my studio back home. Mikhail says I pick up every move faster than anyone he's ever worked with, and he used to work with *professionals*." For most of her life she'd been absolutely sure she was going to be a ballerina when she grew up, until she hit a scant five feet at fourteen, stopped growing, and had to swallow the painful fact that it was impossible—Mikhail had lamented a thousand times that she was too short to meet the minimum height requirements for professional troupes. "I'll be really careful, and Darlena could give me some pointers before we leave? I'm quite sure you won't find any-one more qualified to take her place, in fact, than me!"

June raised her eyebrows. "Come again?"

Birdie's stomach dropped, but she heard herself saying, "I'll make an amazing wingwalker, and you should take me on."

She could do it. She'd just have to wing it, like she did when she got put on stage as a replacement for someone who was throwing up backstage or didn't show up. It happened every other year, practically, and Mikhail had learned to go to her. The girls would mark the steps for Birdie behind the curtains, right before the piece, and then—she'd slap on the costume and remember enough and make up the rest so that the audience never knew she wasn't part of the group.

"Merriwether's pretty picky about who she lets on," said Bennie, giving her a measured look. "But I gotta say, we are sorely in need of somebody like you."

"This could work out!" said June. "You'd be perfect, so long as Merriwether goes for it."

"We'll see," said Bennie. "She had an argument with Darlena last night, and it's got her in a bit of mood this morning."

"I think this is just the thing to sweeten her attitude," said June, motioning for Birdie to follow her.

Merriwether ignored Birdie and June's approach as she put a cigarette between her lips and pulled a match out of her pocket. Merriwether was tall and broad-shouldered, her very short hair pushed off her forehead by goggles, but she wasn't ugly. She had full lips and a lean figure under her duster.

Merriwether leaned down and cocked one foot across her knee, striking the match on the sole of her boot. Birdie stopped a few feet away as June bounded up and slung an arm around the woman.

"Merriwether, darling," June said. "Guess what I found."

The match flared, and Merriwether held it to the cigarette clenched between her teeth. She sucked on it a few times, smoke curling out the corners of her mouth as the tip caught. She dropped the match and crushed it under her boot, then took a long drag, hand on a hip, and looked at Birdie.

"You tell her rides don't start till 11 a.m.," said Merriwether, squinting one eye. "I don't care how cute she is."

Birdie laughed awkwardly, although she wasn't completely sure what the joke might be.

"This is her!" June said. "The girl me and Bennie saw last night? She could get us out of this pickle Darlena's got us in."

"She's too young." Merriwether put her cigarette between her teeth, chewing on it as she looked Birdie up and down. "You telling me you've got wingwalking experience?"

"Yes," said Birdie. If wingwalking counted while the plane was still on the ground—then sure, she had plenty of experience.

"Find who you were looking for yesterday?" asked a voice behind Birdie. It was tattoo-girl, dressed just the same as yesterday, the rose decorating her hair starting to wilt.

Birdie ignored her, and the prickle of irritation that rose along Birdie's spine. "Darlena's a great performer, but I'm a better dancer. I'm quite strong, and I've got experience—"

"With what show?" asked Merriwether.

"Just, um, privately," Birdie said, stumbling over her words. "My dad had a plane."

"Oh, please," said tattoo-girl. "*Every*body's dad had a plane."

"I'd rather do the show with no wingwalker, than a half-baked one," said Merriwether dismissively.

"Come on!" June bounced on the balls of her feet. "What's the harm in giving her a shot?"

Merriwether took a long drag of her cigarette. Birdie tried to look breezy and confident, like someone who walked out on the wing of a plane all the time.

"We'll see what you can do today," said Merriwether finally. "You kill yourself, girl, it's your own damn fault."

"Today?" asked Birdie, with a flutter of nerves. "I thought Darlena—might still? Today?"

"I gotta know you got what it takes before we take you on. You're petite, you can squeeze into the cockpit with Darlena. You'll take turns and she can give us her opinion." Merriwether's expression darkened as she looked around. "Wonder when she's gonna grace us with her presence."

Birdie felt a surge of panic. She'd just joined the circus, as a *wingwalker*. But she was almost as thrilled as she was terrified. She wished she could tell Izzy.

"Oh, she'll show up!" June pshawed. "I don't care what kinda words you two had last night, she's never missed a show." June pumped her fist. "All right! It's almost eleven—I gotta take some rubes on a ride. Excited to see what you do!" She squeezed Birdie's shoulder and headed back to the red plane, where Bennie was turning the propeller slowly, squinting down the length of the blades.

"So." Tattoo-girl eyed her. "I'm in charge of costuming."

Birdie nodded, swallowing skepticism. This strangely dressed girl was in charge of her outfit?

Tattoo-girl sighed as she turned away. A flight of wrens took off from one of her shoulders, across her back. A tiger on the other shoulder swallowed them. "Come on." She lifted a hand and Birdie followed her. "Hazel's got an outfit she barely wore—Merriwether never did get that girl out of the cockpit and onto the wing, but it didn't stop her from trying. I think it might suit you."

"Who's Hazel?" asked Birdie, following tattoo-girl toward the boardwalk, but the girl didn't answer.

"Who are you?" Birdie tried instead.

"Colette."

Birdie gave up, annoyed that she'd even asked, since the girl didn't seem the least bit interested in finding anything out about her.

Colette fished a scrap of sequined material out of a beat-up forest-green Studebaker that was parked on the street on the far side of the boardwalk, then left Birdie in Dad's Jenny to try it on. It was hard to manage, slithered down in the cockpit so no one could see her. Birdie wriggled out of her dress—which was a relief, since she'd sweat so much yesterday—and into the tight leotard. It was a pale pink, ballet-inspired thing that showed plenty of leg and shoulder, with a diaphanous skirt that floated in the breeze. It was a bit big, but she tied the two straps together behind her neck and then it seemed to fit all right.

She thought of Dad reading a poster: Barnstorming Birdie Takes Flight!, with a picture of her smiling in this outfit, on his plane. He would come find her, if he saw a bill like that.

CHAPTER SEVEN

DARLENA NEVER SHOWED.

It was after three o'clock and the crowd was thick on the boardwalk above Birdie's head, roaring as Charlie spelled out "Welcome!" in the air, and Birdie was staring up, picturing losing herself in the crowd. The sand was scorchingly hot between her toes, but Colette had strongly advised against wearing her heels. Birdie would have to make do with bare feet since her ballet flats were back home on her bedroom floor, and the pair Colette offered her were too big and slipped right off.

She could grab her shoes and coat with the money in its pocket and head for the train station. She didn't have to do this.

A young man in a well-tailored leather flight jacket approached, eyes bright blue against his suntanned skin. He smiled hello, his teeth like a horse's, square and handsome. "Hey there! I'm—I *was* Darlena's pilot, so I guess that means I'm yours now." He thrust out his hand. "Oscar."

At any other time she would have been able to smile back at such a keen fellow, but all she could think about was what she was about to do, which made it impossible to unclench her jaw. She shook his hand stiffly. "Birdie Williams."

"So you've really done this before?"

Birdie's stomach did a terrified somersault. "I—well—yes—"

"Hey, hey," he said, putting a hand to her shoulder. "I'll take you up nice and easy, do a couple of level passes in front of the crowd. June said you had some swell moves. You just make sure you keep a good handhold, and you'll be fine." He squeezed, and the steadiness of his grip was reassuring.

She'd rather take the risk that the plane would drop right out from under her than go home to a life that already had. All she had to do was go up the plane and do what she was best at.

Oscar led her to Dad's Jenny and gave her a hand up. She swung her legs into the front cockpit while he hopped into the rear.

"You ready?" called Oscar, all encouragement. Birdie turned over her shoulder and gave him a shaky wave. Oscar pulled his goggles down and gave a thumbs-up, and a boy ran up. It was either John or Henry, one of Merriwether's gangly twins whom Birdie had been introduced to in passing. Birdie couldn't tell the difference between them—they both wore plus fours and suspenders, and both had thick, close-cropped brown hair and dense freckles. They were as tall as she was, but couldn't have been older than fourteen. The boy grabbed the propeller blade, jumped up and dropped all his weight down, pushing the propeller as hard as he could—and the engine caught. The propeller *whoomped* around—then around again—then settled into its rhythm, rattling like a loud sewing machine. *Ticktickticktickticktick*—

Birdie made her mind go blank and focused on the warm sun, the cool spring breeze, the propeller blades flickering. The people crowding the boardwalk, the smell of fried dough. Colette, Bennie, and Milosh, the boy in the striped socks, rattling their revenue boxes—she could almost make it all fade into the background. She'd always wanted to do this when Dad took her flying. She'd gotten the idea in her head once, when she was still very young, to hop out on the wing, spread her arms out, and pretend she was flying all by herself, like a bird—but she'd barely gotten a leg over the edge of the cockpit before Dad lunged forward and pushed her down, yelling. He had landed the plane right away and swore he'd never take her flying again. She'd never seen him so angry with her, not even a bit of admiration for her spunk, and she hadn't tried it since.

The plane lurched forward and Birdie stifled a gasp. The shouting of the crowd swarmed into her head, and the smell of fried dough coated her throat. Birdie's hands gripped the edges of her seat as the Jenny began to bump down the beach. Merriwether roared over the megaphone. "Birdie's first flight, ladies and gentlemen! When she's famous, you can tell everyone you were here for it!"

Birdie's stomach bottomed out as the plane nosed up, the boardwalk on her left suddenly dropping away. She had braided her hair tight to her head to make sure it didn't get in the way, but a few stray strands whipped her cheeks.

She closed her eyes.

Dad is down there on that boardwalk. He's proud of you, and he's sorry. He wants to come back home.

Birdie opened her eyes. She remembered her goggles and pulled them down. The wind up here was just like she remembered it—like a strong wind would be on the ground, noticeable, something to lean into, but not something that felt like it would knock you down. It muffled the sounds of the audience, and Merriwether shouting into the megaphone.

Up until this point, she'd done all this before.

Izzy is down there, her mouth hanging open. She's wishing she'd answered the phone, that she'd come to your house and hugged you and told you it didn't matter what Dad had done, that you were still best friends.

Oscar looped around and leveled out. When Birdie looked over her shoulder, he nodded. Time to climb out. She would be on the wing when he dipped low and buzzed the beach in front of the crowd, so everyone could see her.

She stood up. The wind whipped her skirt, tossing the tulle around her thighs. She leaned back and grabbed the short strut that connected the upper wing to the body of the plane, just behind the front cockpit. Once she was on the wing, she'd have something solid between her and thin air. All she had to do was get her legs over the side of the plane and out into nothing first.

Merriwether and Colette and June are applauding. Merriwether announces that you are amazing. They make you the star of the show.

She took a shuddering breath. The ground teetered beneath her as the plane shifted. The ocean spread out into the distance on one side, churning against the beach.

It didn't make sense that air would hold up a whole plane, but it did. Close to the ground, gravity was a sure thing. But way up here it didn't work the same. They were *flying*, after all. Anything was possible.

All she had to do was step out of the cockpit and onto the wing.

She stuck one leg over the lip of the cockpit and swung it around. The edge of the cockpit dug into her crotch, and she was sure Oscar got an eyeful. Both hands gripped the strut ferociously. Her right foot wasn't that far from the lower wing—how many times had she gotten in and out of this cockpit? She stretched down, then slid a little further, reaching with her whole body, praying.

Her bare toes met something solid. She put her weight on what felt like a wing support, and let the rest of her body slowly detach from the body of the plane. She eased her other foot onto the rough surface.

She was on the wing.

She was up in the air, on the wing of a plane.

The plane gently banked around as she straightened herself. She tried to remember everything her dance teacher taught her. It was all about posture, what made dancing beautiful. Shoulders back, head high, toes pointed. It was all about how you owned the space. Birdie knew how to own it, when the space was a stage. But this was the sky.

The boys are mesmerized. They elbow each other, whisper about how gorgeous you look. They whistle and hoot but you are way up here, inaccessible.

The boardwalk came into view over her right shoulder. She took a deep breath and tried to convince herself to uncurl her fingers from around the strut.

She heard Merriwether roaring over the megaphone, nothing discernible—the crowd roared louder. The plane and the wind roared loudest of all.

It was hard to dance, when there was no music.

She could fail at this.

She could fall.

Birdie jerked a foot, the motion stiff and awkward, hands still glued to the strut.

When she looked back at Oscar, he gave her a thumbs-up, and she knew she was about to disappoint him so terribly.

She looked down at the beach and saw Bennie staring up. She swore she saw his mouth moving.

DUN dun-da-dun, DUN dun-da-dun—Bennie's voice popped into her head, scatting the Charleston like he had last night. Birdie hummed a few shaky bars and felt her heartbeat level out. Her own humming was louder in her head than the rattle of the engine or the shouts of the crowd. It wasn't music, exactly, but it was something.

She let go with one hand and reached for the strut across from her. She ducked through the wires to the back edge of the wing. She crisscrossed her feet as she went. She kicked up a heel. It was clumsy, but it was something. She hummed louder. She lifted both hands from the struts and wires, feet solid on the wing, and waved them. She was dancing. She was doing it. She just had to make it to the end of the wing.

Step.

By.

Step.

Along the wing's thin wooden ribs.

You are perfect. You will never fall, never crash and burn—

Hands skimmed from one strut to the next.

"DUN dun-da-dun, DUN dun-da-dun—buh BAH, buh BAH—"

Her singing was awful and off-key, but by the time she couldn't stand it any longer she was there, at the end of the wing, and the crowd was zipping by, so close below her that she could see every gasp and grin. She pasted a smile on her face as she squeezed the last strut. She blew kisses. She waved.

The crowd believed her smile that said everything was fine. They cheered and whistled and smiled and waved right back. She remembered her posture. She pointed her toes and threw her shoulders back.

She made them believe that she owned the whole sky.

CHAPTER EIGHT

"You!" Oscar was in ecstasy, eyes rolling as he shook Birdie by the shoulders. "You were amaaaaaazing!"

"You didn't see it," she said, grinning as she pulled her coat on over her leotard. She was trying to act smooth, but inside she was giddy with adrenaline. "At least I hope not! You were supposed to be busy with a little thing called flying the airplane?"

Merriwether was loud on the megaphone, introducing Charlie as June took him up in the bright-red Moth for his double-parachute drop.

"Come on! Did you hear Merriwether?" Oscar was gratifyingly impressed, though he seemed like the excitable type. "'*Ladies and gentlemen—the next Gladys Ingles!*' She was going on about how she hadn't seen moves like that outside the movies! I managed a gander or two—and, sweetheart, you looked fantastic!"

"Cool it, Oscar." Colette approached, eyes rolling. "She's barely got her feet on the ground and here you are, trying to sweep her right back off them."

Birdie swallowed her grin and pulled her coat closed over her dress.

"Costume work out all right?" Colette asked.

"It'll do." Birdie's gaze skimmed across Colette's collarbones—a twisting snake glared at her with red eyes. "I'm sure I'll get used to being half naked in public eventually."

43

"Good, because you've got a place in the show and the dress is yours. I know for sure the Incredible Hazel won't want it back."

The Incredible Hazel. Birdie remembered now—that was one of the names on the flyer with Dad's plane on it. Birdie wasn't sure she'd done well enough to get her name on a flyer, but she'd gotten a place in the show!

Oscar chuckled. "Hazel hated that outfit from the start. Pity. She looked amazing in it . . . but you move better than she ever did."

Colette made a noise somewhere between laughing and gagging, but Birdie appreciated Oscar's constant onslaught of praise. She'd walked out on the wing of a plane, for heaven's sake. She'd defied death! Birdie felt like she'd changed the whole world; it was disappointing to come down and find the world—besides Oscar—so unaffected.

"Careful, Oscar," said Colette, pulling a cigarette out from behind her ear. "If I didn't know better, I'd think you were sweet on our little Birdie."

"Come on!" said Oscar. "You know better. This is just me. Just normal, friendly Oscar."

He winked at Birdie and offered his arm. She felt her cheeks warm as she took it.

"Yeah," said Colette, striking a match. "I was afraid of that."

Birdie pulled back from Oscar and gave him a coy look. "Should I be worried about you?"

"Oh, don't mind her." Oscar scoffed as he turned her toward the show. "She thinks anyone that isn't being actively antagonistic has ulterior motives."

Maybe Colette was just being protective of her friend. "I bet Hazel is a lovely dancer," Birdie said, loud enough for Colette to hear. "She got her name on the poster, after all."

Oscar laughed. "Oh, that girl's got two left feet—and she gets too nervous out on the wing. Doesn't like someone else being in control—that's my theory, anyway." Oscar squinted into the sky, following the red plane's movements. A speck separated and began to grow—Charlie, doing his double-parachute drop. "But Hazel's the best fly girl we have. That's why her name's on the poster. That girl's got nerves of steel."

Another lady pilot, then. Birdie hadn't known it was so commonplace.

The sound of the crowd swelled, and a few people screamed. Charlie's first parachute was collapsing—Birdie remembered the response from the crowd the day before. Charlie was plummeting, his parachute trailing behind him. Oscar's fingers tightened on her forearm. Birdie bit her lip, waiting for the second parachute to open. Of course it would.

Charlie—hands fumbling with his second parachute—so close—the ground—

"No—" Birdie choked out as Charlie's body slammed into the sand.

"He's alive," said Merriwether. They all huddled around the bottom steps of the boardwalk, picking at sandwiches and weak coffee that Bennie had picked up on the way back from the hospital. "Doped up good, doctors are taking care of him. His wife is on her way from Philly." Merriwether's face twisted up, and when she spoke again her voice was rough. "They say he might not walk again. Definitely not for a good while. Maybe not ever."

Oscar's eyes were puffy, his nose red. Colette's face looked like stone, lips tight. She had a stubby pencil and was sketching something dark on her sandwich wrapper, with lots of cross-hatching. Tattooed teardrops dripped down her left arm, from the eye of a parrot. Milosh sat beside her, hunched over so far Birdie couldn't see his face. Now that she was close she could see that he had a few tattoos as well—abstract symbols and letters on his knuckles and wrists, the back of his neck. Bennie was holding Merriwether's hand in both of his, cupping it like a bird. The twins had wolfed down their sandwiches and were fidgeting anxiously, their rear ends barely keeping contact with the steps. Smoke drifted up from June's mouth in a thin, shaky line as she stared toward the ocean, eyes unfocused.

After Charlie fell he sprawled unconscious on the sand for an interminable amount of time while the circus folks surrounded him uselessly, Merriwether pleading through the megaphone for someone to call an ambulance. June landed her plane, cut the engine, and tumbled off the wing before it had coasted to a full stop, her voice a hoarse cry. Medics eventually swarmed and bundled Charlie onto a stretcher and they all left in a storm of shouting, trying to clear a path to the street through the crowds. None of the troupe members stayed behind, so Birdie figured that could be her job, to stay and keep an eye on everything.

She tried to summon up what Charlie had looked like before he fell, but she hadn't ever gotten a close look at him. A mustache, a build like Dad's. A horrible twist to his back, one arm bent the wrong way beneath him. She couldn't shake the image of his crumpled body from her mind.

She'd thought the circus folks might be surprised that she was still there when they'd returned, but Bennie had handed her a sandwich without a word.

"Charlie pushed it too far," said Oscar angrily. He shoved his sandwich off his lap, scattering shredded meat into the sand, and ran his hands through his hair so it stood straight up. "I kept telling him—he didn't need to wait till the last goddamned minute to open it!"

"It wouldn't have mattered," said Merriwether. "The parachute glitched. There was nothing he could have done differently."

"Well then he shouldn't have been doing the stupid stunt," raged Oscar. "He kept talking about how everybody had seen a single parachute drop, they were tired of it—well, I think there were plenty of people who thought one parachute was plenty. He didn't need to take those kinds of chances!"

"Charlie knew what he was doing. His stunt got us a shot at the Chicago air show," said June, her eyes still on the horizon, her voice monotone. "It made us a lot of money. It made us a name."

Oscar didn't answer.

"Doesn't matter now," said Colette flatly. "If we don't have Charlie, we're never going to ace that audition."

They were all quiet, swimming in sadness. Birdie felt miserable. She'd soared, only to be brought back to reality in one heart-stopping instant. She'd been one misstep away from the same fall only moments before.

"We're still headed for Chicago tomorrow," said Merriwether suddenly. "Henrieta's expecting me and the boys, and Hazel's going to meet up with us there. Maybe we'll figure something out."

"With Darlena and Charlie gone?" Bennie asked. "That's a tough one."

I'm here, thought Birdie. *You're only down one act.* She couldn't go back to Glen Cove, to nothing. She just *couldn't*. But when she thought about Charlie's body twisted in the sand—his glazed eyes and the guttural animal noises he made as they lifted him in the stretcher—the hungry crowd swelling minute by minute, drawn by the horrific scene below—she wasn't so sure it was a smart idea to stick around.

Bet your bottom dollar you lose the blues, sang Gilda. *In Chicago, Chicago.*

"Everyone, think on it tonight." Merriwether sighed heavily. "This may feel like the end of the world, but it's not. We'll come up with something."

CHAPTER NINE

THE TWINS TOOK OFF DOWN THE BEACH, THROWING ROCKS INTO THE surf, and Bennie and Merriwether left to make sure the planes were all above the high tide mark. Colette and Milosh held hands and went to sit by the water together. Their silhouettes were dark against the sea, their heads bowed together, until the last light went and the moon only caught the barest edges of the waves.

Oscar stared at his hands and June continued to contemplate the horizon. Birdie sat between them in the dark, shivering slightly. The air had chilled now that the sun was gone, and her legs were cold beneath the thin layers of her tulle costume. At least she had her wool coat. She'd put her heels back on, but they didn't do much to warm her feet. The sequins on her outfit dug into her armpits and were beginning to itch. She had furtively rinsed her soiled camiknickers in a public fountain earlier so she could change back into her normal clothes, but they were still damp. Everyone else was still in their flight suits and costumes, too. Birdie wondered where they kept their normal clothes, and where they slept. She was desperate for a good night's sleep tonight.

She hadn't seen her mother since yesterday morning, and Mom would be in quite a state by now. Birdie knew she should get in touch. There was probably a public telephone at the train station, but she felt no motivation to go find it. What would she even tell her? *I'm running away with the circus?* She made herself remember how blank and distant Mom had been since Dad left. Why *should* she call her—so Mom could tell her how disappointed she continued to be?

Birdie felt bad about letting Mikhail down. She was missing another dance rehearsal right now, and he was surely already cutting her from the group numbers. He had little patience for girls missing class, and had even cut people just for being late to rehearsal, if it was close to the performance. She'd never seen a principal dancer let him down, though. If she headed back tomorrow morning she could still try to beg for forgiveness. Then she'd still have dance until the big recital was over. And then what? No dance classes, ever again. She couldn't afford it, and she was getting too old for it, anyhow. She wouldn't be going to Finch's, where she and Izzy had hoped they offered ballet along with deportment and etiquette. She wouldn't even be able to afford to go out dancing for fun unless David took her—and he hadn't been very interested in such things since the bank closed.

"Poor Merri," said June, her face in shadow. "I know this brought up painful memories for her."

"Merri's man died in a flying accident, when the twins were real little," Oscar told Birdie. "Somehow, she managed to keep the show running, and even make it better. Merriwether knows how to go on with the show no matter what."

"That's so sad," said Birdie softly. For the first time since Charlie's accident, she felt tears prick her eyes. She looked down the beach to find the boys, but it was too dark to see them. She could just make out the glowing tips of Merri's and Bennie's cigarettes hovering by the planes on the beach.

"Thank God for Bennie," said June. "He'll help her through."

"I'm gonna hate telling Hazel," Oscar mumbled, wiping his eyes. "She's gonna cry like a baby."

Birdie remembered the flask in her coat pocket. She pulled it out, unscrewed the cap, and took a burning swig, then offered it to Oscar.

He gave her a lopsided smile and took it. The gas lamp on the boardwalk far above gave dim, yellow illumination. "You don't want to come with us anymore," said Oscar. "Now that you know we all end up paralyzed—or worse. It could have been worse." Oscar took a swig from the flask, made an appreciative face, and handed it to June.

June scooted close to Birdie and reached across her to take the flask. Her thigh was warm against Birdie's cold legs, and Birdie was glad when she didn't move away. "We don't have a show anymore," said June. "We don't have enough time to regroup and get another act together. You should back out."

The thought of going with them made her anxious in a not-knowing-what-might-happen kind of way, but thinking about *not* going just made her feel bottomlessly sad, in a no-matter-what-it's-going-to-be-awful way. "So, what's this audition that's in Chicago?" she asked.

"Some guy who's high-up at the Curtiss-Reynolds Airport saw our act and loved it," said June. She tucked her hair behind her ear and the lamplight caught her cheekbone and the curve of her lip. "The second annual National Air Races are happening there at the end of August. We got a call to come show them our stuff next Saturday, to see if we can get a contract for the NAR circus act this year." She sighed heavily, thumb worrying the flask cap. "No chance of that now."

"But you're still going to Chicago, right?" Birdie asked as June tasted the liquor and handed it back.

"We gotta head that way anyway," said Oscar. "Who knows, maybe we'll come up with something."

"We should still try out," said Birdie. A ghost of the thrill of that afternoon buzzed in her veins. Despite what had happened to Charlie, she wanted to get back out on the wing. She took another drink. "Now that I've got the feel of it, I've got a bunch of ideas for my act. And you're both such swell pilots—all those loop-de-loops and dives, flying upside down! We can still impress them."

Oscar shook his head as she passed him the half-empty flask. "You're a great dancer. And sure, we're good at what we do. But it's more than dancing or flying, what they're looking for. They want something that reminds people that what they're watching is really dangerous, like Charlie's stunt."

Birdie frowned. "Yeah, but look what happened. Nobody wants to take it so far that somebody actually gets hurt, right?"

Oscar swirled the flask and stared out at the ocean. "The first time Charlie did his act, I didn't know what he was up to—none of us did. I thought he was going to die. And I thought—God, I thought, 'Wow, this is gonna make us so much money.' I can't believe that was the thought that ran through my head. But nothing helps out the bottom line like a death in the show—"

"And then," June interrupted, "the second parachute opened. Charlie landed, and he was fine. Better than fine—he was a *celebrity* after that. And, get this—the show's been *packed* since then. It was sort of like he died, while also living to perform it again, day after day. That's what defying death is all about."

Darlena was the first person Birdie had ever seen walk out on a wing. She'd been truly thrilled that the girl could fall to her death, but somehow, so gracefully, didn't. But now, Birdie had seen the act. She'd *done* it. She believed the plane would go up, the girl would do her little dance, the plane would land, and everything would be fine—when, in reality, one mistake could mean death. How could she make people remember that?

June leaned in again to take the flask from Oscar, and Birdie caught a whiff of tobacco and engine grease, and a warm scent that reminded her of sunshine. "We're always one little misstep from disaster, aren't we?" Birdie mused as she watched June tip the flask back. "I mean, no matter what you're doing. Flying a plane, walking down the street, sleeping." Going to school, going to dance class, eating dinner with Mom and Dad, thinking every-thing was going to go exactly how you expected it to. "You never know when everything's gonna fall apart."

She accepted the flask from June and took another swallow. Whatever was in it was starting to burn less.

"Thinking about it like that takes the scary out, doesn't it?" said June. "People are so boring and predictable because they think it's safe, but nothing is risk-free."

Birdie was feeling less cold. Maybe it was the liquor. Maybe it was June and Oscar sitting close. She leaned back on her elbows and looked up, and her breath caught in her throat. The stars were endless overhead. The sky looked bigger than it ever had before. It seemed much smaller back at home on Long Island, where nobody walked out on the wings of airplanes. Where no one fell out of the sky.

"I don't know," said Oscar. "I mean, it's definitely safer to keep your feet on the ground."

Birdie giggled.

"Oh please." June reached across Birdie and poked him in the ribs. "If you think like that, you never do anything fun."

Birdie decided. Even if none of them knew what was going to happen once they got to Chicago—even if it wasn't going to be risk-free, or safe—she knew it wouldn't be what she left behind, and right now that was good enough for her.

CHAPTER TEN

BIRDIE WOKE SHIVERING IN THE MIDDLE OF THE NIGHT, UNDER A THIN
blanket on a stiff, narrow mattress that had been Darlena's. She
stared into the pitch-dark of the boarding house room, listening to people breathe around her, and longed for her sleeved
nightgown and thick duvet. But a thrill ran through her when she
remembered that nobody from her real life knew where she was.
She'd just become the kind of person you saw in the movies or
the newspapers. She drifted off again imagining how impressed
Izzy would be when she got back and told her all about it.

Merriwether shook her awake what felt like minutes later.
Headachey and freezing, Birdie fumbled into her camiknickers
and wrinkled lavender dress, longing for a hot bath, her vanity
full of powders and scents, her silver-backed brush to smooth out
her tangles, and her wardrobe full of clean, pressed clothing. At
least her undergarments had dried overnight and felt somewhat
cleaner after their dunk in the water fountain. She buttoned up
her coat and followed the others, shivering, into the still-dark
morning.

They took off as the sky began to lighten. John was flying
Charlie's Jenny, with Birdie in the front cockpit; he had begged
Merriwether to let him fly. June was piloting her red plane with
John's brother, Henry, as passenger, and Oscar had Merri in the
front cockpit of Dad's Jenny. Bennie, Colette, and Milosh would

follow in the Studebaker with most of their things, and would arrive in Chicago the following day.

It became a mild morning with bright sun and little wind. Birdie, exhausted from two nights of little sleep, dozed for the first stretch, until they stopped to refuel from their own stash in a field somewhere in Pennsylvania. Birdie ate some boiled peanuts John shyly offered her, and after they'd lifted off again she stared over the side of the plane and watched towns, fields, roads, and rivers slowly pass beneath them. She pictured climbing out on the wing, an adoring crowd staring up at her. She was ready to try it again. She'd practice like she practiced for dance class, repeating the steps over and over—across her bedroom floor, on the way to school—until she danced the movements in her dreams. She could get really good. Get her name on the posters.

She settled back in her seat and pulled out the picture of Gilda and stared at it, wondering what she might be able to find in Chicago once they landed.

Gilda might have protested Dad's advances in the hangar, but she was back up on her little stage when Birdie came inside with Izzy and Dad, her shoes kicked off, a martini in hand. Birdie hadn't given her a second glance, but if she had, she probably would have seen Gilda stare at Dad with that smoldering look she got when she sang, everything forgiven. But Dad's indiscretion had left Birdie's mind by the time she whirled into the ballroom. The band struck up the first notes of "Black Bottom Stomp," and she shot an adoring look at Izzy as everyone whooped—Izzy must have been the one who told them to play this song for her. Birdie lifted her arms in the air, then dipped into a tipsy curtsy. She could hear the champagne in everyone's shouts, making them holler loud as she raised her arms again.

Unfortunately for Mom, all that ballet training she'd sent her daughter to had prepared Birdie to execute all the latest dance crazes perfectly. Birdie knew all the steps to the Black Bottom.

She'd seen the help that had been hired to cater one of her parents' parties moving their hips and calling out the steps to each other as they cleaned up after, making each other laugh. She'd snuck downstairs, admired them, and asked them how it went, and they'd gamely showed her the moves. Birdie did a quick step, shimmying her shoulders, and Mom's face tightened predictably. Birdie flipped her hair and began to kick up her feet as Gilda opened her mouth and sang.

Girls swarmed the dance floor behind her, trying to copy her moves. Soon enough Dad was out there, highball in hand, tie loosened, asking her friends for pointers and stumbling over the footwork. David came and asked her to dance. Handsome David, that blond curl falling onto his forehead no matter how he slicked it back with pomade.

God, her life had been perfect. Before the bank had failed, David had asked what she'd think if he proposed to her, in a teasing way, and she'd giggled against his neck. She might go to Finch's an engaged woman! How romantic.

After the bank had failed—David hadn't mentioned it again. He'd hardly returned her calls.

Birdie's heart sank as the plane descended. Even if she got a kick out of performing with the circus, she'd give anything to just go back to how things had been.

She stared back into from where they'd come and wondered if she was headed in the right direction.

They landed near noon in a dusty lot with a small hangar. Merriwether went inside to talk to a man with grease on his coveralls while Oscar pulled out some soggy tuna fish sandwiches wrapped in butcher paper, handing one each to the twins, June, and Birdie.

The boys followed Merri into the hangar with their sandwiches. Birdie sat on the wing of Charlie's Jenny—whose Jenny was it now that Charlie was unable to fly?—peeled the paper off her sandwich, and took a ravenous bite. The bread was damp and unappealing, but the filling was delicious.

June plopped down beside her. "Whew, it's gonna be a long day. Coney Island to Chicago in one shot!" She leaned back and massaged her knee, sandwich in her other hand. "My leg was cramping up there, at the end of that last stretch. Good thing the range on these planes is so dang awful, otherwise Merri probably wouldn't even let us out to pee. She's a slave driver, I swear!" *I sway-ah!* June sounded like a Southern belle when she talked, though she looked anything but. Her khaki duster was soiled at the knees, goggles pushed up in her hair, lips and cheeks chapped from the sun and wind.

Birdie swallowed her mouthful and gestured to June's plane. "What kind of plane is that?"

June shot an adoring look at it over her shoulder. "That, my dear, is a Gipsy Moth."

"Never heard of it."

"It's British, a de Havilland. It's like their Jenny—a military training plane that got sold cheap after the war."

"How'd you end up with it?" asked Birdie.

June leaned in close, and Birdie noticed a smattering of light freckles on the bridge of her nose. "I stole it," she said, low.

Birdie's eyes widened, and June grinned as she sat back. "Well, I stole it at first," she admitted. "But after it was clear I wasn't gonna quit stealing it, my daddy ended up giving it to me."

It was almost as hard to imagine someone giving their daughter a plane as it was to picture June making off with one. "Spill," said Birdie. "I need the whole story."

"The whole thing?" June mumbled around a mouthful of food. She swallowed and set her sandwich down. "I wanted to fly since I was little. I was probably nine or ten, watching a parade that had three planes doing stunts—steep climbs and rolls, keeping pace with the parade below. The sun flashing off the propellers, the zoom of the engines, the wide, blue sky—oh my Lord, I wanted to do it right then and there! I didn't know you could want something that bad and never even tried it. But I just knew."

Birdie had had a similar longing when she was a child, but she'd never imagined she could fly them. She'd thought it was something girls didn't do. She took another bite, as a couple of sparrows landed a few feet away and eyed the crumbs at her feet.

"I was determined to fly from then on," June continued. "But my parents are way too highfalutin to let their daughter do anything so undignified. Fortunately my daddy bought that Moth—mostly just for show, I don't even remember him flying it—and I managed to sneak off and teach myself."

Birdie choked on her mouthful. "You taught *yourself?*"

"I couldn't *not!* I was too scared to try the stunts, but I figured out how to take off and land, and the basic in-between stuff. Heard about a race happenening the next town over and took off for it in my daddy's Moth. Believe it or not, I placed! In a regional competition, but still. That's how my parents found out. They were *not* impressed—but they did end up coming around. They even paid someone to teach me, since they figured there was less of a chance of me killing myself that way." June picked her sandwich back up and took a bite.

"How thrilling." Birdie sighed. June's story was so fun—a spunky tomboy taking off in her daddy's plane while her prim parents fanned themselves back on their plantation.

"They might've had some regrets when I took off with a flying circus—but they'll be all right. They're making peace with the fact that I'm gonna do what I want, no matter if they approve or not." June sounded a little wistful as she looked away.

"They don't sound so bad," Birdie said. "They let you do what you want."

June laughed shortly. "I'm not the daughter they want me to be, but they've resigned themselves to that, for the most part. And my sister more than makes up for me." June's face brightened.

"She's the type that screams at mice and won't walk through a puddle unless some fella puts his coat down. My parents get to take out all their fussing on her, and she just eats it up." June gestured with her sandwich. "Enough about me. What's your story?"

"Sort of like yours." Birdie shrugged, a flutter of nerves in her stomach. Anything she could think to say beyond that seemed like too much. "I always wanted to run away with the circus," she managed.

"You fly as well as you dance?" June popped the last of her sandwich in her mouth.

"I've never flown a plane."

June almost choked. "*What?*"

"My dad said it was too dangerous." How silly that sounded now.

"You'll wingwalk on a plane some sap you don't know is flying, but flying it yourself is too *dangerous?*"

Birdie laughed. "That makes no sense, does it?"

June crumpled her sandwich wrapper into a ball. "Bennie said you came asking about Oscar's new Jenny?" She tossed the ball into the air and caught it. Tossed it again.

Birdie fidgeted with the last of her sandwich. "Oh, that. My dad had a plane just like that Jenny, is all." She threw it on the ground and watched the tiny brown birds cautiously hop closer.

"Your dad had a plane, too—that makes you either a rich kid or a poor performer's kid."

Which best described her now? "I grew up well off."

"I figured." June winked. "You don't look like the starving performer type to me."

Birdie put a hand to her messy hair and attempted a coy smile. "Oh really? I was sure I was beginning to make a convincing hobo, three days in the same outfit and no soap!"

June grinned and nudged her with her shoulder, and all of it—the wink, the smile, the nudge—made Birdie feel warm. Of course they weren't *flirting*, but something about their banter gave her the same thrill.

"It's funny how this business is full of runaway rich kids. Every pilot I know is, practically. Except for Hazel." June picked up Birdie's wrapper, tore it in two, and crumpled the two halves into balls. "You'd never guess she grew up poor, with a hundred siblings. I still don't know how she convinced some guy to teach her to fly, then got herself a plane, then got into racing and stunt-flying, all with no money or credit or anything! I'd never have managed, if I had to work as hard as she did." June picked up her wrapper as well and juggled the three makeshift balls. Around once, around twice—"So your folks are rich. Do they know you're here? Or, let me guess. Y'all the type of folks that leave out certain information if it might bother someone unnecessarily."

Birdie's swallowed her smile and had to cough it back up. "Might have left a few details out." She coughed again as she stood up, scattering the sparrows. "Gosh, I'm thirsty. Think they've got some water in there?" She gestured toward the hangar.

"Let's go take a gander." June dropped the sandwich wrappers in the dust. "I'm parched myself."

Birdie followed June toward the hangar, throat tight. It was over two days since she'd seen Mom. No phone here, in the middle of nowhere, but they'd be in Chicago tonight, where there should be plenty of them. Birdie'd call then. She owed her mom that.

The night before he left, Dad had put on the gramophone, twirling her around the parlor after supper while Mom watched from the chaise lounge. He had spun her around and around, until the whole room seemed like it was falling to pieces and she fell over laughing. When the room had stopped spinning everything was still where it was supposed to be. Dad was still there. The room was still there, and the house around it. The bank was still there, still supposedly full of money, just down the street. He had acted like nothing was wrong.

Wouldn't you tell a person that something so terrible and big was about to happen, even if it would bother them? Wasn't that too much information to leave out, just to make sure no one got upset?

CHAPTER ELEVEN

BIRDIE STUMBLED OUT OF THE FRONT COCKPIT ON CRAMPED LIMBS WHEN they landed for the final time. John, his cheeks red from the wind, gave her a hand. They had stopped two more times to refuel, and now the sun was setting.

The others stretched their legs and lit cigarettes. June offered Birdie a drag as she approached, but Birdie shook her head. She was light-headed, having eaten nothing since lunch, and the smoke would make her fall right over. "This isn't Chicago," she said, unable to keep aggravation out of her voice. An expanse of flat pasture and trees was interrupted only by a single house, a barn, fences, and a rough, empty stretch of road. "I thought we were going to Chicago tonight."

"We're just outside of Elgin," said June. "Chicago's within an hour's drive. We're staying here through the audition, with Merri's aunt. The fields are great for practice."

Birdie's irritation flared hotter. An *hour's drive* to Chicago? "We're staying here, in this—this cow pasture? The *whole time?*"

June raised her eyebrows. "My, my, Miss Prissy. The beds are comfortable, and Henrieta's a swell cook. You're gonna be just fine."

Birdie bit back a tart answer. Chicago was supposed to be jazz singers and speakeasies. It was supposed to be bright lights and slick hotels. It was tall buildings and fast cars and big crowds. If Dad was anywhere around here he was in Chicago.

She had been promised *Chicago*.

Birdie was hungry and tired. Hopefully tomorrow this would seem like a fun adventure again, and not just a giant mistake.

Merriwether put her cigarette out and cut purposefully through the field toward the white farmhouse, motioning for them all to follow. As they approached, a woman with wild, frizzy white hair slammed the front door open and starting hollering. She hugged Merriwether and then went for the twins, squeezing them and pinching their cheeks and calling them *"Babisiu!"* and *"Myszko!"* with an accent Birdie didn't recognize. The whole place stank of vinegar and woodsmoke. What looked like a thousand cabbages were piled up against the house, and empty mason jars were scattered on the porch in untidy piles.

The woman introduced herself as Henrieta, Merriwether's *ciotka*, or aunt. She gave them each a sour-smelling hug and exclaimed that they were as welcome as her own family, insisting they help themselves to her cords of firewood stacked on the porch and make a fire while she scrounged up something to eat. Merri ordered the twins to drag the chairs on the porch down next to a pit in the yard as Oscar grabbed some logs. Birdie excused herself to the outhouse, and by the time she came back Oscar had started a small fire and Henrieta, her hair now pulled back in a respectable bun, had brought out a few loaves of fresh bread, a crock of salty butter, and a hard salami. They sat around the fire and munched the bread, lips glistening with butter. June cut off pieces of salami with a pocketknife and passed them around. Birdie had never tasted anything so salty and warm and chewy and sweet as that bread and butter and salami, and it went a long way towards cheering her up.

Tomorrow. Everything she needed to figure out, she would figure out tomorrow.

Henrieta launched into a story about how a couple of girls had stayed with her during last year's Powder Puff derby, and how one tomfool girl had went and crashed her plane into the lone tree standing in the middle of Henrieta's pasture. "You stay yourselves on the ground after you've had some of my *trunek*," warned Henrieta. "Some can barely walk, much less fly, after drinking it—but for some reason people get some daft idea in their head for a stunt, and next thing you know—"

Oscar asked to sample the hooch. Henrieta brought out a jug and then went to shut the chickens in for the night. Oscar tasted it and gave it his nod of approval, then passed it to June.

"We'll meet up with Hazel tomorrow," said Merriwether. "She's at a boarding house near the Curtiss airfield in Glenview. We'll tell her—about Charlie. She might have ideas for a new set, or maybe we could ask the other girls." She popped a piece of bread into her mouth and chewed for a moment, then asked, "Anyone had any thoughts?"

"Nope," said Oscar. "Hazel's brilliant, though. You know she'll come up with something."

"I'll check in with the folks at the boarding house tomorrow," June said. "See what their take is."

"Yeah, June's gonna check in with Ruth first, I bet," said Oscar, teasing. "She's gonna find her so she can just, oh, get her opinion." June didn't respond, just took a swig of hooch and gave him a dark look.

"How about you two?" asked Merriwether, nudging one of the twins.

"If you'd let me fly in the show, I'd find a way to save it," he said, cheeks chipmunked with bread, and the other twin snorted.

"Yeah, John will get us the contract by crashing straight into the stands."

"'Youngest Pilot Ever Allowed by His Own Mother to Fly Dangerous Stunts!'" Oscar swept his hand across the horizon as if gesturing to a marquee. "I bet that would catch someone's attention."

"We flew all day with nothing better to think about, and *nobody* came up with anything that won't get me jailed for negligence?" Merriwether huffed. She looked at Birdie. "How about you?"

"New girl never even saw an air show before ours," drawled June. "She's got nothing."

Birdie shot her a look. "You don't *know* that!" she protested, but she hadn't thought about it all day.

Merriwether sighed and tore off another chunk of bread.

Henrieta came and told them that she'd made up the usual rooms for them—and realizing that she'd forgotten Birdie, Henrieta told her she'd make up the daybed in Merriwether's room, which was right inside the front door. "You are small enough," she said, patting her shoulder reassuringly. "You will sleep very good."

Birdie thanked her. Anything would be better than that horrid mattress she'd slept on last night.

Nobody went right to bed. Merriwether invited Henrieta to share a pipe. June and Oscar passed the gin back and forth, their voices getting louder, while the twins stifled their yawns, fighting their obvious tiredness.

Birdie wasn't ready to go to bed, but she didn't feel much like talking. She stood up stiffly, her antics on the plane the day before catching up to her. She was used to dancing for hours at a time—much longer than yesterday, when there was a show coming up—but adrenaline and wind and gravity all made wing-walking a different kind of exhausting. She walked through the dark field to Charlie's plane, pulled a blanket out of the Jenny, and wrapped it around her shoulders. Sneaking past the fire and onto the porch, she propped herself up against the wall of the house with her ankles crossed.

She tugged the blanket close against the chill and watched Oscar and June gesture by the fire, the twins listening earnestly to whatever story they were telling. She watched Oscar smile, skin gilded by firelight. The sadness that had hung around him since Charlie's accident was gone—or sodden with enough alcohol, at least, that it didn't rise off of him in waves. She watched his striking eyes crinkle up at the corners. His full lips. Thick, short lashes. Big white teeth flashed when he smiled. Broad, strong hands.

She saw how he looked when Hazel was mentioned, the way his face lit up. She got the sense that Oscar was stuck on the mysterious girl they were meeting up with tomorrow, no matter how flirtatious he'd been with Birdie.

June was a strange girl. Birdie hadn't ever met anyone like her. She sat like a boy, and Birdie could swear she flirted like one, too, but she wasn't a tomboy in the way that it was fashionable to be. Birdie had thought there were two types of girls in the world—good ones and rebellious flappers who wore short skirts and smoked cigarettes. She'd thought those were the options. But June was something else entirely. Something tall and challenging and—fascinating, really.

Birdie closed her eyes and imagined June watching her dance across the wing, her green eyes staring into her.

You looked real pretty up there . . .

Charlie was falling again. This time Birdie saw it in slow motion, and she willed the parachute to open. She could make it open, if she just believed hard enough. The parachute would open. Any second, it would pop open. Any second, everything would be okay. Everything would happen like it was supposed to.

She turned away right before Charlie hit the sand. She stared at the ocean and kept believing. He was still up in the air. If she didn't look, he could still be up in the air. There was still a chance the parachute would open.

When she turned back he would be standing on his feet, waving at an adoring crowd.

Birdie woke with a start, her mouth like cotton. June was standing over her, a lean shadow. Smoke was curling up from the fire's embers into the dark sky. Everything below the tree line was black.

Everything was quiet.

June squatted down, and Birdie's breath caught in her throat.

"Hey," June said softly. "Everyone's gone to bed. You want a hand up?"

June extended a hand and Birdie reached out. Their hands caught, and June pulled Birdie to standing. They were inches apart, their toes almost touching. June held her hand.

June turned and led her toward the door. Birdie's heart was thumping in her chest. She couldn't say why. She was on the wing again, and each step she took was one step closer to a drop into the unknown.

June made sure the screen door didn't make a sound as it shut behind them, her hand still clasped in Birdie's as she turned to face her again.

Birdie felt June's fingers loosening. She realized, the dream-fog clearing from her mind, that they were standing in front of the bedroom door Birdie was supposed to sleep in. June had walked her inside to make sure Birdie found her way to bed and didn't sleep on the porch all night.

"Sweet dreams, Birdie," said June softly, releasing her hand.

She turned and walked away. Birdie's hand fell to her sides as June crept down the hall, then up the stairs.

Birdie tried to orient herself. There was the floor beneath her feet, the wall against her hand, and the doorknob within reach. It felt like she had still been sleeping and was just now waking up.

She opened the door. Merriwether was sprawled out on the bed, snoring lightly. Birdie went straight across the room and lay down in the narrow daybed, made up with a blanket and pillow, her eyes wide open.

She imagined June lying in her bed upstairs, her breath coming fast, too.

CHAPTER TWELVE

THE MORNING SUN CUT INTO THE ROOM AT A SHARP ANGLE AS BIRDIE woke. She rolled over groggily, gaze coming into focus on Merriwether's unmade, empty bed. Birdie rose stiffly and shuffled to the door, wiping sleep from her eyes. She heard voices coming from the back of the house and followed them down the hall, raking her hopelessly tangled waves into some semblance of a braid.

At the kitchen door she paused, the disorienting heat she'd forgotten from last night flooding her when she saw June sitting with Oscar, Henry, and John on long benches at a splintered wooden table. They devoured thin pancakes that a red-faced, frizzy-haired Henrieta tossed from the griddle into a great pile in the middle of the table. The griddle sizzled and spat, and the air was filled with a sweet steam. Oscar glanced up at her, chewing. "Birdie!" he exclaimed, around a mouthful of food. He motioned to the bench next to him. "Sit! Eat yourself some food!" His good mood from last night seemed to be lingering.

June nodded to her, but when Birdie sat down across from her the pilot seemed preoccupied, fixing her gaze on her plate as she spread jam on a pancake. Birdie made herself relax and make small talk with the boys. She pushed the feeling of those long fingers intertwined with hers from her mind, and gradually she could look at June again without feeling strange. Nothing had happened—just a disorienting, half-awake dream.

Henrieta turned to throw a few more pancakes on the table. She clucked when her eyes landed on Birdie. "Is that dirty dress the only clothes you have?" When Birdie nodded ruefully, Henrieta shook her head. "My daughter left some clothes here when she married. I'll dig them out and you can see if they suit. And there's a tub in the attic—you look like you could use a bath. Oh—there is a phone as well." Henrieta gazed at her, and she could feel the old woman measuring her—the make of her dress, the youngness of her face. "There's someone you should call, to let them know you're here?"

After breakfast, Birdie lifted the black receiver of the phone in the front hall, then hesitated.

Izzy's face jumped to Birdie's mind. Her wide, dark eyes, her crazy laughter. Izzy would *die* when she knew what Birdie was up to! She'd look at Birdie in that admiring way again, instead of avoiding looking at her at all.

Birdie should call home first, though, and let Mom know where she was.

Mom might accuse Birdie of running away like Dad did. *"I had no husband, and now I have no daughter. You disappear like that, you are dead to me."* She might have already left Glen Cove and headed for Aunt Annie, one-upping Birdie by abandoning *her*. She might have been hoping that Birdie would choose to go upstate so she could escape to England on her own.

She might be glad Birdie was gone.

Birdie dialed Glen Cove with trembling fingers.

"The Fletcher residence, please."

The operator connected her.

"Izabel Fletcher speaking."

"Izz," said Birdie urgently. "It's me."

Silence. Then, "Birdie." Birdie felt no texture to Izzy's voice, no ripple that indicated pleasure or distaste. "You haven't been at rehearsal."

Birdie plowed right in, talking fast—she shouldn't dally long-distance on someone else's phone. She told her how she'd gone to look for Dad at the show, Gilda-from-Chicago's picture, how Darlena had left and Birdie had volunteered to take her spot—

"You didn't!" gasped Izzy. "Birdie!" Birdie thrilled at the note of admiration in her voice. Izzy was warming to her, she could feel it.

"This pilot, Oscar, is sweet on me," said Birdie, low, hoping to hook her even more—without anyone overhearing. "You should hear the sorts of things he says to me!"

"Oh." Izzy's voice sounded disappointed.

"What?"

"Well, David?"

"Oh, well. David hasn't seem so interested since—since school ended." But all of a sudden she remembered the breadth of his shoulders, the assuring press of his kiss. His tone half-serious when he'd teased about getting her a ring.

"Really? He's been going on about you. Went over to your house, apparently. To tell you he didn't care what his parents thought, but then you weren't there."

"He did what?" said Birdie, startled.

"Very romantic, the way he tells it! He's very torn up about it. Monty's made terrible fun of him."

"Oh." Birdie should feel more, shouldn't she? David had been husband in her perfect plans. Columbia and Finch's, the flat in New York . . .

"David's not the only one who misses you," Izzy said hesitantly. "You should come back."

"Oh," Birdie said, hope flaring. She cleared her throat and began again, lightly. "I'm coming back, don't you worry. I just . . . I might as well see if I can track Dad down since I'm here."

Izzy made a scoffing sound. "Remember what my mom called your dad, after we went to see *Peter Pan?*"

"'The boy who wouldn't grow up,'" said Birdie. Of course she remembered. Dad had loved being compared to the star of the show, even if Izzy's mom had said it to dig at him.

"Remember how we almost *died*, watching them fly through the air?"

Birdie remembered how they'd clenched each other's hands so tightly. "And how! It was terribly disappointing, to find out it was all cables and line."

"Mom's called him that ever since. And you 'Tink,' when she's annoyed with you fawning over him."

Birdie grinned. Izzy had told her that before. "I don't mind. Tink doesn't need happy thoughts to fly—it just happens naturally."

The line went fuzzy, rustling. She heard Izzy's voice at a distance—she must be holding the receiver to her hand and talking with her mother. After a moment: "I have to go." Izzy's voice was too loud, too formal.

Birdie sighed. "It was good to talk." *Like we used to. Like we're still friends.*

"It was really good," Izzy whispered. "You're coming back, aren't you? Soon?"

Birdie's heart lifted. "Soon."

"Good." A soft pause, then: "'Bye, now!" Brightly.

The connection went dead. Birdie gasped, like a line had been cut. She was falling through empty air again after a moment of being held aloft, weightless.

When she looked up, Oscar was leaning in the kitchen doorway, looking rumpled and sympathetic. "You okay?" he asked. "You want to go on a walk or something?"

She hadn't said anything untrue. He *had* been flirty. He was flirting right now, whether he was in love with Hazel or not. "That sounds lovely," she said sweetly, feeling revived. "Let me freshen up."

He told her meet him outside, and she put the receiver down as he pushed through the screen door. Her fingers lingered on the phone, heart accelerating. She *should* call Mom, she knew it.

Birdie picked up the phone again quickly, before she could change her mind, and asked to be connected to Glen Cove, to the Williams' residence.

The phone on the other end rang and rang, but no one picked up.

CHAPTER THIRTEEN

"So tell me more about this tryout," said Birdie. She and Oscar walked down a path in a strip of woods that lined a stream. It felt incredible to be clean, her scalp scrubbed and hair damp, wearing fresh clothes. But although Henrieta's daughter's old dress was a pretty cornflower blue, it was homespun and worn, like nothing Birdie had ever owned. It was too big to boot, the shoulders loose and the skirt hanging almost to her ankles. She was sure she looked quite plain. "What's it for, again?"

Oscar scuffed his lace-up oxfords along the dirt path. They were grubby but the leather was fine and matched his belt. His knit pullover had a hole in the pocket but was also well-made. "The NAR—the National Air Races. It's a big trade show for all the airplane manufacturers and such, and there's races of all kinds—speed, agility, those sorts of things. And then—drumroll, please—there's the circus show!" He hopped up and tapped a tree branch as they passed beneath. "You wouldn't believe who's supposed to be there! Lindbergh, Earhart, Louise Thaden . . ." He jumped up and tapped another.

"Wow," said Birdie, impressed. Those pilots were so good they were celebrities. It was crazy to think she could meet them—not that she was staying with the circus that long. She wondered why Mom hadn't answered the phone. "No wonder you're so set on getting that contract."

"It's not just that," said Oscar. "They say there's Hollywood agents that come to the NAR, scouting for stunt pilots for the movies! Can you imagine? It's Hazel's and my dream to do something like that."

"I have an idea." Birdie reached up to brush her fingers against new leaves that hung above the path. "A stunt that might nab the contract." The idea had come to her after talking with Izzy. It made sense in her head, but she had a feeling it would sound pretty screwy if she said it out loud.

"What are you thinking, pretty bird?" asked Oscar. "What sort of stunt?"

Pretty bird. The familiarity of her old pet name made Birdie feel warm, and she decided to run it by him. "Did you ever see *Peter Pan?*" she asked, and told him what she'd been thinking.

Oscar listened, eyes wide, as she detailed the stunt and a plan for a show to go with it. When she was finished, he nodded thoughtfully. "We can get thick enough wire, I'm sure," he said. "I'll take the Studebaker when Bennie and the others get here, and find a hardware store. We can make you a harness out of one of the parachutes." His forehead furrowed. "I've never seen this done before. There's a lot that could go wrong."

Birdie forced a light tone. "It's more exciting if there's a chance I could actually die, right?"

"I did say something like that, didn't I?" He laughed uncomfortably. "Well, if you think you've got this, I believe in you."

They strolled quietly through the bright, almost-summer woods.

"Do you really think you can pull yourself back up?" Oscar asked finally. "I mean, from dangling under the plane? So we can land?"

Birdie grabbed a low-hanging branch. "I got the record for arm strength for girls in school." She did chin-ups, counting as she did it. "One, two, three . . . ten, eleven . . ."

A slow smile spread across Oscar's face. He lunged at her, tickling her armpits. "All right, all right, show-off! I believe you!"

She squealed and twisted, letting go of the branch. Oscar's hands stayed around her waist as her feet hit the ground and she stopped squirming. Their eyes locked and Birdie didn't look away. For a breath Oscar held her, her hands clutching his arms. His eyes were brilliant blue in the dappled light.

He exhaled in a rush and stepped away, and Birdie straightened her faded blue skirt with a last hiccup of laughter, no doubt in her mind that he was sweet on her. "You're right. I'm a terrible one for showing off." She skipped down the path ahead.

"Well, so far I'm impressed," he said. Birdie threw a smile over her shoulder, but he looked quickly and kicked a rock down the path.

Of course he was feeling conflicted. There was Hazel, after all—the *incredible* Hazel, no less. And they were going to meet up with her that afternoon. Birdie stopped to wait for him to catch up, refusing to feel guilty. It wasn't her fault Oscar was attracted to her.

Oscar stopped, squinting into the underbrush. "What in the—" He grabbed her hand and pulled her off the path. She stumbled into the bushes behind him, and for a moment she thought he couldn't resist the pull between them, that he was about to take her in his arms—

He stopped short and whistled low. "You see that? What is it?" he said.

Bones. Big bones crumpled next to a rocky outcropping. Flesh had rotted away, mostly, exposing a white lattice of ribs, a grimace of teeth. A harness. A bridle and reins.

"Holy mackerel!" murmured Oscar.

Harness shredded—reins like worn-out wire—

She fumbled for Oscar's arm, suddenly light-headed and shaky.

"Hey," he said softly. "Hey, it's all right." He pulled her against his chest and squeezed her gently. "It's just a skeleton, Birdie. Whatever happened, it's been gone a while."

She was so heavy, so much denser than air. Wires could snap, the harness could fail. She could fall from the sky.

In stories, people just flew—all they had to do was believe hard enough, and it happened. In reality it took harnesses and wires. It took big wings and engines. It took luck.

It took a lot to fight gravity and win.

She'd pieced the story together from the rumors. Dad had invested a whole bunch of other people's money—her schoolmates' parents' money—in the stock market, so he could make some extra cash for himself. He bought shares, and the price went up, and then he sold them, and he kept the difference.

But then the market crashed, and the money was lost. He didn't even get the original amount of money back. He got less.

Much less.

Apparently lots of people had done it—all sorts of bankers and investors. It was a thing that plenty of upstanding people did. Mom said it wasn't a bad thing to do at all, so long as the market held. Dad had just been unlucky, like a lot of others had been. Even losing all that money—he could have eventually gotten it back and replaced it without anyone knowing, through regular bank business. But someone at the bank found out that Dad lost all the money, and they'd told somebody else—and once it got out, everyone in town went and tried to take their money out of the bank at the same time, and the bank ran out of money before hardly anyone had gotten theirs.

That's how a bank failed.

That's how Dad's bank had failed.

She and Izzy were going to get money from Dad for an egg cream at Henry's Luncheonette before ballet. Izzy's voice trailed off as they came around the corner of Glen Street and caught sight of the bank's shining white columns and gleaming plate glass. A huge crowd surrounded the double doors, shouting and banging and rattling them, their collective voices a roar. It was very strange that the doors were closed and locked during business hours. The people—they seemed angry. Furious, even. Worse—they seemed frightened. Birdie's insides twisted up.

"What's happening?" asked Izzy, her voice high. "Why aren't the doors open?"

"I'm sure it's nothing," said Birdie, forcing herself to keep walking. "Remember when we saw that dog lying in the road last summer, and we thought it was dead? We were hysterical! But then when we rushed up to it, it turned out to be just dozing. It's like that. Maybe the door broke and they can't get it open."

Maybe, but it didn't calm her nerves one bit. They approached slowly. Other girls and boys from school were standing on the outskirts of the crowd, curious.

"It's the Williams girl!" Birdie heard a voice call out. A man broke off and strode toward them, his mouth set. She almost didn't recognize him—Mr. Greene, who owned the grocery around the corner. Every other time she'd seen him, he had a broad smile and a sweet for her.

Birdie drew herself up, trying to mask her sudden panic. "Hi, Mr. Greene," she said, sweet as she could manage, but it came out a squeak.

Mr. Greene bent down so his face was right in front of hers, and she recoiled. "You tell your dad it's no use avoiding this," he spat. "He thinks he can just lock the doors and leave?" His eyes narrowed. "That's *our* money in there. We got a right to it, no matter what. Bobby Williams owes us *all* our money, not a cent less."

"I don't know . . . what . . ." Birdie's eyes went wide as she looked around. Most of the people still crowded around the doors, but a good few were closing in on her and Izzy.

Izzy turned suddenly and strode away, clutching her books, with her head down. Birdie started after her, but a woman grabbed her arm, fingers pinching. "That's why you put your money in a bank! To keep it safe!" The woman was hysterical. "So you can get it back whenever you need it!"

"Izzy, wait!" But Izzy was almost to the corner of her street—and then she was gone. The spring air suddenly felt icy on Birdie's neck.

A crash splintered the air, then a cheer. Birdie whirled and saw that one of the pretty triangular windows beside the doors had broken. A brick sailed through the air, shattering another.

Mr. Greene stabbed Birdie's chest with a finger. "You go find your dad, and you tell him he owes us," he said. "Tell him we're looking for him."

Birdie stepped away from him shakily. "There's been a mistake, I can see that. He'd be happy to talk with you, I'm sure." Birdie turned and pushed through the people closing in.

She'd find Dad and he'd have some way to make everybody happy. He knew how to put a check in anyone's hand, a smile on anyone's face. Birdie broke into a run. She'd find him. She was sure he could fix everything.

But she didn't find him that day, or since—and everything had only gotten worse.

Bennie, Colette, and Milosh pulled up in the Studebaker in late morning, as the boys roasted sausages in a skillet over another fire for lunch. Bennie complained of engine trouble that had begun about a hundred miles outside Elgin, but they had managed to get there all right.

Oscar winked at Birdie as he asked Merriwether if he could use the car to go find a hardware store once Bennie took a look at the engine.

"Sure," said Merriwether. "You run your errand, and then we'll go see Hazel."

"Is Hazel in Chicago?" asked Birdie, licking the last of the sausage off her fingers.

Merriwether squinted against the bright midday sun. "Nope, she's at a boarding house in Glenview, near the airfield. Still about a half an hour outside Chicago."

"When are we going into Chicago?"

"We should go into the city this weekend," called Bennie, his voice muffled on the other side of the Studebaker's windshield.

"I was thinking we would go dancing at the Mayfly again," said Oscar.

"I love that place," said Merri. "Maybe Friday night?"

Friday? It was only Monday now. "Can I get a train into the city from Glenview?" asked Birdie.

Merri gave her a funny look. "Today? You wouldn't make it there and then back to Elgin before the trains stop running for the night."

"You should wait till Friday," said Oscar. "I'll give you the grand tour."

She *had* to go into the city. She just knew Dad was there. But she was excited about her idea for the audition. What if the circus got the contract, and she helped them do it? She could give herself the week. She'd go into the city on Friday and try to find him, and then the tryout was Saturday. *Then* she could figure out what was next.

John and Henry squeezed rowdily onto the blanket next to her, sausages in buns piled with Henrieta's famous sauerkraut in all four of their hands. "Oscar told us about the stunt!" Henry exclaimed in a stage whisper. "I can't wait to see!" She was pretty sure it was Henry—he was the one who always looked shyly away when she smiled at him. She tried it and sure enough, he looked away, cheeks pinking beneath his freckles.

"I'm gonna try it, too, if it goes okay," John mumbled around a mouthful of sausage. He was the one who met her gaze. It was

the most the twins had ever said directly to her, and she grinned
at their enthusiasm.

"You're going to make sure I don't fall to my death before you
have a go at it?" teased Birdie, ignoring the twisted skeleton that
sprang to her mind. She'd be fine. If they could do it hanging
from a rafter above a stage, she could do it hanging from the
landing gear of a plane.

"Mom read us that story, you know!" said Henry, mustard
smeared across one cheek.

"Maybe we can make it a whole act!" said John. "You could be
Wendy, and I could be Peter Pan! Or something?"

"What are you on about?" Colette asked from the other side
of the fire, where she was forking a sausage out of the skillet.

"Shhhhh!" said Henry, elbowing John. "Oscar said not to let
anyone hear, not just Mom!"

"All right, all right, keep it down!" giggled Birdie. Their
excitement was helping shake off the shadows. "Let's make sure
the stunt works before we plan the whole show around it."

John and Henry continued throwing ideas around, but they
kept it to a whisper, and Birdie didn't stop them. Maybe the circus
would end up with a really good show. Maybe she could find Dad
and perform this weekend *and* then go home and find everything
not so terrible as she thought it was.

CHAPTER FOURTEEN

HAZEL'S BOARDING HOUSE WAS NEAR THE CURTISS AIRFIELD WHERE THE auditions would be held. Birdie didn't have to go with the others to see Hazel, but of course she was curious. They pulled up next to a beat-up Model T in the dusty lot out front of a white three-story with porches on the first and second floors. A couple of bicycles leaned against a rack out front next to empty hitching posts. Airplanes clustered in the field beyond the house, brightly colored wings glowing in the late afternoon sunlight.

Everyone else had cleaned up in Henrieta's tub, too. Merriwether was wearing an almost fashionable, slightly tailored dress with a floral print, a hat with a ribbon softening up her square lines. Oscar was clean-shaven, wearing twill trousers and the same pullover, shoes, and belt he'd worn earlier. His freshly washed hair stuck up even more enthusiastically than before. June looked slim and fresh in a clean white button-down tucked into khaki trousers, and short, worn leather boots.

There were shouts and lifted hands from a group of men and women on the porch, and one woman jumped out of a rocking chair, barreled into Merriwether, and swept her into a hug. The girl, perhaps in her early twenties, had a straight, straw-blonde Buster Brown, her bangs hacked off well above her eyebrows, and a cigarette hanging off her lip. "Merriwether, sugar!" the girl said in a raspy smoker's voice. "I heard a rumor you got tapped to try out for the NAR spot, too. A long-shot chance for your lot, but still—I applaud your pluck."

Merriwether laughed and pushed her away. "We're gonna beat your butt, Ruth." Merriwether grinned and slapped her on the back. "It's not even gonna be a contest."

"Oh, we got us some new planes since you saw us last, so I think there might be more competition than you thought," said Ruth. Merriwether rolled her eyes, but Birdie could see her smile tighten. The girl looked at June, and a slow smile spread across her face. "Well, hey there, June," she said. "Hazel said you were coming to see me."

"Howdy, Ruth," June said coolly, but her cheeks flushed pink.

A few others crowded in boisterously, and Merriwether and June gave hugs and cheek kisses all around. Birdie and Oscar stepped aside to make room. "Merriwether and June used to race against some of these girls. Hazel still does," Oscar told her, his eyes darting around. "A bunch of them travel with the Hollbrook Flying Circus. We've competed with them for fair contracts before. We usually land them—at least we did, with Charlie. I think we've still got a shot at the contract this time, if we can get your idea off the ground."

Suddenly Birdie was less certain about her idea. Would putting on a child's play in the sky really make them serious competitors?

Oscar leaned in, lowering his voice. "I got the harness rigged up for your stunt. And we've got plenty of wire and the right gear to secure it to the plane. It's gonna go off without a hitch."

The crowd moved onto the porch, Birdie and Oscar trailing. Birdie got pushed back against the peeling railing and tripped over an empty glass bottle as she sidestepped, scattering a deck of playing cards.

A group of girls hadn't squealed like this for her since her last birthday party. She missed her friends, how they used to be before.

Through the open door, Birdie saw a girl coming down the stairs. Long wavy auburn hair cascaded over one shoulder. She had a full figure in a pinstriped, navy high-waisted dress. Her lips broke into the sunniest smile when her eyes landed on Oscar—

"Hazel!" Oscar pushed through the crowd and sprinted toward her. The girl squealed. He caught her by her waist so that her feet lifted off the bottom step.

The incredible Hazel.

Oscar spun her around and kissed her mouth, hand searching for the banister to balance.

Merriwether grabbed Birdie's hand and whirled her around, talking fast as she introduced people. CindyGertrudeHelenLucy— Birdie couldn't match faces to the names Merriwether was throwing out. None of the ladies looked the least bit like powder puffs, either.

She kept her eyes on everyone's faces instead of looking past them, to Oscar and Hazel sneaking back up the stairs, holding hands.

She looked around for June but she seemed to have disappeared, too.

"Nice to meet you, Birdie," a fellow said. "What do you fly?"

"I don't," said Birdie shortly. "Fly."

"Oh yeah?" he said. "Whatcha doing with these folks, then?"

Good question. "Excuse me," she said. She shoved her way toward the door, feeling like an awkward little sister forgotten while the older kids impressed their friends. Merriwether didn't notice when she slipped inside the house.

She shouldn't have tagged along today. She should have stayed at Henrieta's farmhouse, or gone to find the Glenview train station. She could have made her own way into town and figured out how to find Gilda and get some answers about Dad—

Birdie paused in the empty hallway and took a few gulping breaths. She would not cry.

She *would not* cry.

These people didn't know how much everyone at school used to like her, how handsome her beau was. They didn't know she was the best dancer at Glen Cove Dance Academy. They didn't know about her bright idea to save Merriwether's Flying Circus of the Air.

But after they saw her stunt at the audition—maybe they would.

She would find Dad Friday night, and she would impress everyone at the audition on Saturday, and *then* she would go home, because she didn't need these people, not really. They would need *her* after they got the contract, but they would have to find someone else. Birdie heard clanging and voices down the hall and wandered towards the sound, peering through the doors. She looked in the dining room—no one there. In the kitchen, there was just a harried-looking cook and a couple of young girls wearing aprons.

She heard voices coming from the back porch, through a screen door, and walked down a dark hallway toward the sound.

It was a bright, shiny summer evening, the light still brilliant against the lengthening shadows. June sat on the porch with the girl Ruth, smoke curling around their heads in bright, lazily ascending halos. Birdie paused in the darkness of the hallway and watched them.

Ruth's long, white legs stretched out in the sun. She held her hand over her eyes to shade them as she looked at June. She was bright and lovely, skin radiating sunlight.

June said something tersely, and Ruth looked away as she waved a hand dismissively. June leaned forward as she continued talking, her hand landing on Ruth's thigh.

Her thumb moved, back and forth against Ruth's skin. Ruth said something low, and June's hand tensed and stilled.

They both were quiet, looking at each other. It was a long look—June's eyes sad, Ruth's asking a hopeful question.

Reluctantly June slid her hand up to Ruth's waist and pulled her in, and Ruth tipped sideways, resting her forehead in the crook of June's neck. June shook her head, but then lightly brushed her lips against Ruth's blond hair.

Then Ruth turned her face up, and their lips met.

Birdie crept back down the hallway, heart pounding, not knowing what to think.

Birdie put her hand on the empty wine bottle, giggling. Music seeped up from downstairs. Mom and Dad were having a party, and unbelievably, David, Monty, and Izzy had snuck upstairs with her to her bedroom. A pilfered bottle of wine had been drunk between them, and now they were playing Bottle of Fortune. The game was Izzy's idea. Birdie knew Izzy was sweet on Monty.

She had a feeling David was sweet on her.

She knew she *had* to get the bottle to land on David. She knew Izzy would be incredibly irritated with her if she kissed Monty, when Izzy hadn't yet.

She meditated on the bottle. *Land on David,* she ordered. She wasn't sure if she was feeling anything from the wine. The others had drunk most of it, sucking it down before it had even gotten to her.

She twisted her wrist back, then spun the bottle as hard as she could. The carpet stopped the bottle's spin almost instantly, the neck of it pointing directly at Izzy.

They all laughed. "Doesn't count!" cried David. "Spin again." His cheeks were pink from the wine. He obviously wanted the bottle to land on him.

Birdie reached for the bottle but Monty's hand got there first, blocking her. When she looked up he had a wicked look in his eyes. "What if it *did* count, though?" he asked.

Izzy squealed, "No!" She sounded scandalized, and delighted. Izzy loved being scandalized.

It took a moment for Birdie to follow what he meant.
She looked at Izzy, a smile warm on her lips. Izzy was flushed.
too, her eyes black and inviting, her mouth red and sweet.
"What if?" Birdie asked.

CHAPTER FIFTEEN

OSCAR LEANED OVER THE EDGE OF THE FRONT COCKPIT AS BIRDIE SET-tled into her seat. "You ready?" he asked—the same words he'd said the first time he took her up, but this time she flinched at the note of concern in his voice.

"Sure am." Her harness was on, the straps tight around her shoulders and thighs, chest clasp winking in the sunlight. She'd pinched June's drab flight suit since she couldn't wear the harness over a dress. The suit was a little long for her, bunching around her wrists and ankles, but she still felt rather sleek in it. She'd worn bloomers under skirts for sports at school, but never proper pants—not that the flight suit counted as pants, but it had a similar look. A pair of Merriwether's goggles pinched her forehead.

"Test it first!" Oscar said urgently. "Don't just jump out into thin air, okay?"

"Of course," she said shortly. If he didn't stop, he was going to make her nervous.

"You sure you can pull yourself back up?"

"Oscar! Quit fussing. I'm serious."

Oscar looked like he wanted to say something else, but just patted the cockpit edge reluctantly before hopping into his seat behind her. Birdie fiddled with the carabiner attached to the cable that was fastened to her harness as she went over the plan in her head. She would snap it onto the spreader bar once she'd climbed down onto the landing gear. From the ground, it would be very hard to make out.

She went through all the steps in her head, just like she would before a dance performance, picturing everything going right—but now she was starting to think of all the things that could go wrong. Charlie had been paralyzed from an equipment malfunction. The cable could snap—the carabiner could open—the harness could tear—

She took a deep, shaky breath. Everyone was going to be so impressed when she pulled off the stunt.

Henry started the propeller and it whomped around a few times before smoothing out, sunlight flashing off the blades. Merriwether, Bennie, Milosh, and Colette were sitting on Henrieta's front porch, talking about the upcoming show. They were still trying to come up with a new set. Birdie could barely make them out from the far side of the field.

The plane lurched forward. Birdie stared at her knuckles as they whitened around the caribiner.

The terror she would feel as she plummeted—the cracking sound her spine would make as it snapped—

Maybe she wouldn't die, maybe she would just be paralyzed like Charlie, and then how would she get back home? She'd never find Dad—

The plane surged upward, and in what seemed like an instant, Oscar was turning the plane and leveling out. She closed her eyes.

They'll adore you for saving their show. Oscar will be so impressed he won't be able to help falling for you.

If she fell into the woods instead of the field they might never find her body—and then she'd just turn into dirt and no one would ever know that she'd been alive at all, ever tried to do something amazing—

She stood, planted her rear on the edge of the cockpit, and swung her legs around. Fields whipped by beneath them, then the dirt road, then fields again. Oscar banked around as she got her feet on the wing, the canvas scratchy beneath her bare soles. She should get herself some proper shoes if she was going to keep doing this. She walked slowly to the front edge. The weather was beautiful, the air warm and rushing in her ears. She put a hand to the strut and slid it down all the way to where it met the bottom wing, then sat carefully on the edge of the wing next to the plane's body. The wheel of the Jenny was close enough to brush it with her bare toes.

Henrieta's house was getting closer, the porch-sitters' faces turning up towards them. The Studebaker was pulling up to the house—June had gone back to the boarding house that morning to pick up Hazel for a visit, and they'd made it back just in time.

Hazel's never done something as incredible as this.

June won't be able to stop thinking about you—

Birdie leaned out from the wing, hand holding the strut tightly. The wheel blocked the direct path to the spreader bar, but there was another bar that came back from the wheel and connected it with the fuselage. She planted her foot on it, and it felt sturdy enough. Oscar had said that the landing gear was more than strong enough to hold her. She put her weight on it, swung out on the strut, and put her other foot on the spreader bar, keeping her body tucked to avoid the propeller. Deep breath in, deep breath out. She shimmied around until she was facing forward, the propeller flickering right in front of her face, hands tightly grasping the short bars on either side. She made herself uncurl one hand and grope around until she found the wire connected to her harness and followed it to the end with trembling fingers. She reached behind her. The large carabiner, heavy in her hand, clicked sharply as it closed over the spreader bar. She tugged on it to make sure it was fastened properly, then leaned away from the landing gear, letting her weight settle into the harness. As her arm reached full extension, the harness hugged her torso, pulling back against her. Nothing indicated that it would snap.

She must look crazy. They all must be watching her now, trying to figure out what she was doing hunched in the landing gear.

It would only be a little more weight on the cable and
spreader bar to perform her stunt, but it seemed like an impossible leap from where she was right now. She sat down carefully on
the spreader bar, letting her legs dangle in the wind. She had to
do it now. She'd tested the cable and harness. She had no excuse.

Birdie waved at the people on the ground, projecting a confidence she did not feel. She swung her legs back and forth in a carefree way. The motion almost convinced her that she felt all right.

No one will be able to ignore how fearless and talented you are.

Before she could doubt she pushed off the bar and spread her
arms—

Falling—for one terrifying second she was a breathless
scream—

The cable caught with a harsh jerk, and she flopped on the
end of it like a fish on a line. Her vision swung wildly from blue
sky to green earth until her panic crested and she stopped thrash-
ing. She hung limply, trying to catch her breath as the harness
squeezed her lungs mercilessly. The wind roared in her ears, tears
leaking out the corners of her eyes—but she wasn't falling.

She looked down.

Milosh stumbled to his feet. Bennie's mouth was open, pointing at her. Two figures fell out of the car doors and shaded their
eyes as they looked up—

She was hanging from the harness gracelessly. She probably
looked like a scarecrow tacked to a post. But she was flying, suspended in air, nothing between her and the ground, not even a
thin strip of canvas and wood.

No one will be able to forget you.

Birdie bared her teeth and tossed her head back. She arched
her neck and spread her arms out, kicking her feet up, energy
crackling out of all her fingers and toes.

She was a perfect shape, a half-moon suspended in the sky.

Then it was time to get back on the wing.

She relaxed, and the weight of her legs pulled her into a somewhat upright position, although the slipstream blew her backward a little. She reached over her head, following the cable up. There was the spreader bar. She tightened her fingers around it and flexed. The top of her head caught on the cable. She wiggled her head around it, but then the cable snagged over her shoulder.

She had envisioned doing a pull-up to get back on the spreader bar, but the cable was connected to her back, between her shoulders, and it was getting in the way.

She was stuck.

She grasped the bar tighter and strained, feeling all of the muscles in her arms and stomach burning as her palms grew slippery—

You won't fool anyone.

She let go, panic rising in her throat. Oscar couldn't land the plane unless she got back on the wing. She would be ground to a pulp if he landed with her dangling like this.

They'll remember nothing but how badly you messed up.

Maybe she could somersault forward and tuck her feet into the landing gear. She took a gasping breath, grabbed the bar again, and started to swing her legs back and forth. Back and forth, in bigger and bigger arcs—but the slipstream was too strong, keeping her from swinging forward very far. She wouldn't be able to use momentum to get herself up.

She tried one last big swing and tucked her knees up, carful to avoid the propeller. She contracted every muscle in her body—her arms, thighs, and stomach screaming—she squeezed every bit of air out of her lungs. She flailed her legs, trying desperately to get them through the slipstream until it pushed her in the right direction—she was almost there—

Or maybe you won't be worth remembering at all.

Someone grabbed her foot and pulled. Somehow, her foot connected to the bar. She fumbled her hands around and lifted her head, gasping for breath.

"Geez, that was close!" Oscar shouted. He crouched on the wing beside her, both cockpits empty. "You almost had it—just need a few more tries I think—but thank God I—"

"I could have done it myself," she wheezed. Everyone had watched him rescue her. "I didn't need your help."

His eyes widened behind his goggles. "I'm sure you could, but we might need to tweak—"

"Oscar!" she snapped. "Isn't there something you should be *doing?*"

He threw his hands up, then lunged for the rear cockpit.

She clambered up onto the wing and lay down, shaking as she waited for touchdown.

CHAPTER SIXTEEN

Birdie stepped off the wing once the plane bumped to a stop and was immediately tackled by John and Henry, their double hug tipping her off-balance. "HolymolythatwasINCREDIBLE!" John shouted.

"IthoughtyouwereDEADbutinsteadyou'reAMAZING!" exclaimed Henry.

She could practically see a poster with her face on it already printed. She held the image in her mind, focusing hard on it, trying to calm her nerves. She felt damp all over from a cold sweat, strands of hair sticking her to cheeks.

Colette was standing with her arms crossed, of course, but she looked impressed—a look that, for Colette, Birdie had previously thought impossible. Milosh gave Birdie a lopsided grin and a thumbs-up. Bennie was beaming like nobody's business, running his hands up and down his suspenders. Birdie let all her breath out in the *whoosh* and found herself smiling back. She'd taken a chance and pulled it off.

She squeezed John and Henry and scruffed their hair before turning to find Oscar—she should let him know that everything was all right between them. He was with Hazel, of course, bare-headed, hair pressed flat by his helmet. The air was so warm, Birdie was starting to sweat into June's flight suit again. She unbuttoned the collar and the flap as she walked toward Oscar. She actually hadn't been introduced to Hazel yet. She watched as Oscar pulled the girl in

93

close and kissed the top of her burnished head. The sun shone down on the two of them, the cover of a romantic novel. A fashion plate. A circus poster. Birdie's steps slowed, harness straps swinging.

She detoured towards the Studebaker where June was perched on the dented green hood, wearing the same trousers she'd worn to the boarding house yesterday. "Nice suit," June drawled, nose wrinkling. "Funny, I've got one the exact same make and color, but I don't remember anyone asking to use it."

Birdie shrugged. "I heard you'd gone to visit a friend—Ruth, was it?—otherwise I would've asked."

June's eyes narrowed. "I went to get *Hazel*," she clarified. "Hazel! Come on, I'll introduce you."

Hazel bounded over, grabbed Birdie's hand, and shook it enthusiastically, looking darling in another dress, mint-colored this time, which eschewed fashionable looseness and a drop-waist in favor of a trim line that flattered her curves. "That was incredible! It's Birdie, right?" Birdie nodded. "June told me all about you. I was devastated when I heard about Darlena, but now I see we've got nothing to worry about." She swallowed, eyes welling up. "Except for Charlie, of course . . ." Oscar, who had walked up behind Hazel, grabbed her hand and squeezed it comfortingly.

"I'm sorry," Birdie said. "Nice to meet you. Gosh, I'm all flustered from—I just—sorry." She sounded like a complete goof.

"It's fine," said Hazel, giving her a small smile. "Really. I know what it's like to come down from up there. Don't feel like you need to say the right thing."

"Woo-hoo!" Merriwether clamped a hand on Birdie's shoulder and flipped her around. "Jiminy, girl, give a lady some warning next time you decide to pull a stunt like that!" She steered Birdie toward the porch. "Tell me what you did up there. I figure we can expand the act. We might still just have a chance to pull off some sort of show! Come on, I need details." She gestured for the others to follow them.

Birdie let herself swagger just a little on her way to the porch. The stunt really couldn't have gone better, even if the ending had been a bit sloppy. Everyone had seen its potential.

"Okay, so the boys tell me it's a Peter Pan thing," said Merriwether when they'd all settled. Colette slammed through the screen door holding a sketch pad, and sat with her legs dangling off the porch. "You, Birdie." Merriwether pointed at her. "Give us the shortest version of the story possible, with the least amount of characters. I think a popular storyline might really give our show an edge. Make it stand out, sell it to the NAR people."

Birdie thought of where to start. "There's three children, and Peter Pan comes and takes them to Neverland."

Colette began scribbling furiously.

"Let's make it one kid."

That could work. "It'll have to be Wendy, then," said Birdie.

"Okay. So that's two characters: Wendy and Peter." Merriwether held up two fingers.

"There's a fairy, Tinker Bell."

"Forget the fairy."

"Henry wants be the fairy," said John, snickering.

Henry howled and shoved John off the porch.

"Jonathan and Henry Merriwether," boomed Merri. "Settle down. Now."

"Okay," said Birdie, raising her voice as the boys settled back on the porch, arguing under their breaths. "Wendy and Peter and the Lost Boys get in a battle with the Indians—"

Merriwether held up another finger. "Can we make the Indians just one character?"

"That would work, Tiger Lily's the main one. They also get in a battle with the pirates—Captain Hook. And he ends up getting eaten by a crocodile. And Wendy goes home, and Peter Pan never grows up."

"So we add Captain Hook, and a crocodile. That's five."

"There's ten of us!" said John. "Me and Henry can be the Lost Boys! Or pirates!"

"I'm not flying," said Colette, still scrawling something on paper. Birdie leaned toward her, trying to see what she was doing.

"And boys under fourteen aren't doing anything but helping out like they usually do," said Merriwether. "We've got four planes and the Studebaker. I think it's best if we stick to five characters."

"I'll be Peter Pan," said Birdie. She could see it now, details filling in around her face on the poster. "Me and whoever else is going to fly the plane."

"Of course," said Merriwether.

Bennie stood on the ground beside the porch, looking over Colette's shoulder and nodding. "Yeah, the Studebaker would make a great crocodile! It's already the right color, just needs a few details to get it to read crocodile to the audience."

"That's good," said Merriwether. "I'll be the pirate captain. I've got an idea for a stunt, for when Hook gets eaten by the crocodile—oh, I think this is gonna be good! But I'll need someone to fly my plane."

"I'd love to be a pirate!" said Oscar. "We can paint a Jenny brown like a ship, and paint the wings white for sails—"

"Just this once," said Milosh, then stopped as everyone turned to him, his smooth cheeks flushing. "I c-could, uh, maybe do some pyrotechnics up on the wing of the pirate ship? During a battle scene or something, like cannons firing?"

"Yes! Milosh!" said Merriwether, clapping him on the shoulder. "Now you're talking! Oscar, you fly Peter Pan. I'll pilot the pirate plane while Milosh does his fire thing—nuts, who's gonna fly me when I do my stunt?"

"There's only the four of us with licenses now," said June. "Between the four planes."

"I'll fly the pirate ship!" said John. "I can do it, you *know* I can!"

"No," said Merriwether. "Not at Curtiss airfield without a license, you can't."

"This is going to be *wild*," said Henry.

"Hazel's the best aviatrix here," said Oscar, "so I think she should be Tiger Lily. That way she gets a battle scene, so she can really shine."

"Oh my *God*," said Hazel. "If we get this contract, they're sure to advance me that new Travel Air I test-flew at the airfield last week, so I can show it off in the show. It blew my lame OX-5 engine out of the water!"

Oscar leaned in and kissed her cheek. "Every Hollywood agent there is going to be beating down your door."

"That leaves me being Wendy," said June. She shook her head ruefully. "Of course *I* end up being the girly girl."

"Oh!" exclaimed Merriwether, a light bulb going off. "To make up for it, how about you fly the pirate ship during the battle scene and stunt? Wendy's plane doesn't need to be in the air for that, I don't think. You can switch between the two."

"That works!" said June. "If we get the contract, maybe we can hire one of Hollbrook's pilots to help us out in the real show."

"This's gonna be so neat!" said Henry. "Peter Pan on one wing, Captain Hook on another, brandishing swords at each other—"

"Here," said Colette, turning her pad around. "I've got the beginnings of it."

It was a scribbled line drawing, but every detail was clear. There was Dad's Jenny, only in the picture it was painted with vines and leaves—Peter Pan's plane. Charlie's Jenny had planking drawn on it, like the hull of a ship, with sails for wings. The Studebaker had a crocodile pattern. Hazel's plane was decorated with tribal designs. June's Moth had hearts painted on the wings.

Birdie's pulse accelerated. "We could really pull this off."

"Lord, no," said June. "Don't defile my baby like that!"

"You're so talented," said Milosh, kissing Colette's cheek.

"Thank you," she said, shooting June a dirty look. "This is just the preliminary brainstorm."

"We've got until Saturday to get the bones of a show together," said Merriwether. "That gives us three days. We need to plan the acts into the story—we'll all work on that—Colette's on costuming and design—anything else?"

"If you're Hook," said Colette, "who'll be on the megaphone, telling the story?"

Merriwether broke into a sunny grin. "You, my dear. Of course!"

Colette looked startled, an unsure expression crossing her face. The unmarked skin of Colette's throat caught Birdie's eye, and the unbroken paleness of her hands. Under the scramble of forbidding images covering her skin, she couldn't be much older than Birdie.

Milosh took and squeezed her hand, his big eyes crinkling under the shiny, black hair that flopped across them. "Look at that," he said. "You get to be in charge of how the story's told."

Colette looked at him with such rawness that Birdie had to look away. She stared down at her own hands, wishing that she had someone to squeeze them and tell her she was in charge with such reassuring authority. Of course, she didn't need that like some people might. She looked up, putting on her brightest smile. "Oh my gosh, three days!" she said. "Let's get to work!"

Everyone jumped up, talking excitedly, except for Colette, who hunched back over her pad.

"I didn't know you could draw like that," Birdie said, scooting closer to watch her sketch.

"I designed all my tattoos," Colette replied. "I even inked some of them on myself."

"I didn't know you could give *yourself* tattoos." Colette was the first person she'd seen up close with tattoos. She didn't like how it made Colette stand out in a way that people judged much more often than they admired, but the images were beautiful. She wondered what she would print on her own skin, if she had been the kind of person who did things like that. "Actually, I haven't the faintest idea of how tattoos happen at all."

"You wouldn't like it. It involves needles."

Birdie imagined it like getting a vaccine—someone in a white coat injecting ink into your skin slowly, the ink spreading into a perfectly designed picture—but that couldn't be right. "I'm not squeamish. Tell me how it works."

"There are different ways to do it. An Inuit man showed me first, with a needle and ink."

Birdie didn't know what *Inuit* meant, and *needle and ink* didn't explain much.

"Then I learned how to use an electric tattooing machine, when I was in the three-ring." Colette looked up from her drawings and gave Birdie an appraising look. "I could show you sometime, if you like." Her voice held a challenging edge.

Birdie smiled nervously. Needles were bad enough—an electric tattooing machine sounded horrifying. "I could watch you give someone a tattoo?"

Colette's eyes trailed over Birdie's arms. "Or you could get one yourself."

Birdie shivered. What would Dad say, if she was covered in ink like Colette? "Oh, I wouldn't know what to get."

"I could draw something up for you. It's something I really like doing. I've drawn them up for everyone here except you, actually, but only Milosh lets me give them to him."

The old Birdie would never dream of tattooing herself. But a Birdie who wasn't going to Finch's, had no family, no money, and danced on the wing of a plane? That was the only Birdie that Colette knew, and she was curious who Colette thought that person was. "Well," said Birdie. "Draw me some pictures, and let's see what I think."

CHAPTER SEVENTEEN

BIRDIE LOOKED BACKWARD AS CHARLIE'S PLANE BUZZED AWAY FROM them, following the line of the road. She and Bennie sat in the Studebaker with the top down on the longest, straightest, quietest stretch of road they could find. June was flying the plane with Merriwether in the front cockpit. It was their first attempt at Merri's new stunt idea.

"The timing's gonna be tricky." Bennie's fingers tapped the steering wheel. "We gotta start driving as soon as we see the plane. Keep an eye out for cars coming, okay?"

"Got it." Birdie flipped forward in her seat as the plane disappeared from view.

"We gotta be at top speed when the plane is overhead. Merri will climb down the rope, and we'll try and get her in either the front or back seat. You're here to give her a hand if she needs it." His eyes flicked to the rearview mirror, checking for the plane's approach.

This stunt was going to be the big finale of the show, and ever since Merriwether had explained it Birdie had been breathless with excitement. The two of them would sword-fight on the wings of their planes, and when Birdie-as-Peter-Pan won, Merriwether-as-Hook would "fall" from the pirate ship and into the crocodile's jaws by climbing down a rope and landing in the Studebaker, driven by Bennie dressed as the crocodile.

"I didn't know Merriwether did stunts," said Birdie. "Couldn't *she* do the parachute jumps now that Charlie's gone?"

"Before the twins, before her man died in that accident, Merri used to be *the* stuntwoman," said Bennie. "She got offers from all the major barnstorming circuses, did every parachute jump in the book and then some. Every car-to-plane and plane-to-car transfer. She hung from planes by her hands, feet, and teeth. She did handstands, cartwheels, somersaults, all in the air. You name it, she did it. Once she was left with the twins on her own, though— her priorities changed. She can't risk leaving those kids behind if something happens."

A car came up behind them, slowing as it approached. Birdie leaned out the window and waved them around. A couple stared into the Studebaker, and it occurred to Birdie that they saw a white girl alone with a big, dark-skinned man. She wondered what she would have thought only a few weeks ago, before she watched Bennie play cards with the boys and help Henrieta with the dishes after dinner. She'd never spent any time with someone whose skin color didn't closely match her own, but it felt natural to be here with Bennie. She gave the couple a cheerful wave and settled back in her seat.

"Why is Merriwether doing this stunt, if she's so careful now?" she asked.

"This stunt is actually pretty safe, so long as you know what you're doing," said Bennie. "You never let go of the rope until you got a firm handhold on the car, or vice versa. That's the trick. You *never* risk a jump, hoping you'll make it. That's how you die."

"I'm glad she's giving it a shot," said Birdie.

"It's because she's excited about your show!" Bennie clapped her on the shoulder. "I hope you know, we really think this is going to give us our edge. Everybody loves a familiar story, especially if there's some kind of twist."

"You ever been a stuntman?" Birdie asked.

"Not my thing."

"Have you ever flown a plane?"

"What country do you think we're in?" Bennie asked, giving her an incredulous look. "You gotta get a license to fly a plane, and there's no flying school in the country that'll accept me. Believe me, there was a time when I tried."

Birdie hadn't considered that. She'd thought Bessie Coleman had to go to France to learn how to fly because she was dark-skinned *and* a woman, but it must have been her skin color that excluded her. Turns out, there were plenty of white women pilots. "Merriwether lets John fly around some, and he doesn't have a license," she mused. "Can't you just fly on the sly?"

"Even if someone caught him at it, nobody's gonna throw a white boy in jail for flying without a license. But they wouldn't hesitate to throw the book at me. It's not worth it. It's bad enough—" Bennie stopped, and Birdie saw a muscle jump in his jaw as he checked the rearview mirror again. "It's better, I mean, not to attract unnecessary attention," he finished.

She knew what he'd been about to say: *bad enough that I'm traveling with a white woman and her kids.* Birdie knew why Bennie and Merriwether slept in separate rooms, as well as she knew why Merriwether left the room late at night when Bennie tapped on the doorframe and asked if she wanted to share a cigarette. Birdie may have been naïve, but there were some things she knew weren't safe. A black man and a white woman in love was one of them.

A girl in love with another girl was another.

Charlie's Jenny appeared, a whining speck on the horizon.

"Time to go!" Bennie shifted into gear and floored the pedal. Birdie held on as the car jounced down the road, accelerating quickly.

"I'm glad you were able to fix the Studebaker," Birdie shouted over the wind and the engine. "It's driving just fine!"

"It was just a plugged exhaust! We'll see how it goes."

Birdie kept an eye out for cars coming from either direction, but none appeared as they whipped down the road, the plane gradually gaining on them. A rope dropped from the Jenny, swinging backward in the slipstream. Merriwether appeared, crouched on the landing gear. The plane dipped low, only a few yards above the road. It was almost on top of the Studebaker, the wind and engines a deafening roar. Merriwether grabbed the rope and swung out on it, climbing quickly down. As she got closer the rope dropped straighter, until Birdie could stand and grab the end of it as she braced herself on the front seat. She held tight as Merriwether climbed to the end.

The Studebaker engine coughed, suddenly dropping in speed. The rope dragged Birdie forward until she was hanging over the back of the front seat, her heart pounding in her ears. Merri's boots dangled over the front seat, then the windshield. "Bennie!" Birdie screamed, pulling back as hard as she could on the rope. Bennie's jaw was tight as he stomped his foot down on the accelerator, to no avail. Merri's feet hit the windshield, and she managed to hook them over and slide down the rope until her knees caught the edge. She let go of one hand, then the other. The rope whipped free and snaked over their heads as Merriwether pushed off the windshield and dropped into the front seat with a whoop. Bennie took his foot off the accelerator and their speed dropped dramatically.

"Woo-hoo!" Merri crowed. "Jesus, I forgot what a rush that is!"

Bennie honked the horn to signal to June that the transfer was complete. He didn't look happy. "It wasn't the exhaust. Dang. I'll give it another look."

"You've got this." Merri slapped his arm. "You always figure it out."

"You sure you can climb back up that rope if you need to?" asked Bennie, a worry line deep between his brows. "That really gave me a turn."

"I'll practice in the barn." Merri leaned into his shoulder. "Tie a rope to the rafters and practice climbing it. Don't worry. I'm not going to do anything stupid."

Birdie approached Dad's Jenny slowly. The words *Pretty Bird* scrolled across its yellow flank greeted her as cheerily as ever. She set down the bucket of emerald paint that Oscar had picked up at the hardware store after their big planning session yesterday afternoon. She had instructions to paint the whole plane Peter-Pan green for the tryout, and Colette would go back and add details later, if they got the contract. Birdie hadn't been thinking of Dad as much, caught up in the drama of the show, but now the memory of him calling her *pretty bird*, so affectionately—it was the breath she sucked in, and then it was in her chest, aching.

She must've been seven or eight when Dad bought the Jenny. It had a dull factory paint job. He'd it repainted as a surprise for her. When he showed her the gold and blue paint, the flourishing script meant just for her, she'd been so thrilled.

It was impossible that a father that could do something so sweet could abandon her like this.

There were lots of bankers who killed themselves. Everyone whispered about it. At first it was the Wall Street bankers and investors. She heard stories of them shooting their brains out, or jumping out of their office windows twenty stories up, or hanging themselves by their silk ties. Mom said the tales were nonsense. But there were stories in the newspapers a few times, and then one close to home: only a few towns east, they found the body of the owner of a bank that failed. He'd taken a Model T and driven it out on a country road until it ran out of gas, then shot himself in the head.

It was easy for people to imagine that guilt had destroyed Dad when the bank failed—but Birdie knew better. He was smiling and easy. He ignored what felt bad. He pretended things were all right when they weren't. He would never kill himself.

He would just run away.

The sad ache in her chest turned hard and hot. She dug the paintbrush into the paint, and it came out dripping. He'd promised her everything she wanted, told her all her dreams would come true. He'd said she was the most important thing in his life.

And then he'd run out on her.

She slapped the paintbrush across the pretty script—*WHAP*—spattering herself with paint. She slapped it across again, and again, eyes stinging. Paint struck her arms and misted her face. *WHAP! WHAP!* She dipped the brush again and kept going until *Pretty Bird* was obliterated by angry swipes of green.

She stopped, breathing hard. There. Now it could be any Jenny. There were literally thousands of them out there, all basically the same.

Not one of them was special.

"Say yes," said June.

The sun blinded Birdie as she turned. "What?" she snapped.

June took in the scene. "You sure are getting into that paint job, aren't you?" she joked, but when she registered Birdie's expression her smile melted to concern. "You okay?"

"What do you want?" asked Birdie, her tone more even, though anger still bubbled in her stomach.

June stepped to one side so Birdie wouldn't have to squint into the sun, and said cautiously, "Well, I couldn't believe you've never flown a plane before, so I thought maybe you'd want to take a stab at it?" She held up her hand, goggles dangling, expression hopeful. "We could take the Moth. They're the easiest thing in the world to fly."

Birdie's stomach twisted. She'd never convinced Dad to let her pilot the plane, and he usually gave in to her every request. "We've got a lot of work to do before Saturday."

"You can't paint in this heat. I can tell the fumes are getting to you."

Birdie almost cracked a smile. It *was* so hot. "I need a license."

"Oh, come on! Nobody's gonna fine you for flying the Moth around an empty field."

"I don't know . . ."

"You don't know what you're missing," June wheedled. "That rush you get, walking out on the wing—imagine you're not just along for the ride. Imagine you could go anywhere you wanted, fly so fast and high that no one could catch to you."

Birdie swallowed, mesmerized. "I'm not sure I'd like it," she protested unconvincingly.

"You gotta *try* it to see if you like it," June urged, stepping closer. "I think you aren't gonna be able to get enough." Birdie's eyes fixed on June's mouth, curled in a lopsided smile—*stop staring*—then she locked into June's gaze. In the sun her eyes were so green, lashes dark and short. At rest her brows curved up, so Birdie always felt like June was asking a question she wasn't voicing.

"No," said Birdie, too loudly, and June flinched. Birdie turned fast and jabbed the brush into the bucket. Her breath came short as fumes constricted her throat. "Not interested."

June let the goggles drop against her thigh. "Guess I was wrong." She shrugged. "I'll leave you to it, then."

She turned and was gone, strolling through the tall grass toward the house. She whistled a tune, and Birdie recognized it. *Five foot two, eyes of blue—but oh, what those five foot could do . . .*

Birdie resumed painting the plane in a hot fury. Sweat dripped into her eyes, her thoughts a tangled mess. She didn't know why her stomach dropped and her skin tingled when June touched her hand, or said funny things, or even looked at her.

June was a girl.

June was a girl who had kissed another girl, no games or drinking to excuse it.

Birdie paused and looked over her shoulder. June was a few yards off, bent down, picking a small, white clover. She straightened and lifted the flower to her nose.

Birdie turned away, but in her mind June's lips grazed the flower's slender petals as she inhaled its subtle scent.

What if? Birdie's question hung in the air as Izzy's eyes widened. Birdie held her gaze and leaned forward over the bottle, daring her. Izzy shook her head and looked away, biting back a smile, then suddenly came up on her knees and tipped forward—

Izzy's lips touched Birdie's, soft as Birdie imagined, full and sweet and spiked with champagne. Birdie's hand came up to Izzy's neck and touched the smoothest skin, and Birdie felt heat coiling in her belly, rising through her chest. She tugged Izzy closer and pressed into the kiss, mouth opening, breath against breath.

Monty whistled. David swore softly. Izzy's kiss turned into a laugh and she pulled away. "Oh Lord," she said, putting her forehead in her hands as she sat back down. "I must be drunk." She looked up, perfect bangs askew. "I'm so drunk. Aren't you so drunk, Birdie?"

Birdie's mind was a steamed-up mirror. "Yeah," she said, breathless, pushing hair off her face. What had just happened? "I must be."

"Enough to do it again?" Monty asked hopefully.

Birdie looked at Izzy, but Izzy pushed the bottle aside and crawled toward Monty. She pulled him in, arms twisting around his neck.

The heat Birdie felt, Izzy was putting into a kiss that counted.

David's arm snaked around her waist, and Birdie turned and followed Izzy's lead. She wasn't drunk. She wished she hadn't kissed Izzy because it made Izzy want to kiss Monty and Monty was an ass, and it made Birdie want to keep kissing Izzy all night. Forever.

Necking with David was fine. It felt good. Birdie liked David. He was the boy everybody in school wanted to go steady with. Handsome, that curl falling down on his forehead. She always felt pleased when he caught her hand.

What if?

Now she knew the answer, and wished with all her might she could forget it.

CHAPTER EIGHTEEN

A HORN HONKED IN THE DISTANCE AS BIRDIE STEPPED BACK FROM DAD'S Jenny. It was Friday and she'd finally finished painting it, in between being measured for her costume, having her photo taken for the poster, practicing aerial "sword-fighting," and fine-tuning her acts—she'd done the free-flying stunt over and over, until she was sure she could pull herself up without a hitch. The sun was low in the sky, and its light glowed through the Jenny's canvas skin. It was strange to see the plane's delicate bones illuminated, revealing how the huge machine was really nothing but a wooden skeleton with fabric stretched over it.

June's Moth, Hazel's Waco, and the two Jennys surrounded her in the field like a herd of pastured beasts. Pink hearts decorated the wings of Wendy's plane (despite June's impassioned protests), Tiger Lily's was striped in tribal designs, and Captain Hook's Jenny sported a brown hull and white wings. They weren't as detailed as they would be for the real show, if they got the contract, but the fresh paint helped tell the story. The costumes weren't completely ready either, but Colette had drummed up a few key items—a green leotard for Birdie, a pirate hat for Merriwether, a paper-mache crocodile mask for Bennie. They were ready enough for the audition tomorrow. Birdie's scalp tingled. *Tomorrow.*

The horn blared again, insistent. Birdie wiped her hands on her skirt and looked up, shading her eyes against the sun. The Studebaker's top was rolled back, its green-and-brown alligator paint job almost camouflaging it. June leaned out the back door, waving her hand at Birdie and hollering. It looked like Merriwether and Bennie were in the front seats. Oscar sprinted out of the house wearing plus fours and a V-neck sweater, pulling on his flatcap, the door slamming behind him. Birdie jumped. Tonight! They were going into the city and she'd almost forgotten! She ran toward the house.

The car was fuller than she'd thought. Hazel, Colette, and Milosh were tucked in the back seat. Milosh looked adorable, his black hair slicked back to reveal his big brown eyes, wearing a fitted Fair Isle sweater with a tie and button-up shirt under it. Colette wore a white A-line dress with a few strands of her signature sequins adorning the neckline and straps. Oscar was squeezing in next to Bennie up front, and June stood beside the car, one scuffed oxford up on the remaining back seat. "Come on, girl!" said June. "Time for some big city fun!"

"There's room for all of us?" Birdie asked doubtfully.

"The Studebaker Big Six *officially* sits seven," said Oscar confidently, "but we got at least nine of us in here back in New York one night, when we gave a lift to a couple of birds we met at a club!"

"A couple of *birds?*" said Hazel, mock offended, and leaned forward to slap his shoulder. "A lift better be all you gave them!" She laughed and kissed Oscar's cheek when he protested.

Birdie looked down and was instantly mortified. "Oh my gosh, I'm a fright!" She'd ruined the cornflower blue dress days ago with splatters of green paint. Strands of hair scraggled across her sweaty shoulders, and her knees were dirty from where she'd kneeled to paint the Jenny's underside. She could kick herself for not giving herself time to get ready to go out.

"Run inside and splash off," Merriwether told her. "Hurry up!"

Birdie ran up the steps and tore into the guest bedroom. She fumbled out of the old blue dress and worn, oversized boots that Henrieta had loaned her, and splashed her face and armpits hastily in the washstand. She pulled the dress that she'd worn from home—the lavender one with the cap sleeves and swinging skirt that hit just above her knees—out of the wardrobe. Henrieta had cleaned it sometime in the past few days. As she pulled it on, her reflection in the mirror startled her—the dress clean and pressed but her lips chapped, hair matted and wild, knees still dirty. She dampened her unruly locks and pulled them into braids, hoping it would dry in pretty waves before they got to town, and quickly scrubbed most of the dirt off her knees.

She grabbed a few dollars from her coat pocket, tucked her feet into her kitten heels, and ran outside, half afraid they would have left without her—but there they were. Colette shifted onto Milosh's lap, Hazel scooted over, and June tipped up on one hip, putting her arm over the back of the seat as Birdie squeezed in beside her. June smelled good, like licorice and spice. Birdie slammed the door shut. "Where are the boys?" she asked.

"Henrieta took them to see a movie." Merriwether shifted into gear and pulled out onto the gravel road.

"Oh!" said Hazel excitedly. *"Dawn Patrol?"*

"Lord no, I would've made them wait to see that with me—I'm gonna have too much fun critiquing all the stunts," said Merriwether. "It's just some jailhouse flick."

"How's she driving?" asked Bennie. "I replaced the throttle cable and think that did the trick. Feels better?"

"Good as new." Merri's stunt had gone off without a hitch that day. "I'm sure everything's gonna go smoothly tomorrow."

"Tonight I'm gonna take you where me and my pals used to go. It's a sweet little speakeasy." Oscar reached over the seat to put a hand on Hazel's knee. "A black-and-tan. You'll all like it." He said the last part self-consciously.

Bennie smiled. "I'm not worried." He looked dapper in a crisp white shirt and red tie, his head freshly shaven. "I been around this town before."

"I've never seen anything like it outside Chicago." Oscar raised his voice as the car picked up speed and wind whipped around their heads. "There's *all* these clubs on the South Side that cater to anyone, no matter what your color."

At any party or club Birdie had been to before, only white people ate and drank and danced. Anyone who wasn't white was working. They had to squeeze in their dancing later, while they cleaned up everyone's mess. They had to humor the boss's daughter and teach her the moves she demanded, when their work still wasn't done.

"We won't go anywhere you're not wanted." Hazel reached forward to squeeze Bennie's shoulder. "Or you, bunny," she added, patting Milosh's thigh. Birdie had never met anyone with silky black hair and brown skin like him in Glen Cove, but she had a feeling that if he had been at one of those parties, he'd have been working instead of partying, too.

"I'm not worried," repeated Bennie. "I never feel more comfortable than I do here, besides home in Nawlins."

They drove for a while, until farmland turned to neighborhoods, and neighborhoods to city. Birdie was quiet while the others chatted. She'd never thought twice about how everything was separated along color lines, but the more she noticed it, the less it made sense. Why shouldn't Bennie be able to get a pilot's license? Why shouldn't he and Merriwether be able to get married? It might not have been illegal in New York, but it was in most of the country, and even in New York there were plenty of people who thought it should be—Birdie had overheard many express that opinion.

A huge expanse of water opened up on one side as they drove over a bridge. It reminded her of the Long Island Sound, of loitering with friends down at the landing back home, of going to regattas and dances at the Hempstead Harbour Club. Workers had been pumping sand out of the harbor to create a swimming beach when Birdie left, and she had wanted to sunbathe there with Izzy so badly. Birdie hung her arm over the door, spread her fingers wide, and felt the air rush against her skin. Something didn't feel right, and homesickness rose in her throat unexpectedly. It took her a moment to put her finger on it, but she realized—it was the smell. The water looked like the sound, wide and smooth, but it must be a lake—one of the Great Lakes, maybe. It was pretty, but Birdie longed for the smell of salt in the air.

"June told me you won't fly a plane yourself." Hazel leaned in from June's far side. "I have to say, you don't know what you're missing!"

Birdie willed her cheeks to stay cool. "I—I wasn't feeling well." She glanced at June, acutely aware of the warmth where their thighs pressed together. "Sorry I was so cross with you."

June raised her eyebrows. "I didn't mind you one bit," she said laconically.

"I know wingwalking is this crazy thing," Birdie said, "but—I don't know. It's different than flying—oh, I can't explain it." She'd had a lot of time to think as she finished painting the Jenny, but she couldn't come up with why she wouldn't accept June's offer. Why was she scared? Usually she could talk herself into trying anything.

Dad was probably in Chicago tonight. He might be on the South Side, where they were headed. If he was with Gilda . . . chances were that he was, since it was a Friday night, and she was one of the hottest jazz singers in the city. Her stomach knotted up. She was here to find him—but once she found him, then what? What did she want to happen? She'd been having such a wonderful time, she didn't want to spoil it. She didn't want to remember that Dad had left her—that her whole life had fallen apart—ugh. This week had been nothing like the exciting future she'd pictured the past few years, but it was exhilarating in a totally unexpected way. She couldn't wait for the audition tomorrow. And she'd become very fond of these fascinating people that crowded all around her.

June's fingers brushed Birdie's shoulder as she reached for the window. "Feels good, doesn't it, Peter?" she said.

Birdie felt like she couldn't turn to look at her. June was too close, the tips of her hair brushing Birdie's cheek when the wind caught it. "Sure does, Wendy," she replied softly.

"Tell me the truth." Colette leaned in from Milosh's lap, her black curls swirling wildly in the wind. "Don't you secretly think that whole story is kind of terrible?"

"What? No! I love *Peter Pan*." Birdie was very aware of June casually settling her arm across the back of the seat behind her.

"The girls, though," Colette pressed. "Wendy just wants to mother everyone. Strange for a kid, right?"

"I don't know." Birdie had always adored Wendy. "Don't a lot of little girls want to be moms?"

"And then there's Tiger Lily, and Tinker Bell," Colette continued, ignoring her. "And all three of them are obsessed with Peter Pan, this boy who refuses to grow up."

"I like Peter Pan," announced June. "Who wants to grow up, anyway?"

"You're *supposed* to like him," said Colette. "He's self-centered and boastful and impulsive—but somehow, he's still cute and charming. And Wendy's so boring, always doing whatever's expected of her. Meanwhile, Tiger Lily and Tinker Bell get the crap end of the story. Tiger Lily's out in the swamp, *ruling*, but nobody cares."

"Tinker Bell gets what she wants," said Hazel. "She gets Peter to stay with her forever, in Neverland."

"That doesn't seem like much, though, does it? I wish she wanted something more than a boy too interested in himself to change."

As they approached the city seemed to rise up out of the flat horizon, growing larger and larger. Birdie stared at the buildings, wondering which one might be hiding Dad. "Wendy though," Birdie said, trying to think of something to redeem the story. "She chooses real life in the end. Neverland isn't enough for her."

"Yeah," said Hazel. "She grows up."

"You've convinced me." June laughed. "Peter never changes, and that's boring, so who cares about him?"

"Let's change the title then, what do you say?" said Colette. "'*Wendy: The Girl Who Finally Grows Up.*' Now that's a story I want to hear."

CHAPTER NINETEEN

THE SUN DISAPPEARED BEHIND THE BUILDINGS AS THEY PULLED OFF A busy main street in Chicago and down a quiet alley. The dusky, gray air was still and warm on Birdie's skin as they all piled out of the car. A well-heeled couple, looking out of place in the empty alley, disappeared through a shoddy-looking door as a couple of kids sitting on the curb looked up from their game of jacks to appraise the newcomers.

"The rich folks flock down from the coast at night," said Oscar. "Give 'em a few hours. In the meantime, we'll get the royal treatment."

They followed the couple into a dim foyer where a bored-looking man read a newspaper. Oscar mumbled something unintelligible to him, and he hardly glanced up before waving them up a narrow flight of stairs. Oscar turned left at the top, led them down a dark, dusty hall, and pushed through a nondescript door that swung open to reveal a bright, warm, beautifully appointed room with a massive bar made of polished wood and brass. In plain sight glass bottles full of clear and brown liquids sparkled in the electric light.

"Oh!" said Birdie. "Wow! You wouldn't know drinking's a crime, coming in here."

"Oh, they've got it down pat," said Oscar. "If the police show up, they just let everyone out the back door."

It seemed doubtful that the police didn't know about such an establishment. Couldn't they all go to jail just for being here? "What if the police come in the back door?"

"They just don't." Oscar walked through the mostly empty room and leaned on the bar. "Hey there, Jimmy."

The bartender looked up from the lemon he was peeling. "Oscar!" He set the lemon down and wiped his hands on a crisp white towel that hung over his shoulder. "It's been a while! Great to see you, sir." They clasped hands over the bar. "Where are the rest of your boys?" He looked the girls and Bennie over. "These aren't your usual set."

Oscar laughed. "I haven't seen Nate and them in a while, now. I ran away with a flying circus, didn't you hear?"

The man's eyes widened. "Now that you mention it—I think one of your boys did mention that a few months back. So the circus is in town, is that it?"

"We're trying to convince some people at the Curtiss airfield that we're their guys for the NAR," Oscar said, as Hazel came up and put an arm around his waist. She looked stunning, her red hair pinned up in a messy faux-bob, green cardigan tight against her curves. "Tryouts tomorrow, air show in September. You make sure and come see us!"

The man smiled at Hazel. "Oh, I'm remembering now—the way I heard it, it was a girl you ran away with, as much as a circus." Birdie turned away as Oscar answered, admiring the pretty furnishings, the baby grand piano, the high ceiling that looked like it was made of delicately wrought metal. She had to admit, the fact that they shouldn't be here gave her a thrill. She followed Merri and Bennie to a long table with enough plush velvet seats for them all to sit, and the rest followed a few moments later. A quartet was setting up on the far side of a dance floor. The well-heeled couple was settling into a small table, the woman smoothing her neatly pressed waves as the man set their coupe glasses down and pulled her chair out for her. Oscar and Hazel came over balancing a bunch of old-fashioneds in rocks glasses, and set one down in front of each of them.

"See, Bennie?" said Oscar, nodding at the couple.

"Lord, son, I see," said Bennie, waving a hand. "I feel very comfortable. You can relax now."

"I made pals with a gal at my last race who took me out to a club in Manhattan," said June. Birdie wondered what *made pals with* meant, if June had kissed more girls than just Ruth. "I was the only white girl there."

"June Delaney!" Bennie smoothed his southern drawl to mimick hers. "What a thing for a proper Georgia girl to do!"

"It was so much fun." June stirred her drink with a finger. "I never had such a time! We stayed till the sun rose. She even managed to teach me a couple of dance steps."

Merriwether chuckled. "Says you! You're worse than Colette for standing stiff in the corner while everybody else cuts the rug."

"Not true," said Colette. "I don't stand—I sit, if at all possible."

"I learned a few moves," said June, as Milosh laughed. She looked at Birdie and said saucily, "Maybe I'll teach you a thing or two once the music starts."

They sucked down their drinks, conversation flowing fast, but the music failed to inspire them to get out of their seats and the crowd stayed sparse. June mentioned that some of the girls at the boarding house were going to another club on the South Side, and Oscar said he knew the place. "Did *Ruth* say she'd be there tonight?" he teased. "Is *that* why you're so keen to go?"

"I don't know or care where Ruth is tonight," June said firmly. "It's over and done with."

The way she and Ruth had kissed on the back porch in a halo of light made Birdie think that June cared more than she'd like to admit, and everyone else seemed just as skeptical. "Oh, we haven't heard that one before," Merriwether teased, and Hazel laughed.

They ribbed June like she was sweet on Ruth—and there wasn't any other explanation, was there?

"I'm serious this time." Conflicting emotions crossed June's face that Birdie couldn't parse. It seemed like more than a kiss had passed between them.

"Awww, I'm sorry." Oscar reached across the table and gave her shoulder a comforting squeeze. "I never thought she was good for you. I just thought—"

"I know." June sighed. "I haven't exactly stuck to my word before. But I mean it this time."

"She doesn't deserve you." Milosh nudged her with his shoulder.

June gave him a lopsided smile. "Thanks, friends," she said. "Ugh, enough about her! Y'all ready to get a move on?"

The next thing Birdie knew they'd all piled into the Studebaker again and were zipping through the night-cool air.

She should ask about Gilda. This was her chance to look for Dad. But June's leg was pressed against hers again, arm across the back of the seat behind her. If she pretended to look out the window she could watch June's long fingers tap the seat, then absentmindedly catch and play with a strand of Birdie's hair when it brushed against her knuckles. Birdie looked briefly at June and their eyes met. June gave her a lazy smile that made her look away, cheeks warming. Birdie leaned into her ever so slightly when she turned to look out the window again.

Birdie had had this feeling before—a feeling with nowhere to go, a sucking tide that was hard to keep her head above when she was with Izzy. Most of the time they were best friends, but sometimes the smell of Izzy's hair, the softness of her skin, her passionate proclamations of love and friendship had made Birdie feel crazy. It had been embarrassing, too frightening to even look at unflinchingly within her own mind.

She'd never let the idea that two girls could be sweet on each other—and what might happen between them if they were—fully enter her awareness.

The possibility made her stomach tight, her skin electric.

They pulled up outside a plain brick building where a couple of girls with long feathers in their shiny marcelled hair stood outside, smoking and talking. Merri bought everyone hot dogs from a vendor and they ate them on the street. They went down another alley and in through another unmarked side door. A mixed crowd filled the speakeasy inside: pretty girls with fringe on their skirts and cigarettes in their holders, slick-haired men in suspenders, and boys with wide smiles. There was a five-piece band playing something with a brisk tempo. Pilots from the boarding house dotted the crowd, girls wearing skirts or pants, lipstick or pomade, everyone drinking gin and whiskey. Birdie spotted Ruth, looking lanky and glamorous in a shoulder-baring dress and a beaded headband, and checked to see if June had noticed her. But June went straight to the bar and ordered a drink.

So Birdie followed her.

Dancing, screaming laughter, the croon of the jazz singer, the thick smoke. Birdie hadn't danced or laughed so hard since her birthday. She tried to keep up with the tempo of the music but her feet were starting to lag, her chest burning. She had taken down her braids hours ago and her hair stuck to her shoulders, so much for her pretty waves.

Bennie and Merriwether were dancing like crazy in the center of the floor, a ring cleared around their Carolina shag in the thick, sweating crowd. Bennie was shaking his hips and shimmying his shoulders like nobody's business, everyone clapping and hooting and shouting, "Get hot! Get hot!" Merriwether's cheeks shone red and happy. Colette and Milosh lurked in a booth in the corner, heads cozily together in their own secret world.

Oscar stood behind Hazel at the bar, his hand on her waist, his lips on her neck. Hazel said something into his ear, and he smiled. They were so beautiful. So gorgeous. Oscar's hands slid up Hazel's waist and pulled her against him. Birdie looked away and caught June staring at her through her thick lashes, a halo of smoke around her head. She wore pants and that fitted shirt so well. June was dancing slowly, ignoring the upbeat tempo. Birdie felt her own feet slow. June sucked hard on her cigarette so the tip glowed red. The cherry traveled down toward her fingers, bright and rippling.

Birdie moved her body to mimic June's steps. She'd been taught how to mirror someone else perfectly, to move so similarly that the teacher couldn't find a single difference to correct. She found June's movement quickly—step touch, step touch, a little bit of hip swivel, chin up. June grinned lazily at her, took her hand out of her pocket, and step-touched over to Birdie.

"Are these the moves that girl at the club taught you?" Birdie teased.

June pressed her lips together, holding in a smile. "This ain't the half of it."

Birdie blushed as June bit the end of her cigarette, freeing her hands. "I'll show you, ready? You step back—then cross, then over—" she said through her teeth, fluttering her hands.

Birdie followed her steps, then laughed, her nerves settling. "Oh, I know this one!" she danced a few steps of the Big Apple in a circle around June.

June shook her head, amused. "I shoulda known better than to think I had something on you."

The music ended with a crash of cymbals. The crowd cheered loudly and the band struck up a slow number, a waltz. "Come on. You know you want to dance with me." June tugged on Birdie's hand. She put her cigarette between her lips, caught Birdie's waist with the other, and pulled her in. Birdie had to tilt her chin up to make eye contact, June's shoulders an inch or two above her own. June's eyes were a dark-chocolate color in the dim electric light. The crowd pressed close and sweaty, perfume and cigar smoke thick in the air. Birdie put her hand on June's hip. Her eyes met a man's that was leaning against the bar. He raised his glass to her, and Birdie tripped over her own feet.

"Hey." June squeezed her hand. "What's this? Birdie doesn't know the easiest dance of all time? Ready, count with me—one-two-three, one-two-three—"

Birdie smiled shakily and focused on the music. She didn't know what was wrong with her—usually she never missed a beat. She looked at June again, feeling shy as feet found each other's rhythm and fingers tangled. They danced, not speaking. She could hear Merriwether boom from far away, Bennie's whooping laugh in response.

Birdie thought she was familiar with all different kinds of dancing. There was fun dancing, party dancing—all performance and showmanship, all swagger and flirt. There was the formal kind of dancing Birdie had been taught—ballet, or traditional couples dancing like the fox-trot, every step a marvel of choreography and skill.

But then there was this. June held her a little closer than she had to, and Birdie found she was leaning in, too. They lingered in each sway a breath longer than necessary. Every step and spin trailed into the next as if neither of them wanted to let go, like they wanted to feel each shift against their skin as long as possible. The music was on tempo, but they hardly followed it at all. The music washed around them, and they floated together amidst it.

She had never danced like this.

It was the alcohol, those old-fashioneds. Her head was light, she couldn't quite keep herself on the beat. She had to lean into June sometimes, to keep her balance. She felt the tide rising, and it made her feel nauseous and confused and anxious and woozy like it had before, but this time it also made her feel fluttery and exhilarated and bouyant and reckless—

She leaned into June with her whole body and kissed her. A pause—lips soft and warm, the music fading out, fingers entwined. Barely touching, breathless. Then sensation rushed in—the taste of sugar and bitters, the heat and damp, the swell of music, an inhale of breath, a hand cupping her face, June's mouth tilting, softening, arms pulling her in—

And then June pulled away. "Ruth," she said.

Birdie's mind couldn't register anything but the lingering softness on her lips. She unpeeled herself from June and turned around. Ruth's face was tight.

Ugh.

No.

"Can I talk to you?" Ruth asked June tersely.

"Yeah . . . of course." June looked at Birdie and squeezed her hand. "I'll be right back," she said earnestly, then trailed Ruth as she stalked toward a back corner.

Birdie tried not to watch them go. She looked around, blinking, trying to shake off the fog. It was like she and June had been in a quiet room alone together and then suddenly a whole crowd had rushed in around them and wrenched them apart. The music was too loud, the air thick and humid.

She watched June climb into a booth with Ruth. June took Ruth's hand right away, and Birdie's stomach went hot as she remembered them kissing. The urgency between them.

She could see the same urgency flare between them right now.

Birdie looked away, anxious energy rising inside her. She'd danced with girls before, she and Izzy used to dance with each other all the time. She'd kissed Izzy and it hadn't meant anything. It didn't have to mean anything now.

Birdie had liked kissing David. She'd liked holding the hands of the beaux she'd had before that. June was the one who kissed girls. June was the strange, boyish one—not her.

Hazel and Oscar were slow dancing nearby. Birdie ground her teeth as she watched Oscar's cheek press against Hazel's. Why couldn't that be her? Why couldn't she be dancing with the handsome boy, feeling him against her cheek like that? Those blue eyes; that easy, bright smile; those broad, tan hands.

Why couldn't it be Oscar that made her head go light?

Oscar reach into his pocket. He pulled something out as he talked into Hazel's ear. Hazel's head was bent so that she couldn't see what was in Oscar's hand, but Birdie could.

It was a ring.

CHAPTER TWENTY

Birdie watched as Hazel pulled back, surprise on her face, as Oscar knelt. "Hazel Riona O'Malley—" he began earnestly.

Birdie turned toward the bar, bile rising in her throat, and suddenly the room was spinning. She stumbled and reached her hand out—

"Whoa there." The man's voice sounded far off. She felt an arm around her, then she was being settled onto a barstool. Birdie pushed him away and leaned her elbows on the bar, head in her hands.

"Hey, doll," he said. "You need some air. Let me help you outside for a minute, some fresh air will—"

"I just need a minute," Birdie said shakily. "I don't need your help." She stared down, trying to slow her breath, and after a moment her vision steadied. Birdie straightened and pushed limp hair off her forehead. She was fine. She was tipsy and light-headed and had let herself become momentarily disoriented, but it was nothing a glass of water wouldn't fix.

"Can I buy you a drink, sweetheart?"

She glanced at the man and remembered him raising his glass when June had put her hand on Birdie's waist and pulled her close to waltz, their fingers tangling—she would *not* look over at the booth where June and Ruth sat together. She didn't much feel like talking with this fellow, either, but her throat was terribly dry. She leaned over the bar. "Hey!" She waved a hand at the bartender.

The bartender glanced up from the orange in his hand, then looked back down. He carefully peeled off a sliver of rind and set it on the rim of a full tumbler.

"Nice moves you had out there," said the man.

The bartender leaned over and set the drink on the bar, nodding to acknowledge another man's order. "Excuse me!" Birdie called, and was ignored.

"Let me buy you a drink," said the man.

Birdie took another look at him. Somewhere in his late thirties, she guessed. Not so bad looking. His face was red from alcohol and his hairline was a bit thin, but he was in good shape, blond hair neatly combed. He looked like money—gold cuff links, loosened silk tie and all. He looked one of Dad's friends.

Dad could be sitting at a bar just like this, somewhere close by.

"Fine." She settled back in her barstool.

"Frankie!" The man hailed the bartender, who looked up from the big, square ice cube he was setting in a tumbler. "Can I get a gin and soda for the lady?"

"And a water!" Birdie added. *"See-voo-play."*

The bartender nodded. Maybe you had to address him by name to get him to acknowledge you. Or be wearing a suit.

"You from around here?" she asked the man, smiling pertly.

"Nope, in from Hollywood for a few weeks."

Shoot. "You know of Gilda Deveaux?" she asked anyway.

"I know that name." The man leaned an elbow on the bar. "But I'd rather know yours."

Birdie smiled and forced herself to lean in as well. "You know where she sings in town?" She trailed a finger along the bar.

"Saw her myself just last night at The Midnight," said the man, and Birdie's pulse quickened. The bartender set a fizzy drink at her elbow. No glass of water. Birdie would have sworn at him if she wasn't so focused.

"Now that was a hot show," the man continued. "What I remember of it, anyway! One thing's for sure, they know how to pour a drink over at the Midnight."

"I want to see her," said Birdie. "Gilda Deveaux. I hear she's the berries." She picked up the drink and put it to her lips, holding his eyes as she drained the glass. She set it carefully back on the bar. "I'd go right now, if someone would take me."

"Would you now." The man appraised her, and she couldn't guess what he must make of her—fine silk dress, scraped-up knees, dirt under her fingernails. "I'll take you over to The Midnight, if you like. It's Friday night, and she's their regular act on the weekends."

"Oh, would you?" Birdie's heart started pounding. "Why, that'd be just ducky."

"You gotta tell me your name first," the man said. "I'm Sinclair."

Birdie heard Bennie exclaim behind her, and Oscar's voice raised jovially, but she refused to look. Hazel was probably holding out her hand so that Bennie could see the ring, and Merriwether was crowding in to see it. Colette and Milosh were standing up in their booth to see what all the fuss was about. June probably wasn't even noticing, lost in a dark booth with Ruth.

"Nice to meet you, Sinclair. I'm Birdie." She pushed the glass away and put a hand on his starched elbow. "Let's go, shall we?"

Birdie ducked her head and clung to Sinclair's arm until they'd exited the club, half hoping no one would notice her leaving— and half hoping someone would. But no one came out as they waited, shivering in the quickly cooling air, for the driver to bring Sinclair's limo around, and she was glad she had this chance to track Gilda down.

It was a very nice limousine, the glow of the gas lamps reflecting off its glossy surface. "This is so swank!" Birdie exclaimed as the driver opened the door. She climbed to the far side, and Sinclair followed her in. Its leather smell made her miss Dad's Duesenberg. It made her miss nice cars in general. And drivers to take you places, and dancing, and flirting, and going on dates— all the things she'd been too busy to miss since she'd joined the circus. Sinclair himself might not have been ideal, but it was nice to get a taste of her old life.

"This is fun, huh? I'm glad we're doing this," Sinclair said, and she rewarded him with a bright smile, her sweaty calves sticking to the leather. But as he settled in next to her and the driver revved the engine, a knife-edge of nerves sliced her stomach.

Dad had bought the Duesenberg before her first school dance, and he'd wanted to drive her there himself. It was a magnificent car, sleek and black with big whitewall tires and a convertible top. She was fourteen, wearing lipstick for the first time, and so tickled about the whole thing. Dad looked at her strangely as she got into the car. "You be careful, all right? You don't just hop into anybody's car looking so pretty."

"Ugh, Dad!" Back then, everything always went the way she wanted it to. She couldn't fathom a situation where she would feel helpless.

"I mean it," he'd said. "Not every fellow is the gentleman your old man is, you hear?"

Gentleman. Some gentleman he'd turned out to be.

She felt safe enough with the driver there, and Sinclair seemed relatively harmless, even if he was a bit hoary-eyed. He hadn't tried to touch her. He'd said he was *in from Hollywood,* which was intriguing. "What do you do in Hollywood?" she asked.

He smiled slowly, as if he was considering whether or not to tell her. "I'm a filmmaker," he finally said.

Sinclair. The name sounded familiar . . . she did a double take. "You're—you're not Sinclair *Stevens?*" Aviator, inventor—he wasn't just a filmmaker, he was a *celebrity*.

He shrugged, obviously pleased with her reaction. "Having a bit of low-key fun while I'm in town for the week. Nobody knows I'm here yet."

Birdie thought she'd feel more awed when she met a famous person. "What are you doing in Chicago?" she asked, as if she were talking to any old person, instead of *Sinclair Stevens!* The cocktails must be making her bold.

"Working on my next movie. Got one coming out in November, but *Dawn Patrol* is out right before it, and with everything the way it is—looks like the competition might be rough." His face darkened. "Gotta hit the ground running," he mumbled, almost to himself. "Another war flick, but with more action and romance than ever before! Dogfights, stunt-flying, that sort of thing—"

"You're filming it here?"

His face cleared as he registered the question. "No, I'm here to meet with some investors a week from Monday. You need a lot of money to make that kind of movie."

Sinclair Steven's movies were the sort that hired pilots like Hazel and Oscar. They would just *die* if they knew where she was right now! "Are you going to have stunt pilots?"

"Of course, but I can't worry about that now. Investors first, actors second, then we'll start scouting for stunt pilots." He tapped his fingers on the windowsill, looking pensive again.

"Did you ever hire a woman pilot to do stunts?" The limo slowed, pulling up to the curb.

"Nope." He raised his eyebrows. "That's not a bad thought. It would definitely make a buzz! If she was pretty enough, that might be something, even if we'd have to keep the stunts simple."

He must imagine lady pilots as *powder puffs*. "Not if they were like my friends. They fly better than anyone else—"

"Here we are," Sinclair interrupted as the driver opened his door. Birdie was annoyed that he cut her off, but almost instantly her stomach turned. Here they were, at The Midnight, where Gilda Deveaux was sure to be. Where Dad might be.

Sinclair came around and helped her out, his palm moist against hers. She took his arm flirtatiously—"It's awful nice of you to take a girl out to such a fancy-lookin' place"—affecting her best Zelda Fitzgerald for the occasion and shooing away his ensuing compliments.

The Midnight Ballroom was an imposing old building with broad columns and bright red doors. The ceilings were high and the patrons white. The five-piece band was hitting all sixes on stage, and standing behind the long, silver stem of a microphone, her lips to the bud on top—

"Gilda Deveaux," Birdie breathed.

She shone, the grail Birdie had been seeking. Her chestnut curls were sculpted into a carefree wave, a few wisps falling over her forehead, long strands of pearls swinging to her waist, one strap of her dress slipping off a shoulder. She was as seductive as Birdie remembered, her voice as sweet and throaty, but there was something else about her that Birdie understood now. It wasn't the beauty of her voice or body that made her so compelling. It was like Gilda had all the intensity Birdie felt inside her building up, only Gilda was somehow able to fill her lungs with those feelings and pour them out into the microphone so they resonated deep in Birdie's guts. The aching, the sadness, the longing. Who couldn't help falling in love with her?

"She's something else, isn't she?" Sinclair's hand on her lower back guided her toward the dance floor. "How about those moves I saw over at the Hot Toddy? I want to see more of that!"

June pulling her close, hand on her waist—Birdie's skin warmed. She turned away from Sinclair, not wanting him to think she blushed for him. "Of course," she said. Her tone was flat and didn't come out as coyly as she'd wanted, but he didn't seem to notice.

The dance floor was just below the stage, and the band was playing a hot number. The words of the song, "I'm in the Market for You," were simple, but Gilda's sultry rendition hinted at unspoken meanings. It wasn't as crowded as it had been at the last bar, but there were plenty of people dancing in expensive suits and fashionable dresses, limbs loose and careless, cheeks flushed and lips parted. There was a current in the air.

Sinclair wasn't much for dancing. He stood at the edge of the floor, sucking down a drink as he watched Birdie hungrily, motioning for her to go on when she paused. He didn't touch her, but the way he stared was uncomfortable—especially after he'd finished his double. Birdie put more distance between them, inching closer to the stage, and fixed her eyes on Gilda.

Gilda's red-nailed fingers trailed on the microphone, her eyes making deep contact with some unknown *you* in the back of the room. Birdie turned her head, her heart in her throat—what if Dad was standing there, bourbon in his glass, staring back?—but no one was there. Gilda was staring at the wall like it was the only thing in her life that she'd ever cared about.

Birdie could see how someone might see that look, and want it for themselves.

In what seemed like no time at all, the set ended with a great crescendo of sound crashing beneath the highest, longest, loudest note that Gilda had sang all night. The crowd clapped and whistled and stomped, but the clock read three a.m. and Gilda and the band ignored their request for just one more.

Everyone hung off each other's necks and complained about having to leave. Gilda, a delicate sheen on her brow, turned to laugh with the bassist. Birdie felt Sinclair's arm snake around her waist. "Whaddya wanna do now, sugar?" His sour breath was hot on her neck. He'd definitely gone downhill since they'd left the Hot Toddy.

"I want to talk to her." Birdie nodded at the stage. Her heart was in her throat, her head light.

"Sure, doll." He patted her hip. "Go chat her up, then we'll go. I'll wait at the bar, sugar."

A few gentlemen fans were standing around the base of the stage as Birdie approached, hands in their pockets or holding cigars. Gilda crouched down to listen to one speak, her knees neatly together in her tight skirt, then laughed and answered in a throaty murmur before she stood again. Birdie pushed her hair back and tugged on the hem of her own dress. She was sweaty and rumpled, and Gilda would have no idea who she was. She probably wouldn't believe Birdie when she told her.

Birdie squared her shoulders and put on her smile. "Gilda Deveaux?" she said, raising her voice.

The men turned. They smiled when they saw her, so maybe she didn't look so terrible.

Gilda squinted into the stage lights. A jolt of recognition flickered across Gilda's face, her pleasant expression hardening.

"Jimmy?" said Gilda, putting a hand on the bassist's sleeve. "Does that look like Bobby Williams's girl to you?"

CHAPTER TWENTY-ONE

"I'M BIRDIE WILLIAMS." BIRDIE WAS UNNERVED BY GILDA'S QUICK ASSESS-ment and cold tone. "Do you have a moment?"

Gilda looked around the room lingeringly, a frown creasing her forehead. When her gaze came back to Birdie, she put a hand on her hip and cocked her head to the side. "Make it quick." Her voice had lost the hint of exotic accent, her face the softness of her stage persona; she looked stern and uncaring.

"You sure, Miss Deveaux?" The bassist squinted at Birdie. "I can escort her out if you like."

"It's okay, Jimmy," said Gilda. "I can handle this."

His eyes searched the room like Gilda's before he turned away.

"You must know why I'm here." Birdie meant to sound accus-ing as she said it, but instead a rush of sadness crawled up her throat and made her gasp.

She would not cry. She *wouldn't*.

Gilda pressed her lips together. "I think I might have some idea."

Birdie hugged her arms around herself. "He's here, then?" Her voice came out hopeful and high, and she wished she'd never come here. "Forget it," she gasped. "I thought maybe you could tell me where he is, but it's fine, I just—"

Gilda's brows raised. "Oh Lord, you came to me looking for *him?*" Her eyes softened. "And here I thought you were gonna dress me down like your momma did on the phone." She looked over her shoulder. "You hang on, let me give the boys a hand breaking down. Be right back."

Birdie watched her walk away, startled out of her sadness. Mom had *phoned* Gilda? The revelation simmered in Birdie's mind, heating her up. Mom had known all along where Dad might have gone and she had told Birdie *nothing?*

Gilda helped move a few things off the stage but the men waved her away after a moment, and Gilda stepped down and sat on the edge of the stage and patted the spot next to her. Birdie was seething already and she'd only learned one thing—but she forced herself to sit down next to her. Her stomach was aching, and her head was light.

"You poor thing," said Gilda, patting her knee. "Out so late. You hungry? Thirsty?"

Birdie shook her head, unnerved that Gilda was treating her like a child. She'd gone from seductive to stern to sympathetic so quickly. "I just—I was hoping you could tell me where my dad is."

Someone handed Gilda a cloudy martini and she thanked them, took a sip, and swirled the toothpicked olive around a few times. "Well, he's not here now, if that's all you were after."

Birdie had gathered that. "But he was?"

Gilda laughed shortly. "Sure was. He'd never come to see me in Chicago before, but it's not too hard to track me down. Said he couldn't stop thinking about me. That he was divorcing your mother, and that he wanted me to break off my engagement and marry him instead. Of course I wasn't touching that, but I was flattered." She paused to take another sip, and cleared her throat. "Took me a minute to track down the newspapers from your town. The bank failure? He didn't tell me about that. What did he think he was doing? Did he think I'd marry him, no questions asked?"

She glanced at Birdie and her tone changed. "I'm sorry, bunny. All that—it must've been hard for you."

Birdie shrugged noncommittally, not trusting herself to answer. Gilda watched for a moment with limpid eyes, then said softly, "You know, your dad's always been one of my biggest admirers. Has been ever since he saw me on tour in New York— lord, it's been two years almost since then. He came up and talked to me after the show. What a charmer! He sent two dozen red roses to my hotel room the next morning. They weren't signed, but I knew it was him."

Fine, she could handle this. She'd known already, or guessed, at least, that Dad was in love with Gilda. "So, Dad and you—two years?" That was tough to swallow.

"Oh, no—I mean, he pursued me, and I'd flirt with him after the shows, but we never were an item. I love that kind of attention, the roses and gifts and everything, but I don't let it mean more than it does. These men . . ." She waved a hand around the room. "They see a slicked-up, showgirl version of me, singing all these songs about what I'd do for a man, and that's who they think I am." She shook her head. "I can be that girl for a few hours every night, up on stage, and it makes me a pretty fine living. But it's not who I am."

Dad wouldn't be so foolish as to think a stage act meant something special, just for him. Gilda must have led him on a *little.*

"He started showing up at all my shows when I came through New York. He was persistent, but I knew he had a family—he talked to me about you, though he never did mention your mother—and I wasn't getting caught up in that. Plus, I was engaged. Married, now. I might look fast, but I'm a one-guy kinda gal."

Birdie looked down at Gilda's hand and saw the band on her finger. She believed her—but surely she had made it seem like she *might* run away with Dad? She clearly liked the attention. But up close, with the act turned off and the walls down, Gilda didn't seem like the type to lead somebody on.

"Then I got the request from him to sing at your party. I had a bad feeling from the start, so I named a crazy price for me and my boys to come out there. And when he said he'd pay it and then some, I thought, what the heck. Of course, soon as I got there I knew it was a mistake. Your momma staring daggers at me all night. Bobby drinking, hanging all over me, not caring who saw. Not caring if *you* saw. I couldn't get out of there fast enough."

Birdie tried to think back. She'd been so caught up in her own head in that moment that she hadn't really understood. She and Izzy had caught him, right in the act of kissing Gilda, and he really hadn't seemed to care.

"He telegrammed me after that, but I never answered. With the market crash all my regular work in New York dried up, so I thought that'd be the end of it. Imagine my surprise when he showed up here a month ago!" Gilda looked at Birdie, and must have seen something on her face. "You okay, bunny? Is this all too much?"

"I'm fine." Birdie swallowed. "You aren't saying anything I hadn't guessed." It was hard to hear it all plainly, but what she was hearing sounded just like the sweet father who showered her with gifts and attention—and always assumed money and charm would get him what he wanted.

Gilda looked concerned, but continued. "I turned him down, but that didn't change anything. He kept coming to all my shows, approaching me after every set. I told the doormen to keep him out, but then he'd chase me on the way to my car. Three in the morning, and he'd be running after me! Jimmy and the boys finally had to knock some sense into him, I'm sorry to say."

That didn't sound like Dad at all, but Birdie had never seen him thwarted.

"Haven't seen him since. Two weeks it's been, at least. I was starting to think he's gone for good. Finally got some sense beat into him, and he's gone home with his tail between his legs. Back to you, I thought. But now you're here, and that's got me worried."

"He could be there," Birdie said slowly. "He could've gone back home." She wondered what Mom would do if he showed back up in Glen Cove, when she knew about Gilda. Birdie was furious with Mom for not telling her what she'd guessed. She was furious with Dad for proving Mom right. *If he's alive, and he just left us like this—he doesn't deserve for you to wait around for him.*

Instead of finding Dad and getting the assuring explanations that she so desperately wanted from him, she'd gotten the bald, unflattering, depressing story from someone else. Dad was a callous, no-good two-timer. He'd been the good guy so many times in her life—but in this story, he was the villain.

Her head was starting to throb.

"I'm so sorry, bunny," said Gilda gently, a troubled expression settling on her face. She reached out and squeezed Birdie's arm. "How'd you get here, child? You got a way home?"

Birdie blinked furiously. "I'm fine." She jumped up and backed away from the stage. "I came with friends."

Friends. She looked around to see where Oscar and June and the rest were—and remembered that she'd left them behind.

"You sure, bunny?" Gilda reached out to touch her arm again.

The proposal, running off—she needed to get back to the Hot Toddy. How long ago had she left?

The audition tomorrow!

"I have to go," she blurted, lunging away from Gilda's concerned look. She should thank her, and probably apologize, but then she'd cry in earnest, and she had to hold it together and finagle a way back to her friends before it was too late—

Sinclair was hunched on a stool, eyes mostly closed, tie loose, a lax hand around a drink sweating on the mahogany bar. He jumped when she grabbed his shoulder. "Hunh? Oh . . ." His eyes focused on her, then a slow smile spread across his face. "Hey there, sugar."

"I'm ready to go." It was easy to pretend she was fine with him. She gave him a half smile as she tugged on his sleeve. "I need to get back to my friends."

He processed that for a moment, then wagged a finger at her. "Oh, sug'r, don' you know the Hot Toddy closes at two? Your friends's long gone."

She watched him stumble off his chair, her heart constricting to a tiny pinpoint inside her chest.

She was alone. Really, truly, one hundred percent on her own.

But hadn't she been all along? It was only that she was just now realizing it.

There was a way she could pull this off. There was a way that she could save the day, rescue herself from this seemingly untenable situation, find her friends and smile and laugh and get a good night's rest before performing perfectly tomorrow. But she was lost and sad and tired and her head hurt, and she couldn't figure it out right now. Sinclair's car was nice and warm. The seats were rich and soft. She accepted his arm as he slung it over her shoulder, exhaled and said, "Why don't we just go to your place, then?"

CHAPTER TWENTY-TWO

BIRDIE DREAMED CHARLIE'S FALL AGAIN, HIS BODY CRUMPLED IN THE sand. This time she ran up and rolled the body over, confident she could wake him. She pumped and pumped his chest. She looked at his face and saw—it was *Dad*. Dad had fallen from the sky. Her confidence shriveled into panic. She pumped and pumped, screaming at him to stand up but he refused, his blank eyes staring up, his chest juddering beneath her angry fists—

Birdie woke disoriented. Her hands found a velvet couch beneath her, a light blanket draped over her legs. Her stomach churned as she sat up slowly. Heavy curtains were drawn, but the light seeping around the edges was glaringly bright. She was still wearing the dress she'd worn out.

The Hot Toddy, dancing with June. The taste of bitters and sugar on her mouth.

Leaving with a man with moist palms, a gold watch. The Midnight Ballroom.

Talking to Gilda. Finding out—about Dad—

Leaving with that man again.

Sinclair Stevens. She was in Sinclair Stevens's hotel suite.

A headache roared in, and she pulled her knees in and pressed her fists into her eye sockets. She had no idea where she was. Somewhere in downtown Chicago? Probably far from where she'd started out last night, on the South Side. It had taken forever to drive to the hotel from the Midnight Ballroom. Sinclair's head had lolled as the driver swung around corners. They finally pulled up as the sky was starting to gray.

She'd calculated the next moments carefully.

Up the steps and through a big set of glass doors, Birdie's teeth chattering in the early morning air, a doorman with averted eyes helping them in. A wave from a pretty lady at the front desk— "Good morning, Mister Stevens"—her gaze sliding quickly away. An elevator with an operator that kept his eyes on the door and his expression pleasant. Sinclair taking forever to find his key. Through another door. As it shut behind them Sinclair groped for her, but she pushed him away and flicked on a lamp, saying she wanted one more drink. Vodka in hand, she'd followed him to the bedroom. He'd lain back on the bed, drinking straight out of the bottle. He'd cooperated perfectly. His eyes had drooped, then closed, in no time at all.

She'd found a warm bottle of soda water and a bowl of nuts on the wet bar and finished them off, then made herself a nest on the couch with a blanket. She'd squeezed her eyes closed and fell into a disoriented half dream. Gilda, lips kissing the microphone, a ring on her finger—Mom's hands shook as she packed her suitcase—that was Mom's wedding ring on Gilda's finger. No, Oscar was pulling it from his pocket, offering it to Hazel while June and Ruth glowed in a dark corner—silver light a ring around them—

Birdie had tossed and turned, buried her face in the cushions— Dad, falling.

She was desperately hungover on Sinclair's couch with a raging headache and a sour stomach, and it was Saturday, and she had a three o'clock audition.

She stumbled to her feet and pushed the curtains back. The blinding light sending a wave of nausea through her. She stumbled to the marble bathroom and slurped water from the faucet with a cupped hand, then splashed her face. She wiped her face with a plush towel and tiptoed to the bedroom.

Sinclair was passed out. Her stomach crawled up into her throat as she stared at the top of his thinning hair and his rumpled, half-unbuttoned shirt. She was an idiot. Anything could have happened.

She gingerly picked up his wrist and turned his watch around. Almost noon.

She ran back to the sitting room and frantically tugged her shoes on, wincing as they scraped last night's blisters. She dashed around, desperate for something to eat, and uncovered a half-eaten tin of sweet biscuits beneath a throw pillow. She shoved one in her mouth, grabbed a few more, and ran for the door. Down the elevator. Past the front desk, as fast as she could go. A doorman raised his eyebrows at her. She thought about asking him where she was, but decided against it.

Her breath was ragged, the biscuit dry and sticking to her throat as she squinted up and down the road. People in well-tailored summer clothes sauntered wide, clean streets. Downtown Chicago, she would bet on it. Curtiss airfield was north of the city. Henrieta's farmhouse was near Elgin, about forty miles northwest of the city—she didn't have time to do anything but head straight for the airfield. Someone would have brought her costume.

Birdie's hand went to the dollars tucked in the band of her camiknickers. She'd seen the train lines running overhead last night, and the bright yellow taxis on the street. In New York, taxis were fifty cents a mile—which meant she could get about four miles before she'd run out of change. She probably couldn't even afford a taxi to the elevated train station.

She'd *never* had to worry about such things before.

A big, beautiful, shiny car slowed, the window rolling down. Nothing but boys in their summer best, hair parted and slicked, grins on their faces. Four boys, one seat still open. She realized how she must look. Bedraggled, last night's dress and kitten heels wilting in the hot midday sun.

"You look like you need a ride, sweetheart," said the driver, leaning over.

"Oh my gosh." Birdie recoiled, wiping sweaty palms on her skirt. Her heart was pounding. "No. You boys got me all wrong."

She hurried back to the doorman. "Excuse me," she said shakily. "Can you point me toward the nearest train station?"

"Yes, ma'am," he said carefully, not making eye contact. "Union Station is that way, on Canal Street. You can get just about anywhere you want to go from there."

She hastened down the street, the reality of her situation setting in. All of her circus-mates would be scrambling to figure out where she was. No, they'd given up trying to figure out where she was. Now they were desperately trying to figure out how they were going to pull off the show without her.

They'd probably been panicking all night, since they discovered she'd disappeared.

She'd wanted to make a point. June, walking away with Ruth! After Birdie had *kissed* her. Her stomach turned. She had felt discarded, saturated in embarrassment. What had Birdie been thinking? She'd wanted June to know that she couldn't care less, that the kiss had been a foolish, fleeting whim. She hadn't meant to be gone this long. If she ruined today's audition they'd never forgive her.

Birdie's steps slowed. She could go home to Glen Cove. She'd have to go back to Henrieta's and get the last of her money, but she probably still had enough to make it home. She wouldn't have to see any of the circus people again. Curtiss airfield felt just as far away as Long Island right now, full of just as many people she didn't matter to.

Why stop at Glen Cove and the airfield? She could go *any-where*. She could disappear right into thin air.

In this moment, it felt like she already had.

The dreadful feeling she had been ignoring since last night threatened to crawl up her throat and out of her mouth in ugly, gasping sounds—she stopped moving, pressed the heels of her palms against her eyes, and clenched her teeth against it.

Everything used to work out perfectly. It was so unfair, that she had to try *so* hard now, and even then she couldn't make things work out right. She took deep, shuddering breaths and pictured herself leaping from the wing of the plane that afternoon, every-one looking up in awe.

She squared her shoulders and picked up the pace. She would get to the airfield in time. No one would be angry, so long as she showed up and really wowed them. Performing well was her only chance at feeling like she wasn't the most worthless person on earth.

It only took her a quarter of an hour to make it to Union Station.

She limped up to the ticket counter and asked how to get to the Curtiss-Reynolds airfield. The woman behind the counter squinted over her thick spectacles. "The North Shore Elevated will take you within about a twenty minute walk of it. Make sure you get off on the Glenview stop."

Birdie shoved her money across the counter. Her hands wouldn't stop shaking.

"One way, please."

CHAPTER TWENTY-THREE

Birdie limped through the Curtiss-Reynolds Airport entrance and stumbled toward the hangar. It had to be after three. She was soaked in sweat, stinking of last night's smoke and booze. The hangar was massive, cavernous, and endlessly long, with fields on either side. A plane—one she didn't recognize—buzzed across the field to the right, and she headed that way. The plane zipped in and out around pylons set up around the field. People were scattered across a second-story promenade that ran the length of the hangar. She recognized two of the pilots from the boarding house hanging over the railing, whooping as the plane flipped upside down, narrowly managing to avoid hitting a pylon, then another. A row of serious-looking men with their shirtsleeves rolled up stood on the field in the shadow of the hangar, leaning in to talk with each other. They were probably the men who would decide who measured up enough to perform in the second annual National Air Races.

She'd measure up fine, if she could stop shaking.

There—past those men, stood Colette, holding a megaphone and shading her eyes, watching the plane as it flipped right side up and came in for a landing on the paved runway that ran the length of the hangar. A smattering of applause from up on the promenade, then someone yelling—"Go, Ruth!"

Ruth climbed out of the cockpit in a fitted navy flight suit and keen white leather cap, grinning from ear to ear. The group of men walked out onto the field to talk with her.

Birdie looked back up at the promenade and saw June and Hazel leaning over the railing, watching. Hazel's shoulders were hunched, teeth worrying a fingernail. June stared down, hands clenched on the railing. Birdie tried to decipher June's expression, but distance and the shadow of the hangar made it impossible.

She turned and walked hesitantly into the cavernous mouth of the hangar.

"Birdie, Jesus!" Merriwether came running toward her, her pirate coattails flapping behind her. "Thank God!" Merriwether pulled her into a hug, then drew back and looked at her. The twins barreled into her seconds later, their strong, gangly arms wrapping her tight.

"No time to talk," Merriwether said at last, perhaps determining that Birdie was well enough to perform despite her disheveled state. "We switched out with the Hollbrook folks and let them go first, but they're about done. Thank God you made it. They're already not impressed that Charlie's out of commission. I told them what happened, that of course we couldn't help it—long story short, we really gotta wow them."

"Got it." Birdie clenched her hands into fists and tightened all her muscles, but she could still feel herself quivering.

Merriwether ran outside to let June, Hazel, Colette, and the NAR guys know that they were ready. Bennie appeared and put a crocodile-clad hand on her shoulder. "You all right, little bird?"

"We were up all night," said Oscar, coming up with Milosh. "Drove around for hours after the club closed. Couldn't begin to think of where you'd went." His eyes had dark shadows under them.

Milosh flipped his pirate eye patch up onto his forehead. "You're okay?" he asked softly.

Birdie swallowed, unable to hold their eyes. She didn't deserve their concern. "I'm fine. Everything's fine."

Hazel and June ran into the hangar. Hazel threw her arms around Birdie, her new ring glinting on her finger.

"Hey, you." June took her hand and squeezed it. "Come with me. I'll show you where to change."

June's fingers slipped from hers as she headed toward the cluster of their planes. Birdie followed to a somewhat private area between the Moth and a Jenny. It was hard to look at the height of June's shoulders, her dark lashes and questioning eyes, and not forget her resolve to put their kiss out of her mind. She wanted to fall against June's shoulder and feel her arms tighten around her. She wanted to tell her everything that happened last night, everything that had ever happened. About Dad, about Izzy.

But who knew what had happened between June and Ruth after she'd left? June handed over her costume, and she snatched her hand away when their skin grazed.

June turned away to give her some privacy. "I can't believe we lost track of you last night." Her back was to Birdie, but Birdie could hear the tightness in her voice. "I went to talk with Ruth— next thing I knew, I couldn't find you anywhere. And I'd seen that jerk talking to you!"

Birdie had convinced that jerk to leave with her without a thought to the show the next day, and how important it was to everyone. She pulled her filthy dress over her head. "It's not your fault—" she said. Her voice broke, tears threatening.

"No, you don't have to explain anything," said June. Her hair was pulled into two Wendy pigtails, her hair short enough that wisps had come free and were tickling her neck. Her voice was soft. "You sure you're okay?"

June wasn't judging, defensive, or angry. Birdie wanted to tell June how sad and stupid she felt, but she was barely holding it together. Who knew what might happen if she cracked. "I'm fine," said Birdie. "Everything's jake."

She sounded convincing, but her hands still trembled as she pulled on her costume.

Birdie didn't have to do any stunts in the first scene, just climb out onto the wing and wave at the stands while the story began to unfold. The wind tore at her so hard that she stumbled. It pushed and pulled her, whipping smoke-dirtied hair across her face. She couldn't find her balance, no matter how she tried to focus.

Everyone adores you.

She'd thought Dad adored her, but he'd left without a backward glance.

Her hands refused to leave the struts, her feet refused to leave the wing. Her eyes caught sight of the ground and she gasped involuntarily, her fingers tightening around wire until she could hardly move. The grass of the field, the concrete of the runway, the hard arch of the hangar roof, CURTISS spelled out in big white letters against the dark tar paper. The word ran through her mind over and over: *Curtissssss, Curtisssss,* the hiss of a snake. Birdie couldn't think of what she was supposed to do.

Everything is perfect.

It could have been, but she'd done her best to mess it all up.

Oscar glanced at her worriedly. Birdie gave up on letting go of the struts and slid down them until she sat on the wing. She just needed a moment.

She squeezed her eyes shut and tried to breath deeply, but all she felt was the empty space around her. The plane was not in her control; it could jerk or dip and throw her off. It could fall like a stone from the sky. Just because it stayed up in the air every time before, who could say if it would this time? She'd thought she knew how everything would go—but she had no idea which way life would lurch.

You will never fall.

She bet Dad never thought he would fall, either.

"You okay?"

When she pried her eyes open Oscar was crouched beside her, looking so concerned her heart wobbled.

"Now is the sword-fight," he said.

The show. She couldn't let everyone down. She nodded, her stomach dropping out.

"You've got this," he said. "You've done it a bunch of times. You know exactly how it goes." Coaching her gently, Oscar took her hand and lifted her to standing. He guided her to the edge of the wing.

"I'm getting back in the cockpit," Oscar said. "I'm gonna bring the plane around, then it's your turn to shine."

He left her side. After a moment the plane banked, and she glanced out over the airfield. They were coming into position.

She looked straight down and tried to convince herself.

The ground below is home. Life like it used to be is waiting for you. You would jump off the wing of a plane for that.

She would do anything.

But that was just a story she'd been telling herself. That life was gone. She knew it was gone for good.

"No." She gasped and backed away, fumbling for something solid. "No, no, no—"

There was nothing there but empty air, an impossible distance to fall and survive.

CHAPTER TWENTY-FOUR

BIRDIE DIDN'T ARGUE WHEN HENRIETA LED HER TO A STEAMING BATHTUB. She had never felt dirtier, and she couldn't bear to be around anyone. Now she sat on her bed in the front bedroom, damp and exhausted, in a threadbare robe that Henrieta had lent her, as the show's spectacular failure replayed in her mind.

It had all fallen apart after Birdie panicked. She remembered little except for the gasping, harsh sound of her own breath as she struggled to keep her throat from closing up. The gusto had left Colette's narration as she scrambled to make it seem like Peter Pan had saved the day, when it was clear that he had not. Birdie had been able to look up from her own clenched hands only after Oscar had landed, just in time to witness the final catastrophe. Merriwether had crawled down the rope hanging from the Jenny as Milosh flew it, into the open mouth of Bennie's crocodile costume as he drove the Studebaker speeding below. It started out spectacularly, but this time the Studebaker couldn't quite get up to speed, and the Jenny passed the Studebaker a hair too soon. Merriwether had flailed around in the air for a few moments before she realized she wasn't going to make it, then had to pull herself back up the rope ignominiously as Milosh circled the field and the Studebaker came to a rattling stop.

The NAR guys had left the field tight-lipped and unimpressed. The audition had been an absolute *disaster*.

And it was her fault. Birdie had been so stupid, thinking she could just will everything to work out all right.

There was a knock on the door. She stared at the door a moment, willing whoever it was to go away, but there was another soft knock.

She stood up, body like lead, and shuffled over to open it.

Oscar's smile filled the doorframe, a plate in his hand. "I thought, if I was you, I'd like some dinner," he said. "But I also thought, if I was you, I might not want to be fussed over any more. I might be hiding in my room."

Birdie stared at his mouth. He said something else but she couldn't hear it—her exhaustion was a roaring wave. He stepped inside the room and put the plate down on her side table. She caught her pale, hunched reflection in the mirror and fluffed her hair over her shoulders, trying to put a pleasant expression on her face, but when he turned and met her eyes, his smile faltered. "It's okay, if you're not okay," he said quietly. "I don't know what happened last night, but don't feel like you need to pretend."

She could feel tears welling in her eyes. If she tried to explain, it wouldn't make any sense. She was falling apart because a pretty lady told Birdie she *didn't* have an affair with her dad?

She sank onto the edge of the bed. "I'm just hungover," she mumbled. She didn't deserve his sympathy.

Oscar came and sat beside her.

"*I'm* hungover," he said. "You, on the other hand—you didn't make it home last night." He paused. "We were really worried about you."

He was so sweet. They all were. "You asked Hazel to marry you." Birdie's voice rasped, and she swallowed to clear her throat. "I'm sorry I made a mess of your big night."

"Come on, Birdie," he said. "Don't beat yourself up about that, or the show today. It wasn't just you. We weren't ready."

Birdie stared at the floor, hugging her arms around her ribs. It was getting harder to pretend she was fine.

"We were really scared when you didn't come back last night," he said. "I wanted to tell you that. I wanted you to know we care about you."

She closed her eyes and leaned into his shoulder, trembling.

"C'mere, pretty bird." He pulled her into a hug. "You must've had some night."

She breathed him in for what felt like minutes. His breath was steady and deep, and it calmed her. The itch of tears receded from her eyes, and she became aware of his cheek against her forehead. She could feel his chest rise and fall. She tilted her head up and breathed against his neck. He smelled like Henrieta's handmade soap and tobacco. She remembered his hands lingering when he'd tickled her on the path.

He inhaled and pulled away. Sadness washed over her, all the breath left her body. She felt like she was drowning. Tears slid down her face as she caught his cheek and pulled him in—his full lips brushed hers, salt and warmth and sadness. She felt him resist but she clung tight, she'd go under if she let go—

A gasp sounded from the doorway. Birdie looked up and June was standing there, her mouth open. A plate, identical to the one Oscar had placed on the bed stand, tipped toward the floor. A pierogi fell and hit the rug, rolling under Merriwether's bed as they all stared at each other.

Oscar was on his feet in a second, hands wavering, unsure.

Tiredness surged though Birdie.

"You," said June, staring at Birdie. She blinked. "You," she repeated, this time with venom. She looked at Oscar, who's open mouth held unsaid explanations. "You bastard!" Her face reddened as she flung the plate at him. He ducked, and the plate clattered to the floor as sour cream and bits of onion slimed the bedspread behind him.

"June, it's not—it's—" Oscar stuttered.

"You *just*—" June stabbed a finger at Oscar, words failing her. "Hazel—"

"Oh my God. This is a mistake," he said low. "This is an accident."

"It's my fault," said Birdie wearily. *It's all my fault.*

"You don't get to say *anything!*" June whirled on her. "What are you even doing here? What were we even *thinking?*"

Birdie pulled her robe tight, wishing she'd headed home this morning. She should've gone straight back to Glen Cove after she got the truth from Gilda. Then she wouldn't be here, this wouldn't be happening.

"What's going on here?" asked Hazel, swinging into the doorway playfully.

No one answered. Hazel took in Oscar and Birdie standing next to each other, the plate of food smeared across the floor. "What's going on?" Hazel repeated, straightening and smoothing her skirt.

June looked at Birdie with utter contempt. "You've done nothing but mess things up. You have no experience, no sense. It should've been clear to us from the start that you're just a spoiled girl looking for attention."

Rage was a raft, lifting Birdie out of her stupor. "Me?" said Birdie incredulously. "*I'm* spoiled, Miss My-daddy-gives-me-everything-I-want? You don't know *anything* about me." None of them would understand what she was going through.

"You're right," said June quietly. "I don't. I sure did want to, though, for some crazy reason."

"You don't say," said Birdie, alive now. Hot and electric. "Sorry if I gave you the wrong impression, I was just *looking for attention.*"

Too late, Birdie remembered them dancing together. Slow, hip-to-hip, fingers entwined. She remembered the tug of that strange thread between them.

She felt now how quickly it was unraveling, as June shook her head and looked away.

"Please tell me what happened." Hazel was staring at Oscar, hurt dawning in her eyes. "Oscar?"

"I—I don't know what happened." Oscar reached out to catch Hazel's hand. "I came in here to—" His voice trailed off. "I was just—"

Hazel pulled her hand away. She looked at June.

"They were kissing," said June flatly.

The color left Hazel's face. The air left the room. Birdie felt like screaming.

David had come around, Izzy had said. He wanted to marry her. She should have gone home as soon as she'd heard that.

She should have known, since the bank failed. Things failed. You could smile and party and dance and pretend like everything was okay, and you would still fail.

Everything was one big disappointing failure.

"Don't worry," Birdie said bitterly. "I'm going home."

CHAPTER TWENTY-FIVE

Birdie eased the door of the guest bedroom open, feeling a pang as she listened to Merriwether's whistling breath behind her. After the terrible audition, Merriwether had been her usual gruff, practical self. *Life never goes according to anyone's plan, that's for damn sure.* When she heard Birdie was leaving, she'd given her five dollars in payment for the Coney Island show. Birdie took it, even though she didn't deserve it. With that and the last of the money she'd brought with her, she figured she'd be able to make it back to Long Island if she was careful.

Birdie quietly shut the door behind her. She had her old coat on. She'd tried to put her old dress on, too, but it stank so badly of smoke and alcohol that she couldn't stand it. She wore Henrieta's daughter's dress. It wasn't clean either, but it smelled like dirt and fresh paint and sunshine.

She would make it to Union Station in Chicago by morning. Henrieta had given her directions. Bennie had said he'd drive her in the morning, but Birdie couldn't stand the thought of being at the house when they all woke up. She couldn't face any of them again.

As Birdie crept toward the door, her elbow caught paper on a side table and swept it to the floor. She cursed quietly, and risked flicking on the hall light. A draft of a poster lay on the floor, fallen from next to the phone. Birdie squinted in the dim light as she picked it up. It proclaimed, Birdie, the GIRL who wouldn't

GROW UP! There was a picture of her and Hazel smiling in short skirts and flying caps, arms around each other, smiling sweetly with painted lips.

No new Travel Air for Hazel. No Hollywood agents. As if that wasn't bad enough, Birdie had taken the thrill of Hazel's new engagement away from her, too.

She heard a tap from the kitchen and turned her head. A candle in a holder burned on the kitchen table, illuminating a steaming mug and a few other objects. Her stomach tightened, bracing for another confrontation. So much for slipping away unnoticed.

"You ready for your tattoo, bird girl?" Colette's voice came out of the darkness that pooled on the far side of the candle.

Birdie felt like she was communing with an invisible spirit. "I can't," she answered. "I'm leaving."

"Train won't leave till morning." Colette's hand appeared next to the candle and patted the table. "Come on, I drew you some pictures. All you have to do is look."

Birdie set the poster next to the phone and walked into the kitchen. Colette materialized, hair piled wildly on her head, a homespun nightgown looking incongruous on her inked, lanky body. Milosh sat next to her, looking equally out of place in a striped nightshirt.

"What do you think about these?" Colette pushed a piece of paper across the table.

"I helped come up with some ideas." Milosh leaned his elbows on the table, hair falling into his face.

A few images stood out. A pattern of stars, all different sizes, like a night sky you could get lost in. It looked like the first night she'd sat on the beach with June and Oscar, staring up at the sky and thinking anything was possible. A trail of musical notes looked like they were dancing, a few of them entwined like lovers kissing. The silhouette of a bird in flight—wide wings and spare lines, light and strong all at once.

When they had thought about her, they'd thought of winking stars, dancing music, soaring wings. Birdie ached for what she was leaving, all of the unexpected experiences she'd never even imagined were possible. "This one." Birdie pointed to the bird silhouette. She felt bold, excited, and frightened all at once. Would it hurt? Was she crazy for doing this?

"That one was my idea!" Milosh's dark eyes were proud.

Colette leaned closer, the planes of her face illuminated starkly in the sideways light. "I thought that one was too obvious at first, but it came out really beautiful." She traced the lines. "I don't have the equipment for anything fancy, not like I used to have when I was with the three-ring, but something simple like this won't be a problem."

Birdie looked at the table. A needle and thread, and a bottle of India ink. Her stomach fluttered. Colette picked up the needle and held it in the flame of the candle until the tip darkened. "Where do you want it?"

Birdie unbuttoned the collar of the dress and pulled it down over a shoulder before she could change her mind. "Here." She reached back to touch her shoulder blade. Milosh stood and wet a rag at the sink. Colette wound string around the needle, then dipped it into the ink.

"Sit with your back to me," said Colette, and Birdie turned a chair and sat sideways in it, nervous. She was a girl who walked out on wings and warmed to a soft, forbidden kiss, but somehow this felt wilder. Milosh wet her shoulder with the rag, rubbed soap into her skin, then wiped it clean. Birdie tensed as Colette placed a hand against her shoulder. She felt the prick of a needle on her skin. Another prick, and another. It hurt, but not badly— like ant bites. Birdie relaxed into it.

"I can keep it covered," she said, reassuring herself. "I'm not putting it where just anyone could see it."

"You never know." Colette's breath tickled Birdie's skin. "These things can change you. You might find you want to show it off."

Birdie was sure it *would* change her if she was covered with tattoos like Colette, but she would never. "What made you get so many?"

Colette was quiet for a moment. "The first time I saw someone covered in tattoos, I saw the way it gave him power. They were runes, protecting him from being hurt. I was sick of being hurt."

Colette as a scared little girl materialized in Birdie's head. "That sounds so sad." She wasn't sure if she'd ever really been frightened when she was young. If her childhood had been different, would she still be the same person? What things made you who you were? Even since the bank had failed, Birdie felt like a different person than the girl she'd been before. Somebody she didn't understand.

"I started drawing everything that was inside of me on the outside." The prick of the needle was starting to feel more intense, and Birdie pictured the images on Colette's skin to distract herself. Lions and tigers with teeth and claws, cowering mice, tangles of vines choking flowers and trees. Birds fleeing skyward. Balloons leaving the earth behind. "I felt powerful when people couldn't ignore me anymore, whether I drew them in or repelled them."

"That's when I met you," said Milosh. "You were fearless."

"But I still let the wrong people, the wrong stuff in close," said Colette. "My tattoos had no actual power to protect me. They were just a way for me to turn the pain into something beautiful. But at some point they became a reminder that I had to protect myself, and that was powerful. And now they remind me of what I overcame on my own, without any kind of magical protection."

"You have power to give pain the meaning you want it to have," said Milosh. "Even if what happened was beyond your control."

Birdie didn't want to give it that much weight. "I'm just getting this—it's just for fun."

"That's fine." Colette touched Birdie's arm lightly. "Some of
mine are just for fun, too."

"I don't need all of that *reminding*." Birdie shook her off before
she remembered that she was in the middle of being tattooed.
She held still again, but now it felt hard not to jump every time
the needle touched her. "It's not the same for me."

"You know, you seemed so perfect when you showed up. 'My
dad had a plane. I dance so pretty, everyone loves me.' But after
spending time with you I've realized, that person—it's not really
you, is it?"

Birdie gritted her teeth against the irritating pinch of the needle. "I suppose I've made that obvious."

"I think I like the girl hiding under all that prettiness," said
Colette. "You should stay, instead of running away, so we can get
to know her."

"I'm not running away." It felt like Colette was digging the
needle into a sunburn. "I'm going home. That's the opposite of
running away."

Colette didn't respond. Birdie watched the candle sputter as
she finished in silence.

"There," Colette said finally. "It's done. You want to see it?"

They went into the hallway and stopped in front of the mirror. Birdie looked over her shoulder. The hall light illuminated
not the single silhouette that Colette had drawn on paper—

"I thought it was just going to be one bird." Winged silhouettes spread across her shoulder in a delicate arc.

"I love what you did with it," Milosh marvelled.

"I started with just one," said Colette. "But I realized when I
was done—it looked pretty, alone, but so abstract. It needed a
flock, to see what it was."

"It's incredible." Milosh smiled at Colette through the mirror.

Birdie stared silently. It was as if Colette had combined all three images she'd drawn—the sparkle of the stars, the dance of the music notes, and the graceful bird. It was stunning, but now all Birdie could think about what it would always remind her of: not just when she'd soared, but finding out Dad was gone for good, kissing June and having her walk away, kissing Oscar and making everyone hate her, failing the audition. She'd never be able to scrub any of it from her skin.

"It needed to look like this," said Colette brusquely, after a few tense moments. She turned and stalked back to the kitchen.

Birdie felt like crying. She waited as Milosh put ointment with a strong herbal scent on her skin, then pulled her dress up and made sure none of the tattoo was visible. As soon as Colette and Milosh were distracted, washing their mugs in the sink and murmuring to each other, Birdie hurried into the windy, dark night. She'd waited too long as it was, and she didn't know what else to say to them. *Thank you* wasn't right. Neither was *goodbye*.

She headed up the gravel road toward the suburbs. She walked for miles and saw no one. The sky was just lightening as houses grew up around streets that became paved, and Birdie made it into downtown Elgin. She found the train station and boarded the first streetcar of the day along with a few bleary-eyed workers heading into Chicago for an early shift. She debarked at Union Station but she didn't have quite enough money to make it back to Glen Cove. It took her most of the day to find a pawnbroker that was open on a Sunday and would give her a reasonable amount for her tartan coat. Then she purchased the cheapest ticket to New York.

She was on a train back to Long Island early the next morning, staring forward, toward a point in the distance that constricted tighter and tighter in her mind every second she got closer.

CHAPTER TWENTY-SIX

BIRDIE WALKED OUT INTO THE PARK-LIKE GROUNDS OF GLEN COVE Station blinking, disoriented. It was Wednesday morning, barely two weeks since she'd found the flyer with Dad's Jenny on it. The country club on the hill across Saint Andrews Lane looked exactly the same, stately brick and columns and clipped green grass, but she had returned a stranger in a secondhand dress. She felt like she'd entered suspended time and lived two years' worth of adventure while home patiently waited for her to realize that she never should have left.

It was a short walk to the village from the station. Cars that passed slowed curiously, and Birdie kept her head down and hoped no one recognized her. She'd freshened up as best she could in the powder room, but three nights in coach couldn't be washed off that easily. She'd eaten only when the train stopped at a station and slept fitfully, day and night, with her head against the window. She'd gotten into Penn Station late the night before and had to wait until morning to take the train home, so that had been another night of dozing on a wooden bench in the women's waiting room without getting real sleep.

She meant to go straight to David's house, but instead found herself standing outside of the bank gritting her teeth, tears welling in her eyes. The bank was already desolate, the whitewashed columns dirty, the broken windows boarded up. A couple of posters were pasted to the side of the building, something Dad never would have allowed. Before it failed it had been all bright white columns and handsome brick and clean glass, more than plenty of money in there to send Birdie to dance classes and piano lessons and finishing school. She could always count on Dad being there when he wasn't at home, his waxed mustache curled up at the corners, taking care of his customers.

She'd been stupid to chase after Dad, looking for answers or adventure when David was right here, the last part of her old life that had a chance of getting her out of this whole mess. It was a week since Izzy had told her he wanted her back; anything could have happened since then. Birdie hurried on her way, tilting her face up as she walked. The sun was bright, a slight breeze, a clear sky. A good day for flying. Birdie wished she were above the treetops.

She saw movement at the parlor window as she stepped off Forest Avenue onto David's drive, and felt a bolt of nerves. She could have waited until tomorrow to come and find him, she felt so unbalanced right now—but this had seemed like the first place to go. She didn't know if the bank had taken the house. She didn't know where Mom would be. And she didn't want to see Izzy until she saw David so she had a story to tell, a way to get back in cahoots with Izzy. Hopefully David would cooperate. Otherwise it was straight off to England—if she was lucky, and Mom hadn't already left without her. Then she supposed she'd have to make her way upstate to her grandparents, the only people left who would take her in, until Mom sent for her in England.

The door swung open before she reached the front porch steps and David bounded toward her, his face angelic, his shoulders broad. Birdie's heart jumped into her throat and she couldn't breathe. "David—"

He came right up to her and pulled her into his arms. He dipped her back and kissed her. He kissed her like the movies.

He kissed her until she was breathless. He kissed her like she'd always wanted to be kissed.

In her mind, June put a flower to her lips.

David pulled away. "Birdie," he said breathlessly, beaming. "I thought I would never see you again."

She blinked. "David." Her voice sounded flat. She should be in her body after a kiss like that—but her mind danced somewhere else, miles and miles away. "*David.*" There, she sounded more like someone who had just been kissed. She put her hand to his face and felt the soft stubble of his cheek, the warm sun on her hair. She was here, in her hometown, on a bright Wednesday morning. Far away from Chicago. "I missed you," she tried.

"Me too." He pressed her hand with his. "I couldn't stop thinking about you since you came by last time."

"I thought you never wanted to see me again after that." The words came out more bitter than she'd intended. If only she'd gotten some sleep, she'd be her usual flirtatious, coy self. She already had the beginning of the story for Izzy. *He kissed me, just like in the movies! So romantic.*

"Birdie, I'm so sorry." He looked pained. "My parents made me think maybe they were right, that we shouldn't see each other—but they're wrong. It's terrible that your dad lost a bunch of their money, but you're not him."

"Izzy told me you came looking for me," Birdie said, melting a little. *He said he wants to marry you.*

David looked over his shoulder, at the parlor window. "Come here." He pulled her quickly off the path and around the side of the house.

He was so excited to see her—Birdie swallowed the fact that he was pulling her out of sight of the house, probably so his parents wouldn't see them together. He led her to the back garden and hurried down the stone path that cut through the flower beds, ducking beneath the branches of a weeping willow tree. They'd kissed on the stone bench beneath its branches, an awkward kiss when he first asked her to go steady around a year ago. "You remember?" He drew her down on the bench. Trailing, thick-leafed branches hid them on all sides.

"Of course." A cool morning breeze ruffled her sleeves as she sat down. She couldn't have scripted this better. *Then he took me to the spot in the backyard where he first asked me to go steady with him . . .* She wished she felt more like her old self, but she could embellish this all in exquisite detail to Izzy as soon as she saw her.

"Birdie." He cupped her cheek and looked into her eyes. "I missed this. I missed being with you."

She was finding it hard to maintain eye contact, but she managed to. She made herself smile. "I missed being with you, too," she tried. She'd been caught up with other things. Distracted. Otherwise she was sure she'd have missed him more.

David looked in the direction of the house. "They've been crazy lately! Just because they lost a little money—they're using it as an excuse to come down so hard on me." He sounded petulant as his hand dropped from her cheek. "They're holding Columbia over my head. But I'd like to see them not send me, after they see I'm not going to give you up."

"I'm sure they'll still send you to school," Birdie said, leaning into him. "Your father's wanted you to join his practice since forever."

He turned back and his face softened. "As soon as I saw you walking up to the house, I knew I was right. I can't ignore how I feel about you. Monty's giving me hell, too, but I don't care."

"Oh, David." She missed someone saying this kind of stuff to her. She missed having what Oscar and Hazel had, or Colette and Milosh. Whatever had happened between her and June was not the same kind of thing.

"I went to come find you the next day, to get you back—" He shook his head. "And then you weren't there. I heard your mom was moving into the village a few days later, so I went there, thinking maybe I'd find you, but she didn't know where you were, either. I thought I'd never get a chance to kiss you again."

He leaned in, but she pulled back and put her hand to his chest.

"My mom—she's moving?" Not to England—but downtown?

"It's over near the school. You haven't seen it? I've got to warn you, it's *tiny*. Hardly a yard, much less grounds than you used to have. Still, people are wondering where in the world she got the money, even for a place that small."

Birdie's stomach clenched, but she put her arms around his neck and leaned in. "Izzy told me something, when I called her. She said you said—" *You said you wanted to marry me.*

"I wish you'd called *me*." His voice sounded a little hurt.

She kissed his cheek. "You know, you *did* tell me you never wanted to see me again."

"I regretted saying that so much. I'd take it back in a heartbeat, if I could."

Birdie looked away. It had hurt, but as part of the whole mess—Izzy's coldness, Dad's disappearance, the collapse of all her dreams. "Once I knew you wanted me back—it was pretty easy to forgive you."

"I don't want you to feel like I might drop you on a whim." David's voice was soft and suddenly, he was kneeling before her. Birdie's hand went to her throat. "I never want you to doubt us again."

She'd thought she was ready for this, but—

"Elizabeth Williams," he said.

She hated when people used her proper name. It made her feel like David was proposing to someone else.

"I know what I want, and it's you. Us."

This was happening too fast. "David," she choked, heartbeat pounding in her ears.

"Elizabeth Williams," he said again, and took her hand. "Will you marry me?"

Say it. Say it. Don't hesitate. If she hesitated she'd lose her chance, and then she'd have nothing. Nothing, no life, no friends, no future.

"You—you don't have a ring," she stuttered.

"I'll get you one! I've got one. My grandmother's ring," he said eagerly. "I didn't ask Mom yet but she's always told me it's mine, to give to whomever I want. She'll get over the fact that it's you." He squeezed her hand impatiently. "Come on, Birdie. What do you say?"

One word, tethering her always to David Ebington—but tethered was better than completely unmoored.

"Yes," she said.

"I love you, Birdie," David said hoarsely.

She leaned in quickly and kissed him. He put his hands around her waist and pulled her down into his lap, so they were sitting in the grass. His hands slid down her back, breath catching in his throat. He pulled her tight against him, and she didn't draw away. She was his fiancée. She could tell by the sound of his breath, by the way he touched her, that he wanted her—and she really was thrilled about that, so she did her best to match him.

CHAPTER TWENTY-SEVEN

SURE ENOUGH, DAD'S SLEEK BLACK DUESENBERG WAS PARKED OUTSIDE A trim, small, two-story house on School Street, looking entirely out of place. Mom was still in Glen Cove, but in a part so different from their old house it was another world. Birdie had never given the houses on this street a second glance. It was nowhere anyone Birdie had associated with lived.

She'd wanted David to come with her to see Mom and let her know the news—and to be a buffer, in case Mom was livid when she saw her—but he'd evaded her. "Lunch is any minute. My mom would kill me," he said, and gave her vague directions to Mom's new place, which had irritated Birdie. He hadn't even taken her inside his house to announced their engagement. "We'll tell them soon, I promise," he said. "I just want the moment to be perfect. You understand, right?"

The perfect moment. She imagined he'd get in a fight with his parents over something, then throw it in their face—*yeah, well I'm marrying Birdie Williams, and you can't stop me!*

But he *had* asked her to marry him. She'd left with a promise to come and see him the next evening, and he'd sworn he'd be waiting for her.

Birdie wanted to go see Izzy next, but she was running on fumes, jittery and exhausted. She'd wait to see Izzy until she was rested and clean and dressed in her real clothes, and tell her the news of her engagement. Izzy would be thrilled! She'd overlook the fact that Birdie lived in this nondescript house in the village now, and everything could go back to normal between them.

The house had bright white siding, a white picket fence skirting the small yard, and a small porch. Birdie pushed the gate open and saw the the front door was ajar. She walked onto the porch, put her hand to the door, and peered inside.

A gramophone played faintly somewhere: "Singin' In the Rain," by the Lucky Strike Orchestra. One of Dad's favorite songs. Maybe Gilda was right, maybe he'd come back. Birdie slowly stepped into the hall, her skin prickling. What if Dad *was* here? She had no idea what to expect. She couldn't guess what Mom's reaction would be when she saw her.

The hardwood floors were worn but clean, and it smelled unexpectedly like fresh flowers. The first door on the left was slightly ajar, and though Birdie could hear a sweet voice singing along to the song lyrics clearly drifting down from upstairs, she paused to push the door open. A huge bouquet of multicolored roses flourished on a coffee table in the middle of the room, and another bloomed on the mantel. The room was small but plenty of light streamed in through the windows. It was spotless, and Mom had decorated with a few of the smaller pieces of furniture from their house—the pink divan that Mom had always loved, a gold-and-cream sofa, the lacquered coffee table. It actually looked cozy and pretty, and Birdie's nerves settled a bit.

The voice singing quietly upstairs was clear and light. Mom didn't have Gilda's smolder, but she had something. She could harmonize really prettily with the voice of the man singing. The door squeaked as Birdie pushed through it back into the hallway, and the hardwood groaned beneath her feet as she approached the stairs. The singing turned to humming, then stopped. "Back already?" Mom's voice sounded happy and girlish and unlike Birdie remembered. "You can set those things right there in the parlor!"

She heard Mom rustling around and smelled cigar smoke. Birdie followed the sound up the stairs and peered through the doorway of a bedroom. Mom had her back to Birdie, hair braided simply down her back, her shoulders curved forward. She looked young. When Birdie caught the profile of Mom's face, it was like she was looking at her own reflection—the same straw-colored hair, although Mom's was beginning to gray. The same round cheeks. Without her mouth set so unhappily, Mom looked like the person Birdie remembered when she was little, sitting on the divan in the living room, laughing as Dad whispered something against her neck. She was holding a record, examining its title. A few more sat on Dad's desk from his study, which was tucked against a wall. Another stack sat in an open valise on the floor. A cigar smoldered in an ashtray.

Mom turned to set the record on the desk, humming a few bars. She reached for the cigar and picked it up. She straightened, and her eyes met Birdie's.

She dropped the cigar back into the ashtray, her hand going to her heart. "Oh my God." Her eyes welled, and she stumbled around the desk, knocking records to the floor. "Oh my God. Birdie." She caught Birdie up in her arms. The tobacco smoke made her smell like Dad, but she also smelled like herself, baby powder and Chanel No. 5. "Mom," Birdie whispered into her shoulder, squeezing her hard. She hadn't missed the Mom who had been so hard on her recently, but she had missed the one who would hug and hold her.

Mom pushed Birdie back abruptly, tears rolling down her cheeks. "Birdie, I could *kill* you." She grabbed her shoulders and shook her, looking sternly into her eyes. "Don't you *ever* run off like that again!"

"Mom," Birdie choked. What could she say? Everything from the past two weeks clogged her throat. Every revelation, every emotion. "I—I'm sorry I—I was trying to—" Her voice trembled.

"Oh dear." Mom wiped her eyes, went to the desk and stubbed out the cigar. "Come here, sit down. Or—maybe we should have some tea? Or something to eat."

Birdie warily followed Mom down the stairs into a tiny, neat kitchen. Mom put a kettle on the stove, then opened the refrigerator and pulled a glass bowl out, sniffling a little as Birdie sank into a chair, bracing herself for more reprimands now that Mom had gotten over her shock.

"When you didn't come back that first night, I didn't worry." Mom cleared her throat. "I figured you'd gone to that air show from the flyer, and I knew you were angry. But then the next day, once it got late—I got a bit hysterical."

Birdie had wingwalked for the first time that day. She'd seen a man fall from the sky. She had been a whole different person before she'd left.

Mom put the bowl on the counter. It looked like chicken salad, and Birdie's stomach growled. She couldn't remember the last time Mom had fixed food for anyone; there'd always been someone else to do it. "I'd been so afraid since your dad left." Mom opened a bread box and pulled out half of a white loaf. "I was so ashamed he'd left me, and of everything that happened with the bank. I just wanted to disappear. But when you ran off—nothing else mattered. And when I started reaching out it was such a relief. People came to check on me, tried to help find you." She took a bread knife from beside the sink and began slicing, tears clearing from her voice. "Then Izzy called to let me know you'd phoned. I was furious, of course. But it was good to hear you were okay." She paused and said softly, "She said you'd gone to find Bobby."

"You knew where he went," said Birdie, anger welling up. "Gilda told me you called her."

Mom turned away and opened a cabinet. "I'd rather people think he was dead, than know he just ran out like that." She pulled down two small plates from a shelf and put them on the counter.

Mom picked up a piece of bread and fidgeted with it. Then she said tentatively, "Did you find him?"

"No."

Mom sighed, and set the bread on a plate. "I don't know why that's a relief to me."

Birdie didn't know either. She'd still give anything to see him again. "Gilda thought he'd come back here."

"I'd confronted him about—things—before, and he would never, ever admit a fault. If he came back here, he'd be forced to acknowledge that he's done some less-than-perfect things. I think he might prefer running for the rest of his life."

Mom scooped chicken salad onto the bread and pushed a plate in front of Birdie as the kettle began to whistle. Birdie dug in ravenously as Mom put tea bags and hot water in a pot and set it on the table with some cups. She pulled out a teaspoon for sugar.

Someone rapped at the door. "Oh!" Mom's spoon clattered to the counter.

"Betty?" A man's voice came from the front door.

Mom pinked and went into the front room. "You can put those right there, thank you so much! Are you hungry?" Then Birdie heard her murmur, and the voice exclaim.

Mom came back into the kitchen, followed by someone Birdie recognized vaguely. It took her a minute to place him. It was Dr. Bridges, Birdie's childhood physician, grayer at the temples than the last time she'd seen him. He looked strange—perhaps because he wasn't in his white doctor's coat. He was dressed in a button-down shirt and slacks, sweating slightly. "Birdie!" He stuck out a hand, smiling with warm brown eyes. "Thank God you're back safe. Your mother's been a wreck."

Birdie didn't know how to respond. She looked at Mom.

"Thank you so much for helping me up with those boxes, Dr. Bridges." Mom looked flustered as he awkwardly lowered his hand. "I so appreciate it."

"My pleasure, Betty." He took her hand instead and squeezed it. "Anytime. It's always so lovely to see you." He nodded to Birdie. "Hope to see you again."

He let himself out.

"What was *that?*" asked Birdie, incredulous.

"He came by with flowers this morning, to brighten the new place up." She fidgeted with a teacup. "And yesterday, too. A friend had him check on me, when I was so upset about you. He's been just incredibly helpful."

Birdie squashed down more questions. Helping her with boxes, really. Wasn't he single, a widow, his wife dead in childbirth years ago? She took another bite of chicken salad.

"Who told you to come here instead of the house to find me?" asked Mom.

Birdie's stomach buzz nervously as she swallowed. "I went to see David."

Mom's eyes widened. "Oh, I thought you two had called it quits?" She gave Birdie a questioning look.

"Actually, he asked me to marry him," said Birdie, with as much excitement as she could muster.

"Oh, honey." Mom's tone was reserved, brows lifting. "And what did you say?"

"Yes."

Mom bit her lip, skepticism clear on her face. "I know you were so excited to go to Finch's while he was at Columbia, to meet people, to go on adventures. I know you *like* David, but— this isn't something you should rush into."

"It's what I want." Birdie's voice rose. "I'd just end up marrying someone else. Someone *without* a good family and education."

"Sometimes I think you take right after your father. Then I realize, in some ways, you're just like me." Mom crossed her arms. "Just because the so-called perfect boy is interested in you, doesn't mean everything is going to be magically okay."

"Oh that's great, coming from you—after fawning all over Dr. Bridges!"

"I'm fond of Dr. Bridges," said Mom sharply. "But I know he's not going to solve all my problems."

"Dad could come back tomorrow, you don't know!"

"I wouldn't need him to solve all my problems, either, if that was the case." Mom smiled slightly. "I should tell you, Annie's buying this place."

So that explained it. "What happened to moving to England?"

"I just couldn't leave when you were missing, and when I told Annie that she got a flash of inspiration and started making inquiries into Glen Cove real estate. She couldn't believe how cheap property is right now, so she decided it was high time she bought her own place over here, now that she can't just stay at our old house when she visits. I'm going to live here and take care of the property. But it'll all be in her name, of course."

"Why didn't she decide on something nicer, since everything's so cheap?" She felt bad as she said it, disparaging the warm light coming in through the windows, the beautiful roses. But she knew what Izzy would think of it.

"I picked this house out. It's big and nice enough to suit the two of us, plus Annie when she comes. I told her, I'm not expecting her to support my old lifestyle." She gave Birdie a proud look. "I was a singer before I gave it up to marry your father. There's a larger room up front that'll just fit the baby grand, and I'm going to try teaching piano and voice out of the house." Mom actually looked pleased at the idea. Birdie tried to wrap her mind around it. Mom, working. She thought she'd be drinking martinis and hosting dinner parties for the rest of her life.

"Goodness, I can't believe I've been going on about myself!" Mom picked up the teapot. "Tell me everything that's happened with you."

"Oh, let's see." The sooner she could forget the whole thing, the better. "I ran off. I didn't find Dad. I came back. There. That's it." Hopefully soon that's all her memory of Chicago would be: a brief detour on the road to a future she'd always been headed toward.

Mom's mouth tightened as she poured them both a cup of tea. "Before you left, you said something about how I wished you were gone." She set the pot down and took Birdie's hand, looking into her face with serious eyes. "I'd never for one second wish that, do you understand? No matter what happens."

Birdie nodded, the knots inside her chest easing. She'd been away for two weeks, but this Mom had been gone for years. Birdie might be able to live here, even in this little house that was nothing special. At least long enough for David to graduate.

Izzy would welcome her back, too, and then everything would be close enough to right again.

CHAPTER TWENTY-EIGHT

MOM HAD BROUGHT OVER SOME OF BIRDIE'S THINGS, AND A TWIN BED
from one of the spare rooms at the house. It wasn't made up, but
Birdie pulled pillows and blankets out of a box and collapsed into
dreamless sleep early that evening.

She woke up restless early the next morning. Mom let Birdie use
the phone after breakfast, so long as she kept it short. Phone calls
were a luxury now, apparently, at least until Mom started working.

"I'm back," said Birdie breezily.

Izzy squealed. "Did you see David?" she asked.

"Yeessss . . ." Birdie let the word drag out.

"Well, did he ask you?"

Birdie squeezed her eyes shut. "Yes."

Izzy squealed again. "Oh, I want to hear it all! But dammit
I have to get to dress rehearsal. Oh—I should have told you.
Mikhail took you out of the group pieces, when you didn't show
up at all last week."

Birdie had forgotten. She counted days in her head—it
was Thursday. Tomorrow was the big recital. "Well, that's to be
expected."

"He cut your solo, too, of course."

Birdie's tutu was gorgeous, a real one that came straight out
from her hips, and she still knew all the steps by heart. "I don't
care a bit."

"So I can't meet up with you, unless—oh, you should come and see me at the theater! I'll be backstage within the next hour, until rehearsal begins. You wouldn't feel too strange, would you?"

"I suppose not." She did feel strange, though. Mikhail might throw a fit when he saw her. The other girls would whisper. She looked down and felt a twinge of panic. She'd found a nightdress in one of the valises full of her things, but she hadn't come across any of her good outfits. Mom had probably only emptied out one of her dressers. "See you there!" she said, and hung up.

"Are most of my things still at the house?" Birdie called from the front parlor. The new bank that was taking over the assets from Dad's bank, including their mortgage, was still in the process of foreclosing on the house. Mom had been going back and forth, taking what she wanted for her new life and leaving the rest.

"Yes," Mom answered from her bedroom.

"Can I drive the Duesenberg over there?" Birdie asked hopefully. Mom was trying to sell it for cash before the bank could take it, but nobody had extra money lying around right now.

"I don't think so, young lady, but nice try. I can take you later, but I've got plans for lunch."

"Izzy wants me to go to the studio rehearsal, but I can't go looking like this," Birdie wheedled, walking to the bedroom door to demonstrate her deshabille.

Mom was rummaging in a box full of stockings and underthings, dressed in a slip, and didn't look up. "You don't know how to drive."

"I do, though." She'd driven Dad's car twice. Once, David had shown her how to drive while her parents were away, and she'd driven it all the way to the beach. It really had been easy. The second time was to show off for Izzy, late at night after she'd snuck out to meet her. She'd driven it all the way to Izzy's house and back in the dark, very slowly. "I've driven it a bunch."

Mom looked up, eyes narrowed. "I should have assumed that." She sighed, and waved a hand in surrender. "Fine. Key's in the ignition."

Birdie changed quickly into one of Mom's Chanel-inspired jersey outfits, clattered down the stairs, and slid into the front seat of the Duesenberg. It still smelled like leather, the steering wheel smooth beneath her palms. The sky looked like it might storm, a gray wind whipping the trees, so she left the top up. She stalled out twice, but once she got it going it was easy to drive to the house, the massive engine purring much more smoothly than the circus Studebaker's as she drove down Red Spring Lane. Dad had always said the Duesenberg would be hers when she went to Finch's. She'd imagined tearing around the wide city streets with all her friends crammed in tightly. She would have been so popular.

She drove slowly down the tree-lined road. Dad hadn't managed to claim waterfront property, but their house was close enough to the massive cottages that lined the eastern shore of Hempstead Harbor that he had considered them practically one of the lucky elite. Birdie's family were members of the same country club; they made sure to attend their lavish parties, and sometimes the Gold Coasters deigned to come to theirs; her best friend had a view of the harbor from her bedroom window.

The sprawling two-story house looked the same as the day she'd left, the overgrown grass the only sign that something was amiss. She followed the circle drive around and pulled right up to the door, bouncing out of the car before it shuddered to stillness. The sky growled above. As she put her hand to the door she imagined finding a maid cleaning the stairs and delicious smells wafting from the kitchen where the cook prepared a meal. Mom and Dad inside, together again. Dad would give her a big hug and a kiss on the head, and Mom would greet her with a smile, and they'd all go in and have lunch.

Birdie turned the door handle and pushed the door open. The high-ceilinged foyer and hall were deserted and dim. All of the drapes were open, but it was dark from the low clouds outside. Some furniture and pictures were missing, but almost everything looked the same. She went straight up the stairs to her room and tried to flip on a lamp, but the electricity was off, so she pulled the curtains open. In the dim illumination she saw that her room was untouched. All of her dresses were still in her closet, her powders and jewelry still on the vanity. She could take these things with her when she and David married, and slip right back into some version of her old life.

She paused in front of the vanity and ran a hand over a perfume bottle shaped like a seahorse, a flowered paper powder box, a boar bristle hairbrush. What would happen, when she and David married? She'd always pictured it as happening in some vague, distant future. After school. But now—would they really wait until he graduated? She could probably convince him that it should happen sooner than later.

They would move into a nice house. David would drive to work in a new car. They might have a butler, a maid, a cook, a gardener, depending on how well David did. Birdie would go to things. Events. Teas. Luncheons. She would entertain. Children would happen. She would drink cocktails and listen to the gramophone, and not be one bit bitter about any of it. Birdie could picture their whole life perfectly.

It was just hard to picture herself as Mrs. Ebington.

She pulled out the tutu she was supposed to have worn in the recital that weekend. It was a beautiful shade of lilac, with a lovely stiff skirt that went straight out in layers of tulle. She shed Mom's separates and pulled on the tight leotard. She grabbed her toe shoes and wound the ribbons around her ankles. She tested the toes, flexing her feet back and forth, and then stood up on them and got a rush of excitement. She *bourré*-ed across the carpet and marked through the steps of her solo, humming some of the bars. This would be very daring on the wing of a plane, wearing pointe shoes, doing real ballet. Would dancers on pointe on multiple planes read to an audience? A ballet in the air—she bet no one had ever done *that* before. She could bring her tutu to Colette, who could replicate it well enough. She'd have to find other dancers that were classically trained, or could at least fake it. *Swan Lake*, with planes! It would work almost too easily. They could paint a plane white, another black—Birdie did a swan-like arabesque, checking her lines in the mirror, and a smudge of darkness on her shoulder gave her a shock of adrenaline.

She stumbled out of the pose and over to the mirror, turning her back to the vanity. *The tattoo.* She couldn't believe she'd forgotten it. An arc of birds was dark blue against her skin, flaking a little. She traced the lines she could reach with a finger. She scratched at them with a fingernail but they didn't budge.

She unwound the ribbons and discarded the shoes in a corner. She shoved the tutu back in the closet.

She chose a pale pink dress, flat shoes, simple gold drop earrings and a thin gold chain necklace, a few gold bangles. She rouged her cheeks and painted her lips a pale pink color. She wasn't any good at styling her own hair. She attempted to mimic what Mom had always done, winding up her hair and shoving hairpins through it, but failed miserably. She settled for brushing it and pulling it over one shoulder, and putting a clasp in it so that it stayed. It looked nice, curling over her shoulder. When she and David were married, she would insist on a maid that could help her with it. *Insist* on it.

She turned her back to the mirror and was relieved that no hint of ink showed. In the half-light she was a colorless, shadow version of herself, but otherwise she looked just like the old Birdie Williams, like nothing had changed.

She walked out the front door looking her best. Everything felt right, despite the big empty house behind her that wasn't hers anymore. Someday—maybe soon—she would have a house of her own, and it would be even better than this one.

Birdie felt calm as she drove over to the Cove Theatre. She looked terribly modern, driving and all. She was back on track, heading in the direction she'd always been supposed to go.

It hadn't begun raining, but the wind had died down. The clouds hung low and dark in the still, hot air, holding everything back.

CHAPTER TWENTY-NINE

BIRDIE POKED HER HEAD AROUND THE CURTAIN, INTO THE WINGS OF THE stage at the Cove Theater. She'd only performed here a few times since it opened. It was dim and cool, a relief from the heat outside. Girls sat around mirrors in dressing rooms, or stretched on portable bars, but the backstage area was still mostly empty.

Izzy barreled toward her, bangs slicked back into a tight ballerina's bun, cheeks chalky with powder and lips rouged red, wearing a darling robe with an Oriental print. "Birdie!" she squealed, hugging her. It was just how Izzy would have greeted her before. Birdie inhaled Izzy's familiar scent—Shalimar—and squeezed her familiar angles, sagging with relief. Izzy kissed her cheek, and Birdie felt the lipstick leave a mark as she pulled away. "I'm so thrilled you're back! Oh my gosh, did you do your own hair?" She touched Birdie's hair, palm just skimming her cheek.

Birdie lifted her hand to the spot that Izzy had brushed. "Yes, I—"

"Oh, don't worry a bit about it! You can hardly tell."

Birdie felt a flash of annoyance as Izzy turned away and led her to a skinny, mirrored side room with chairs lined up in front of the mirrors. "Tell me everything." Izzy shrugged out of her robe. Birdie watched the lean muscles play over her bare shoulder blades through the mirror. Izzy leaned down and pulled pink tights up over her long legs, and Birdie swallowed.

She knew now that what she felt for Izzy wasn't friendship. The surging lift and ache in her chest had a different name, whether or not she ever said it.

But she could never say it.

"Well, David asked me to marry him."

"And of course you said yes!" Izzy was beaming when she turned around, an arm over her chest as she reached for her costume.

"Of course." Birdie averted her eyes as she settled onto a chair.

"Ugh, how romantic!"

"It *is* romantic," Birdie reminded herself. "Everything's going to be just like we'd hoped. Well, I won't be going to Finch's, but— I'm sure I'll move into the city, to be with David while he gets through school."

Izzy squealed. "Ugh, I can't *wait*, I'm dying for class to start already! I was worried about who would be my roommate when you weren't going anymore, but Hope is going, so everything is working out perfectly." Izzy picked up her tutu and shook it out. She stepped into the leg holes and wiggled the royal-blue leotard onto her torso.

"We haven't worked out the whole situation yet," said Birdie. "When we're getting married, where we'll live, that sort of thing. But I'm sure it'll work out perfectly. Me and David, you and Monty, just like we planned."

"Ugh, Monty," Izzy said dismissively, adjusting her straps. "He's been driving me crazy lately. Maybe I'll trade him in for a cute Columbia boy." She gave Birdie a coy smile as she turned her back. "Here, help me lace up the back."

Izzy's flippancy usually delighted Birdie, but this time it shook her. "I thought you wanted to marry Monty." She pulled the lacing tight.

"Oh, probably I will. But nothing's set in stone!" Izzy said over her shoulder. "Who knows how I'll feel once I get out of here."

Birdie looped the laces, pressing them into Izzy's skin as she knotted them again. "Yes, but Monty will ask you to marry him, and we'll have perfect babies, and summer homes in the Hamptons—remember?"

Izzy turned and gave her a funny look. "Of course I remember."

Silence settled over them. Birdie could hear the tinkling of piano keys as a musician warmed up. Izzy leaned into the mirror, checking her makeup as Birdie watched unhappily. She hadn't minded the idea of getting married too much, even if it was sooner than later. It was just that she had always pictured Izzy there as well, doing the same things, making everything fun.

"I'm so happy, anyway, about you and David," said Izzy suddenly. "That's really the best way it could work out, right? I mean, considering everything."

"It really is," said Birdie.

"It's not going to be so different from how it was before." Izzy stood imperially, surveying her reflection. "I'm so relieved. Ugh, I hated what happened with the bank. It was like—all of a sudden, you were someone different than I thought. I didn't know how to think of you. But now—I feel like I know you again. Like you're still the same old Birdie. Mostly, anyway."

"Of course I'm still the same," Birdie scoffed, with just the right mixture of dismissal and playfulness. Pretending she was the same seemed to be working, anyway. She'd settle into it eventually.

"Birdie *Williams!*"

Birdie turned to see Mikhail run-walking across the backstage area, flapping his hand at her. "Is it true? Could it be? You're *here* for the rehearsal?"

Birdie flushed. "Oh, no. I heard—you took me out of the numbers, and of course you should have!" She hated disappointing Mikhail so much. Meeting his high expectations and receiving his praise had always buoyed her up no matter what else was happening, even after the bank had failed.

He swept in and embraced her. "You gave us all a turn, young lady," he said in her ear, then pulled back. "Now it's too late for you to be in the group numbers—I changed all the blocking, and it would just confuse everyone—but I really must insist that you do your solo. Come on, you know all the steps. Birdie Williams hasn't forgotten a single step I ever taught her, her whole life. I know that for a fact."

Birdie's stomach turned. *The tattoo.* "I don't have my shoes—my outfit—"

"It's only a dress rehearsal, my dear! You know half the girls will have forgotten to bring everything. I'll let the light and music people know we're adding it in, and we'll give it a go. Oh dear, better go tell them now, give them *half* a chance not to mess the whole thing up!" With that he swept back across the backstage and disappeared through the curtain. She could hear him exclaiming to the pianists.

Birdie looked at Izzy. Izzy's eyes widened, and Birdie giggled despite her nerves, and then they were laughing together. It made Birdie feel like everything was going to work out fine.

Birdie watched girls from school and dance class enter the backstage area with hair pulled tight and lips painted. Some of them smiled when they made eye contact with Birdie. Others looked away. A few little girls whose classes she'd helped with called her name and waved excitedly, and she waved back. Then Izzy announced to practically everyone that Birdie was engaged to David, and everyone warmed up to her instantly. She got hugs and hand-clasps from practically everyone.

Everything was going to be okay.

She closed her eyes and went through the steps of her solo in her mind. Izzy had pulled Birdie's hair back into a bun to get it out of her way. She'd have to dance in her dress, with bare feet, but at least no one would see the tattoo. She'd be in costume for the actual show, so she'd have to figure something out. Pancake makeup would probably do the trick. Between makeup and clothing, she could keep it hidden for the rest of her life.

She pictured wearing her pretty tutu and pointe shoes. She would stretch on the bar, chalk her toes, and check her reflection a thousand times. She went through the choreography in her head once, then again, as girls chatted and giggled around her. She remembered every step. She'd chosen the culminating piece from *The Rite of Spring* for her solo. She'd picked it because Mikhail thought it would challenge her, but also because it was terribly controversial and hopefully it would shock some people, particularly Mom, and because that pleased Izzy. The song was about a pagan ritual where a girl, chosen as a sacrificial victim, dances herself to death.

When she opened her eyes again the lights were dimming as the girls quieted. She peeked out through the wings. As the music came on, the curtain lifted to reveal a parade of the littlest girls. Birdie grinned at the unsure look on their faces as they pointed their toes and wandered around in tiny, confused circles with flowers in their hair. Birdie couldn't remember her first dance recital, but Dad used to love to talk about it. Birdie had apparently ignored all the choreography and decided to do her own dance out in front of the other girls, smiling broadly at the audience. *I knew then you were going to be a star*, he'd say proudly.

The groups of girls got older, their dance numbers more polished. Birdie's chest tightened as her solo got closer. It was supposed to be her biggest performance yet—but that was hardly true now. She'd danced on the wing of a flying airplane. These girls had no idea what it was like for a crowd to cheer for you.

They had no idea what it was like to fail in front of everyone, to just fall apart.

She watched Hope and Izzy and the others take the stage and begin the piece that she was supposed to be a part of. She could feel the movement in her body. Her brain sent every signal. It was impossible that her arm wasn't extending, right where Izzy's arm was. It was impossible that her back wasn't arching elegantly. She knew exactly what movement every girl was going to do before it happened. She knew exactly how to move so that she would have fit right in with them, blending in perfectly, seamlessly.

The tightness in her chest turned into an ache as her cohorts filed offstage and the first notes of the next song struck up. A spotlight came on, and Birdie walked to the center of the stage, pointing her toes, arms held above her head, leading with her chest. Her muscles tensed as she took her pose.

The first mournful notes sounded and she pulsed to life. She was sad, a coerced victim, but as the power of the rite gradually overcame her she would become joyous and powerful, even though the dance meant her death.

The soft music gained energy, notes swirling and tangling. Birdie took control of every corner of the stage, filling the room with her presence. Elongated, stretching poses contrasted with quick, energetic movement. Her breath came faster as she executed each sequence perfectly. She was performing well—but something didn't feel right. She couldn't quite connect to the power and energy of the piece though she was trying with all her might.

The music became more frantic and she took great leaping pirouettes and jetés, spinning and spinning as the music spun. She hit every mark. She nailed every step—but she began to understand the wrongness in her body. She was supposed to put her foot there, and so she did. She was supposed to spin, so she did. She couldn't connect to the music because her movement wasn't coming from the music. It was just a pretty sequence of steps she'd learned.

The music became more and more frenzied until she collapsed to the ground at the end, just like she was supposed to. She pressed her forehead against the chalky floor as the stage went black, arms outstretched over her head, and squeezed her eyes shut as she gasped for breath. A smattering of clapping broke the silence, and Mikhail's chirping voice exclaimed, but she didn't want to look up. She didn't want to force a proud smile or curtsy. She'd done everything right, but it felt all wrong.

CHAPTER THIRTY

DAVID BENT DOWN TO THE CAR WINDOW, ANGEL FACE GLOWING IN THE gas porch light. "I thought you'd never come!" he whispered. He opened her door, and she looked up at him, confused.

"I'll drive," he explained.

She slid into the passenger's seat, feeling edgy as David got behind the wheel. He pulled away from his house without kissing her. "Let's go to your old place, what do you say?" he asked. "It'll be fun to creep around in the dark—and we can get some privacy." He reached over and squeezed her knee, and Birdie felt a tingle of apprehension.

She and David had spent plenty of time alone, but they had always been in close proximity of other people—an empty room at a party, the hangar before Dad came out to give them rides in the Jenny, in the back garden while his parents were home. Nobody was anywhere near her big empty house. But David was driving there already, and she didn't say anything.

She felt out of sorts after her performance. Mikhail had been even more over-the-top than usual—not only had she remembered every step, he had never seen her dance with such passion and feeling! She should have been delighted to be praised in front of everyone. Instead she kept thinking that there was no way she deserved acclaim for such a rote performance.

David pulled up in front of the house. It loomed in the darkness, barely visible against the cloud-darkened night sky. Birdie couldn't remember ever seeing her house with no lights on at night. It looked like a stranger's house, dark and sad. David shut the car off and turned toward her. He looked like a stranger in the shadows, too. "It feels so good to have everything right between us again."

She smiled faintly. "I'm glad you missed me." The words felt wrong coming out of her mouth, but she *was* glad. She needed him to be glad.

"Let's go inside," he said. "I've got something for you."

She took a deep breath. "David—"

He leaned in and kissed her, and her insides recoiled even though she returned it. With June, she'd felt like all of her nerves were warm and reaching. Kissing her—she remembered how it made her ache—

She felt herself responding to her heated thoughts and pulled away, ashamed.

David's mouth found her ear. "Let's go to the courthouse tomorrow. We can drive into the city, somewhere they don't know us."

She tried to find his eyes, but in the dark all she saw was a faint glittering. She should say *Yes, let's do it. Let's go tonight!* "You haven't even told your mother yet."

"I'll tell her after it's done. That way they can't stop us." He drew her across the seat toward him.

"David, wait—"

He paused, hand resting on her thigh beneath the edge of her skirt.

"I need a few days," she said finally.

"Friday, then?" he prodded, tugging on her hem.

"Maybe Friday."

"Fine." He pulled her in again. "I'm fine with that. I guess I just got so excited at the thought of being married to you—" He kissed her again, and she fought the urge to push away. She was just so tired from her long day.

"You ready to go exploring?" he whispered, smiling.

Getting out of the car sounded wonderful. She fumbled with the door handle and busted out into the cool air, taking gulping breaths, but she still felt claustrophobic. Her ribs felt tight. She wished she heard the buzzing of a plane engine above her. She wished June was landing in the long grass outside the hangar, here to pick her up and take her flying.

David took her hand gently, and it felt nice.

"So, where did you go when you left?" He led her toward the house. "I bet it wasn't all because I hurt your feelings."

"I was trying to find my dad." She tried to keep her mind blank. She'd never told June about that.

Why did June keep filling her mind?

"Why?" he asked as he walked up the steps to the front door, Birdie one step behind. "Isn't it better if nobody finds him?"

"I thought if he could just come back and—I don't know—he could fix things . . ." It sounded so stupid.

"My parents say he's giving your mom money, *their* money he owes them. That's how she can buy that house." David paused with his hand on the doorknob and looked back, a serious expression on his face. "All I'm saying is that there are people who will never forgive him."

Birdie knew he was right. Dad wouldn't be able to fix anything. It would just make things worse, now that she was pulling her life back together. She should try pretending he was dead like Mom had. Maybe that would make her feel better about never seeing him again.

David pushed the front door open and led her into the pitch-dark foyer. "Jeez, it's creepy in here. So dark," he whispered.

Birdie shivered. "I don't know." Her feet stalled in the doorway.

"Come on, let's check your dad's study," David said, a smile in his voice as he tugged her hand. "Maybe there's a couple of bottles still in the liquor cabinet."

"Ugh, David." She was wound so tight.

"Oh, come here." He pulled her into the foyer and hugged her stiff form. "I'm sorry," he murmured into her hair. "Here I am, talking about filching his scotch and how people hate him, when you two were so close."

Birdie relaxed against David and squeezed her eyes shut, sadness flooding her chest. Happy times she had with Dad flickered in her mind. Flying, dancing, playing, laughing.

"You didn't find him, huh?" David said gently. "Wherever you went."

She hadn't found Dad, but the flying, dancing, playing, laughing—new adventures blazed as bright in her mind as any memory with Dad. All of it lost when she'd screwed up so badly.

Maybe this was what Dad felt. Maybe he felt like he couldn't come back, or reach out to her even though he loved her, because he'd screwed up so badly. Maybe he was embarrassed and couldn't face her after what he'd done.

She sniffled and realized she was crying.

"Oh, Birdie." David fumbled around in the dark until he found a couch and sat her down. He handed her his hankie. "Everything's going to be okay." He put an arm around her.

"I made a mess of everything," she said, muffled by the hankie. She'd let them all down so hard, and then she'd just left without even trying to fix anything or explain.

Light caught a glittering in David's hand. She squinted, but it was too dark to make out.

"You didn't do anything wrong." He took her chin and lifted it. She tried to find his eyes, but could see nothing but the dimmest outline of him. He could have been anybody. "Hey, whatever you're sad about, I've got something to make it better."

He held up his hand, out of the way of the shadows. The bit of light coming in through a window showed that his fingers pinched a ring. A ring with a diamond in a Tiffany setting. "See?" he said. "I told you I had a ring."

David found her hand and slid the ring on her finger. It felt warm and clammy against her skin. "David." *Not this. Not now.*

He took the hankie from her gently. She felt the cushion shift on either side as he planted his hands on the back of the couch above her shoulders. "Everything is going to be perfect." He leaned in.

"Oh my God." She turned her face away. She should agree, she should cheer, this was the thing that would make it all better—

"Come on, Birdie." He nuzzled her cheek. "A kiss to seal the deal."

"I can't." Her body heated up, pulse accelerating as she pushed him away, but he didn't budge.

"Why wouldn't you want a kiss?" His voice hardened slightly.

"No." She fumbled with the ring, pulling it off her finger. "I can't *marry* you."

"What?"

She held the ring up to his nose, hoping he could see it in the dark. "I told you, I messed up." Her voice was shaking. "I'm sorry."

She couldn't read his gaze in the darkness. He didn't move for a moment, then collapsed on the couch beside her and ran his hands through his hair. "Are you serious?"

She held the ring out steadily. "I am."

He snatched the ring and shoved it into his pocket. "God dammit." he said softly. "Thank God I didn't tell my parents."

Suddenly she couldn't fathom why she'd ever considered marrying him. "*That's* all you have to say?"

He put his hands on her hip and tugged her towards him. "Come on, Birdie. Let me try and convince you one more time."

Birdie leaned back warily. "I'm calling that stuff off, David."

"You don't think I'm so bad." Another tug, harder this time.

"Stop it." She ducked away to get off the couch, but he grabbed her wrist.

"We can still date, can't we?" He drew her in. "It could just be like before."

"Let go, David."

They were still for a moment, Birdie trying to keep her breath steady as his fingers tightened on her wrist.

"I don't get it." He put his other hand to her thigh and slid it slowly up. Her heart hammered against her ribs. "The way I see it, you should be begging me to take you back."

She hauled back and slapped him.

He yelped, letting go and putting a hand to his cheek.

"Oh, now I'm really sorry," she jumped to her feet, pulse pounding, "that I even *considered* marrying you!"

"God, Birdie! You don't have to be such a bitch about it," David said petulantly.

She stalked toward the front door, trying not to look scared. She could hear him stumbling to his feet behind her. "Birdie!" he called, his voice sweetening. "Birdie, Jesus. Wait, I was kidding!"

She flung the door open and raced toward the car. She pulled the door open and slammed it shut behind her and locked it. He pounded against the door as she turned the key in the ignition. "Come on, Birdie!" His voice was muffled. She spun in her seat and locked the back door when he reached for it.

Birdie looked up as the engine purred and bared her teeth in a smile. "You're gonna to have to find your own way home," she said loudly, so he could hear her through the glass. "Dad told me not to let creeps into my car."

She shifted into gear and accelerated quickly. David hung on to the door handle and ran alongside the car, an outraged look growing on his face, until finally he stumbled and let go. She peeled around the drive and onto the road, tires squealing. She rolled the window down and screamed into the wind, hair whipping around her face. She felt like she was flying. Her heart was still thrumming in her chest but it felt good now, exhilarating, the RPMs high enough to get her somewhere with a good view.

CHAPTER THIRTY-ONE

Birdie was backstage again, and this time the audience was full of people. She peeked out through the curtain as dancers stretched and talked in low voices behind her. Mom was in the second row, sitting next to Dr. Bridges and wearing one of her favorite dresses. He said something to her and she laughed. She wore lipstick, and her hair was curled and pinned. Birdie put a hand to her own hair, slicked back into a neat bun. She wore her tutu, tights, and pointe shoes, with a cardigan buttoned up over everything.

She'd gone back to the house that afternoon to get her tutu and pointe shoes. She'd put on her makeup and done her hair. She'd filled the Duesenberg with her favorite things: dresses and shoes, things from her vanity, a pillow and throw she'd had since she was five, her prized records. The things she wanted to keep.

She'd called David, but he hung up on her as soon as he heard her voice. She was glad he'd gotten home all right, although part of her hoped he'd had to walk the whole way.

The lights dimmed and Birdie headed for the wings. The music of the first number began as the curtain lifted, casting bright, sideways light backstage.

Izzy came up beside her and nudged her with a shoulder. "I talked to Monty." Her tone was smug. "He told me David was going to give you something last night?" Izzy grabbed her hand and frowned at it. Then she grabbed the other one, turning it over. "Where is it?" she asked, her face falling. "He didn't give it to you after all, did he?"

"Oh, he did." Birdie shrugged out of her cardigan and carefully pressed the toes of one foot into a box of chalk, turning her back to Izzy. "I just decided I didn't want it after all."

"Are you kidding? You're trying to tell me that—" Izzy gasped. "What in the world is *that*?"

"What? Oh, that?" Birdie pressed the toes of her other foot into the box. "A tattooed lady in a circus gave it to me. You like it?" She half hoped that Izzy would squeal with delight and ask her all about it, and Birdie would tell her everything that had happened when she was gone and Izzy would love it, admire her for it—

"Oh my God. Birdie. Tell me you're joking." She pressed her fingers against Birdie's shoulder, then scrubbed at the skin. "Holy cow, it's real!" Birdie turned, smiling cautiously, but there was no delight on Izzy's face—only shock, hardening into disapproval. "You're really going to go out on that stage like that? Your mom is out there, Birdie. *My* mom is out there."

"Of course I am," said Birdie, too loudly, and a stagehand hushed her. She continued quietly, "Wouldn't want to break poor Mikhail's heart again." She kept her tone flippant and carefree, but tears were crawling up her throat. Birdie had known what would happen as soon as she said no to David, but it didn't stop it from hurting. She was becoming someone different, someone who kissed girls and rejected rings and tattooed her skin and wasn't rich and would probably never be rich, and their friendship would not survive it.

Izzy stood silently as they both watched an intermediate group file on stage. The space between them filled with questions, but Izzy didn't ask her anything. After a moment she turned on her heel and walked away, and when Birdie turned to look Izzy was whispering with Hope. They both glanced at Birdie, distaste on their faces, and talked behind their hands.

Sadness rose, filling every space inside of Birdie. Instead of making a plan to fix it or pretending she didn't feel it, she held onto her anguish and dug into its texture. The overwhelming ache in her chest, the clench of her fists, the terrible burn behind her eyelids. Izzy and Hope swept past her, onto the stage with her other old friends, for their number, and Birdie didn't watch. She closed her eyes and let tears slip down her cheeks.

The dancers jostled backstage when their dance ended, breath coming fast and excited. Birdie walked onto the stage, feeling worlds away from them as the first notes of her piece cut through her dejection. She didn't pose. She stood in the spotlight and closed her eyes. The audience coughed and shifted in their seats as she stood there inelegantly, head bowed, tears on her cheeks. She listened, hearing threads of yearning that tugged at her muscles, pulling movement out of her. She held still until the music wove deep into her and electricity pulsed through her whole body.

She came to life, letting the music and her own emotion fuel her. Her sadness was overwhelming and terrible, but somehow it poured out of her as she danced and became beautiful and ugly and aching and powerful. She wasn't dancing because she was supposed to, because she was good at it, because it was pretty. She was expressing something true.

She was dancing in the air, the power of her movement enough to lift her skyward without an engine. She jumped so high she could imagine leaving the ground. Izzy and her old life wasn't continuing without her, she was leaving *them* behind. The wings Colette had inked on her skin spread, growing larger and larger, a flock lifting her where she couldn't raise herself. Drums pounded and horns became frenzied and she tried with all her might to sever the ties of gravity, refusing to collapse to the ground in the final throes of the piece as planned.

When she opened her eyes, arms thrown up, panting as the music faded and applause began to swell, she felt transformed.

"Birdie Williams." Mikhail fluttered up after curtain call, cheeks flushed with fury. "Don't you *ever* perform something I haven't approved, do you hear me? I have *never* in all my *days* been so offended. *Never* have I heard of such a thing. This sort of thing is absolutely un*heard* of."

Over his shoulder, Birdie saw Izzy give her a that's-what-you-get look. A few younger dancers surrounded them, eyes wide. Most of her cohort didn't look over at all, making self-conscious small talk as they strained to overhear.

Birdie had never disappointed Mikhail, but she didn't care. She still pulsed with power. "It was my solo. I wanted to try something different."

"It's a choreography," Mikhail insisted. "You have to follow it or it's—it's *nothing*. It's just a complete *mess*."

"It felt right."

"Well," he sputtered. "I just never thought we would end on this kind of note."

"I didn't do it to hurt you," she said quietly. "I could never thank you enough for everything you've taught me."

Mikhail gave her one last squinting look, his mouth tense, then spun around to congratulate other dancers on their well-executed choreography. She knew he'd forgive her. She'd call him from the road and say she was sorry for surprising him, and he'd apologize for yelling at her.

Birdie hopped off the stage and found Mom.

"That was something else!" said Dr. Bridges. "So modern. I've seen something like that before, but only in the city, at this new school. You heard of Martha Graham?"

"What is this?" Mom exclaimed, putting hands on Birdie's shoulders and turning her around. Her fingers touched her shoulderblade tentatively. "My goodness," she said, after a pause.

Birdie wasn't going to get approval, so she didn't try. "The Duesenberg is mine, isn't it?" She turned around to face her. "Dad always said it was mine once I was old enough."

"I was thinking," said Mom, flushing excitedly. "Even at half price, it would pay for your first year at Finch's. I bet we could find someone who'd buy it for that. And maybe we could find a way to manage the second year somehow."

"I don't want to go to Finch's," said Birdie.

"You should be a professional dancer," said Dr. Bridges. "You've got the talent for it!"

Birdie's heart constricted. "I'm too short. They have height requirements."

"Now, I don't know everything about it, but I think the new modern dance school is sort of against having those kinds of rules," said Dr. Bridges.

"Really?" said Birdie, sidetracked. "What school, again?"

"They might let short girls in," said Mom, "but surely they don't take girls with—*things* on their shoulders!"

Birdie shook her head, reorienting. "So if I'm not going to Finch's, I can have the car?"

"You don't need that car, Birdie. Honestly, nobody needs that car. The money would be far more useful."

Birdie took Mom's hand and squeezed it. "Give me the car, and the bank won't be able to take it, right?"

"What in the world, Birdie." Mom's jaw clenched. "It's not up for discussion."

Dr. Bridges cleared his throat. "I'm going to give you two a moment." He walked away to congratulate a few of his young patients.

Mom's gaze followed him. "I've got a lot going on," she said distractedly. "I really don't need you giving me a hard time."

"I'm leaving, Mom. With or without the car. But the car would make it so much easier, and I think Dad would want me to have it."

Mom turned and looked at her. "Nonsense, where would you go?"

"I—I have a place at a show. In Chicago."

Mom's eyes widened. "A show in *Chicago?*"

"Yes. Well, I might. I don't know. I messed things up—I need to take the Duesenberg." If she went back with a new car that went faster than the Studebaker, and a promise to jump off the landing gear, and maybe a few more stunts—they could put the show on for a crowd, like the show they'd done in Coney Island. They could make some money, and get the show back on its feet.

She had to go back and fix the mess she'd made.

"You can't run off. A single girl—you know it's not safe—"

Birdie's hands clenched. She'd wasted so much time already. Days had gone by with June and everyone else hating her. "I can't stay here," she said. "I won't stay here."

Mom's eyes welled up. Birdie grabbed her hand. "It'll be different this time. I'll call you every day, and I won't be gone forever. But I have to go."

Mom looked over at Dr. Bridges, and Birdie could see worry and fear and excitement about their new lives on her face. That's how it was right now. Every feeling all at once, more intensely than Birdie had ever experienced them. Mom probably felt that, too. "We can discuss it further, I suppose," her mother said reluctantly. "You'll tell me more tonight."

Birdie felt her starting to let go. "Sure," she said. "I'll tell you everything before I go."

CHAPTER THIRTY-TWO

BIRDIE PULLED UP TO HENRIETA'S FARMHOUSE MIDMORNING ON SUNDAY. A gentle sun shone down through the open top of the Duesenberg, but the air was cool. It was one of those strange summer days that felt like fall even though it was still months away. She'd thought she could make it all the way from New York in one day since it had taken that long when they'd flown from Coney Island, but traveling by plane was definitely faster than even a nice car—she'd had to pull over to sleep in northern Indiana and continue on the next morning.

The crocodile-painted Studebaker was parked in front of the house, the hood lifted. Milosh was sitting on the porch steps, legs wide, bent over a paperback. He looked up and took in the sleek lines of the Duesenberg and his mouth opened slightly, eyes widening when they landed on Birdie. She waved timidly as she turned off the engine, expecting his expression to harden, but Milosh broke into a smile, closed his book, and ambled up to her door.

"Well, what do you know. You leave with nothing, us worrying what on earth was gonna happen to you—and here you come back looking like you just won a lottery." He bent down and took in the interior details. He whistled low and ran his hand over the steering wheel. "Mind if I get in and take a gander?"

Relieved, Birdie nodded and scooted over to the passenger's side as Milosh opened the door and folded himself into the driver's seat, setting his worn book on the seat between them. He wasn't screaming at her to leave—but then again, she couldn't imagine Milosh ever treating anyone unkindly.

"Bennie's gonna lose his mind." Milosh put his hands on the steering wheel. "I didn't know anybody but celebrities could afford something like this! How fast does she go?"

"It's supposed to go over a hundred, but I've never tried."

"And it's a breezer and everything," he marveled, looking up at the sky through the open top. "Man. Bet she never has engine trouble. The Studebaker's still broke, though Bennie's been fiddling with it all week."

"Here's the thing." Birdie's heart picked up speed. "I came back, and I brought Dad's car with me—I know I messed the audition up big time, but I was thinking we could still put on a great show, like at Coney Island, only right here, in Henrieta's field! We could make a bunch of money with this Peter Pan thing. We can flyer the city, get it together, and wow everybody—" Birdie's hands twisted in her lap. "I could make up for ruining the audition—"

"Oh, man." Milosh looked at her with mournful eyes. "You know, the tryout—nobody blames you for that. Merriwether's transfer was the real nail in the coffin. And—I don't think the others are gonna be too keen on getting the show back together."

Birdie said in a quiet, strained voice, "I know. I really messed up and everyone's so mad at me that they won't work with me, but I was thinking—"

"No matter if they won't work with you. Hazel and Oscar—Hazel gave him back his ring."

"No." Birdie's heart sank.

"Oscar's up north of Chicago, staying with an old friend of his. He's been coming around, inviting us out. Hazel and June are staying at the boarding house. They're thinking of trying for the National Air Races individually, maybe get a spot in a race or demo. They'll hang out till then, give rides to rubes, that sort of thing. Ruth offered them a spot in the Hollbrook circus, too."

"The *Hollbrook* circus?" Birdie hadn't considered that she might come back and find . . . "Everyone's gone?"

"Merri, Bennie, and the boys are still here. She's been giving rides to the local kids, and Bennie's been trying to fix up the damned car. He might end up having to trade it in. They're planning on moving on, but haven't figured out a plan yet."

"But—what about Merriwether's Flying Circus of the Air?" The determination that had driven Birdie all the way from Glen Cove evaporated. She had been fired up to fix everything and make the circus take her back—but there was no circus.

"It's over, I guess. A lot of stuff's coming to an end these days, for lots of people. It's not just us." He patted her knee. "Don't fret. We'll figure out something."

She sank back against the leather seat. "What are you and Colette gonna do?"

He gave her a lopsided smile. "We need the circus more than the rest of you, or something like it. I'm hoping we'll find something here in Chicago, at a theater show or something like that, or maybe head back to New York."

"I guess I'm heading that way," Birdie said bitterly. "I can give you a lift."

"Who knows, maybe we'll try to track down a Ringling train and get in with them. We ran into some trouble in a three-ring before, but it's also what we know best. Who knows, maybe it's time to give it another shot. Maybe we won't have a choice."

Birdie felt numb and drained. "This is all my fault."

Milosh sighed and let his head fall backward, closing his eyes against the bright sky. "Well, sitting around blaming yourself isn't gonna do much good."

She didn't know where to go from here. Sometimes a wobble turned into a crash that you never recovered from. "Suppose there's nowhere to go but back to Glen Cove." If she even could. She didn't think she had enough money for gas to get back to New York. She looked sideways at Milosh, watching the light flicker on his amber skin as a cloud passed overhead. "Where is home for you?"

He kept his eyes closed. "Home is not 'where.' It's 'who.'"

That wasn't much of an answer. "But where did you grow up?"

"All over the place. My family never stopped moving."

"So you *grew up* in the circus?"

"Not exactly." He paused. "My folks are Roma," he said carefully.

"Roman?"

"*Roma*. Travelers. My grandparents came from Europe, but they were from somewhere else before that. We are always from somewhere else."

Birdie had never heard the word *Roma* in her life. "Colette, too? Is she—Roma?"

"No." He opened his eyes and straightened, and sad look on his face as he stared out the window. "I—there's rules about that. That's why we left the three-ring where we met. Well—she had other reasons for leaving. But my family would not acknowledge us."

So many rules about who you should love in this world! All of them ridiculous in the face of the care she saw between him and Colette, or Bennie and Merriwether. "So Colette is home for you now."

He drummed a beat on the steering wheel, his face clearing. "One day I'll try again with my family, if I can find them. I like to think they'd act differently if they had another chance. They are good people." He smiled. "But yes. If I'm with Colette, that's enough for me."

Birdie's eyes welled. Glen Cove was no longer the home she longed for in her mind. Dad was gone. Mom was still there—and she'd made it clear that she'd prefer that Birdie stayed, though she'd given Birdie the car once she promised to call from the road every chance she got—but Birdie couldn't imagine going back right now.

She missed the circus, the family of sorts that took her in with curiosity and kindness. What an adventure the past few weeks had been. Dancing and performing and feeling like she might have a future doing what she loved best. And kissing June, spending time with her—that sense of falling and longing and never wanting to leave—

An idea blazed in her mind, desperation throwing one last switch. "If I could get Hazel and June and Oscar back," said Birdie slowly. "If I could convince them to do this show, do you think you and Colette and everyone else would still want to do it?"

"I bet we all would," said Milosh. "But I don't see how you'll work that. Hazel's not gonna work with Oscar. And neither of the girls are happy with you—they'd probably say no just to spite you. A small-time show might make them a little bit of extra money, but it won't be enough to entice them. Fact of the matter is, most folks that come and see an air show don't pay for it. It's nothing like the NAR contract would have been."

"I've got an idea that would make our show a thousand times better than the NAR." Birdie was energized again. It was a long shot, but it was the only idea she had. Sinclair Stevens was making a new movie that would need stunt pilots. He had said he was meeting with the investors a week from Monday.

That was tomorrow.

Sinclair Stevens was still in Chicago.

CHAPTER THIRTY-THREE

BIRDIE PUSHED THROUGH THE DOOR OF THE MAYFLY CAFÉ IN THE EARLY evening. Milosh had told her Oscar had stopped by that morning and invited him there for a drink, and sure enough Oscar was standing at the bar with another guy. He looked simultaneously more disheveled and more rich than she remembered him, sleeves rolled up to his elbows, loose tie, hair standing on end.

Oscar had always been sweet and friendly, but she had a sinking feeling she might have tainted his attitude. She walked across the black-and-white tile, heels clicking softly in the vast room, and stopped a few feet away from his back. "Oscar."

He turned. "Whoa!" He looked almost frightened, which took her aback. "Birdie! I wasn't expecting to see you."

Birdie smoothed her skirt with twitchy hands. "Can I join you?"

Oscar's jaw clenched as he dropped her gaze and stared into his drink.

Oscar's friend eyeballed her, then stuck out a thick hand. "Nate, nice to meet you."

Birdie shook it. "Birdie."

The guy nodded, a smile twitching his lips. "Figured." He looked at Oscar. "I'm gonna head outside for a smoke. Back in ten."

Oscar breathed out heavily. Birdie could smell liquor on him, but he didn't seem drunk. "Thanks, Nate," he said.

Birdie took a stool, and Oscar ordered her a gin fizz. Birdie commented on the weather. Oscar didn't respond. They sat in awkward silence until the drink appeared. "What are you doing?" he asked tersely, handing it to her. "I'm going to try to be civil here, but never seeing you again was my best-case scenario."

Birdie took a deep breath and watched her tight grip on the glass whiten her knuckles. She deserved that. "You can't imagine how sorry I am," she started.

"I'm pretty sure *you* can't imagine how sorry *I* am." He pinched his lips together and looked down, tapping his tumbler against the bar.

"I heard about—that Hazel—" She stopped when she saw his face twist up at Hazel's name. It felt too cruel to finish the sentence. "Listen, Oscar. I'm gonna make it up to you."

"You can't," he said, clenching his hand around his drink. "The only thing you can do is just leave me alone. Please." He looked like he had right after Charlie fell, like the wattage inside of him had dimmed. She couldn't bear the sad slope of his shoulders.

"I'm going to get the show back together," she said, trying to sound confident, and not like she'd thought of the million ways it could all go wrong. "And I'm gonna convince Hazel to give you another chance."

"You're nuts." His voice was hard. "We lost our shot at the NAR. Nobody's gonna work with you, and Hazel's not going to work with me. You've got nothing."

She leaned in. "Listen, if I could get Hazel to do the Peter Pan show as our own barnstorming circus, and she was willing to work with you, would you do it?"

"God. Yes. I would do it." The pain in his eyes lifted a little. "Please, don't mess with me. You better have some plan!"

"That man I left the Hot Toddy with that night—it was Sinclair Stevens."

Oscar's eyes went wide. "Says you!"

"It's true! He was talking all night about how he was putting together his next film—a war flick, Oscar. He was talking about casting men *and* women in the flying roles, and needing tons of stunt pilots." She wasn't lying—he had talked about all of those things—but just in passing, just making conversation.

Oscar was right, she was nuts to think she could make this into something.

Oscar dimmed again. "It was Hazel's dream to head out to Hollywood and do something like that. And I always thought we'd go, you know, after we got married, and try our luck."

Birdie made her pitch. "What if I could guarantee that Mr. Stevens was at our show, and that he was considering hiring us? Do you think Hazel would do it then?"

Oscar stared at her. "Oh my God. Yes. I think she would." He beamed suddenly, enthusiasm lighting him up like a bulb. "Birdie! Is this a sure thing?"

"No," she admitted, "but I know where he's staying, I know he's still in town, and I know he thinks I'm cute." She smiled tentatively. "How could he resist an invitation to the best air show Chicago has ever seen, when he's looking for the best stunt pilots in the country?"

Oscar shook his head, his expression grave again, though the light in his eyes remained. "Me and you can't even talk to each other, Birdie. Tell Hazel we won't so much as *look* at each other, if she agrees to do it."

Birdie giggled, relieved that he was feeling hopeful enough to joke. "Whatever it takes!" She looked down. "Thank you. I hope you'll be able to forgive me, if I pull this off."

"Oh, I'm terrible at holding a grudge." He ran his hands through his hair and gave her a lopsided smile. "Consider yourself forgiven."

"Oh, don't go too easy on me now."

"Listen—I know I flirted with you some. I—you know, I really did like you. I just—what me and Hazel have—"

"I know," Birdie said softly. "You did nothing wrong. And I'll convince Hazel of that if it kills me."

Birdie almost lost her nerve when she pulled up to the boarding house lot. It was late in the evening, the sky full of stars. The front porches were dark, but she could see lights and hear voices coming from the back of the building. She thought she heard the buzz of a plane in the field, but it was surely too dark to fly at this hour. Birdie killed the headlights and sat in the car for a few minutes before she got out and made her way hesitantly toward the sound of people, tripping over a bicycle in the dark. Around the corner, a crew of girls and guys sat on the back porch under the glare of a single hanging bulb, laughing and smoking and gesturing out toward the field.

These people had seen her ruin the tryout, and they'd surely heard what she'd done to Hazel by now. Birdie lingered in the shadows of the house. She could just leave. She could come back in the morning when they wouldn't all be sitting in ranks, lined up to face her down.

There was June, leaning on Ruth's knee, hair tucked behind her ear. Birdie felt a jolt in her chest, like a propeller trying to catch. She had forgotten the perfect line of June's jaw. How smooth and tan her skin looked above the collar of her shirt. Ruth passed June a cigarette, and Birdie watched her hands take it, her lips touch the paper. Ruth's hand was on June's back with a casual touch and something twisted up in Birdie's stomach, something that made her want to walk up and slap Ruth's face and turn to June and ask her to dance.

Hazel was curled next to June, her long legs tucked up on the step beneath her, hair hiding her face. Someone exclaimed loudly, a few people stood up, and Hazel's head jerked up. She stared out at the field, then looked away distractedly, her smile fading. The overhead light made the shadows deep beneath her eyes.

Birdie deserved whatever judgment this crowd held for her. She was here to fix things with Hazel, not because of the way June had danced with her, or the way her mouth touched a blossom or the paper of a cigarette. Even if June never kissed her or touched her or even spoke to her again, Birdie needed to try to make up for what she'd done.

The unmistakable hum of an airplane engine grew louder. And Birdie squinted out toward the field. A couple of lights bobbed around in the darkness, people holding flares of some sort. Then flares appeared in the sky above the field, very low—coming in fast—a plane was flying *in the dark*, with only a few flares to illuminate its path. A few people shouted, then someone screamed. The plane hit the field hard, flares bouncing in between the jostling lights out on the field, but then it coasted to a relatively smooth stop and everyone cheered.

Birdie left the shadows as everyone ran up to the plane in the darkness. June and Hazel stayed on the porch, but June was leaning in to say something to Ruth and didn't notice Birdie approach.

"That was really neat," Birdie said to the guy who had climbed out of the plane—he was the one who had tried to talk with her at the boarding house the first time she'd been there. "I didn't know you could fly at night."

"Thanks." His eyes flitted to Hazel, and she knew he'd heard what she'd done. "Ah, just working on a stunt for our NAR show. Preliminary trial."

Birdie took a deep breath and turned. Hazel had spotted her and had the same, almost frightened look on her face that Oscar had when he recognized her. Birdie felt like a monster. Then June looked up, and only anger registered in her eyes. Birdie's heartbeat sped up, lifting off in uncertain weather.

"Hazel." She met her eyes, even though it was so hard. "Hi. Can I talk to you?"

"Well, look who it is," said June sardonically, as Hazel looked away. Ruth pressed her lips together to hold back a smile.

"I want to apologize." Birdie couldn't look at June as she walked up. She would be contrite. She was the one at fault.

"You don't have to apologize to these people." June made a sweeping gesture, and Birdie noticed the open flask in her hand. "It's because of you that they'll be performing in our stead at the second annual National Air Races. That's quite a gift you've given them."

June's words threatened to throw her off course. Birdie clenched her fists and kept her eyes focused on Hazel. "Hazel. Just for a minute. Please."

"Oh, you want to apologize to Hazel?" June took a deliberate swallow from her flask. "Yeah, nothing you can say is gonna make up for that."

Hazel looked at Birdie suddenly, her expression pained. "Fine," she said. "Let's talk."

June stood up.

"No." Hazel caught June's hand. "It's okay."

"I'm coming."

"June." Hazel waited.

June looked like a wire strung taut, but she gave Hazel's hand a squeeze and sat back down, Ruth putting a hand on her knee.

Hazel stood up, walked down the steps, and came to a stop right in front of Birdie, arms crossed. "So, what is it you want to say to me?"

She was very intimidating, even when she looked so tired and sad. "Let's um—come here for a minute." Birdie was relieved when Hazel trailed her away from the porch into the gloom outside the bare light bulb's glare. Birdie faced away from the boarding house. Hushed chatter and muffled laughter continued behind her—everyone was watching, everyone was judging her.

"What happened was absolutely my fault, not Oscar's." Birdie took a deep breath. "Oscar was just being nice, he was just bringing me some food and—"

Hazel's hard laugh cut her off. "Yeah, he was being nice all right. He was doing his best 'nice guy.' I've seen it before, though it had been a long time. I thought he'd changed."

"No! He just brought the food and I—"

"You guys spent some time together before I met up with the show. I knew he liked you but—I thought—" Hazel's dress still showed off a full figure, but her face had a hollow look to it. Her eyes were enormous, her cheekbones sharp. "How could he do that to me? It makes me think—I don't know. Maybe I don't know him as well as I thought." She hugged her arms around herself.

"You gotta trust that he's a good guy. I know that he would never hurt you. I'm the one who did this. *I'm* the bad guy."

"I want to believe it," Hazel said. "I want to just scream at you and forgive him but—it's too hard to believe."

Fine. If Birdie couldn't convince Hazel of Oscar's innocence right now, she'd have more time if she could convince Hazel of her plan. "I have something else to tell you," she said, switching tracks.

Hazel waited, arms still crossed around her middle, as Birdie told her the plan. Sinclair's movie. Inviting him to the show. Putting on the show at Henrieta's exactly how they'd wanted to perform it at the NAR, and convincing Sinclair to give them a spot in his next flick. Hazel bit her lip and listened, eyes wide.

"If you think you can work with Oscar—and me—I think we could make this work. I think you could get your chance at Hollywood right here."

Hazel was quiet.

"All you'd have to do is work with us. We don't have to be friends."

"She's never gonna to be your *friend*." Birdie whirled and June was standing there, pulling her hair back into a ponytail, the shorter pieces falling around her face. "Some half-baked apology isn't gonna cut it." She looked adorably disheveled. Milosh had said she was staying here, she was probably staying with Ruth—Birdie's stomach turned over.

"I was just telling Hazel, I've got a plan to make things up to you—"

"Not possible. I don't care what you got."

What a *jerk*. She wouldn't even let her talk. "I see you let Ruth make up for whatever *she* did."

A muscle in June's jaw twitched. "This ain't about me and Ruth, it's about you and Oscar." June raised her brows at Hazel. "Sounds like she's mixed up about what the problem here is."

"It's *me*, just me. I'm the problem," Birdie said. "There's no me and Oscar. There never was, I promise."

Hazel shrugged, but pain flared in her eyes. June stepped between Hazel and Birdie, arms crossed. "Hazel's worked hard for everything she's got. You can't just waltz up here and think one 'I'm sorry' is going to fix things. Life ain't as easy for some people as it is for you."

"You don't know what it's like for me," Birdie insisted, but she remembered how June had said, *I sure did want to*, and how she had thrown that back in her face. Birdie swallowed. "Listen, I—I need to apologize to you, too."

Hazel bit her lip and watched June.

"What for?" June said carelessly, but her eyes flicked away.

Hazel sighed. Birdie felt herself wobbling off course. She couldn't risk being shot down right now. She turned to Hazel, trying to hold back tears. "I'm going to talk to Sinclair tomorrow. If it's a go—would you do the show?"

"Who's Sinclair?" asked June. "Another *boyfriend?*"

"Go talk to him," said Hazel. "Let me know what he says, and we'll see."

"Fine." Birdie glanced at June.

June turned back toward Ruth and the others without responding.

Birdie managed to hold it together until she got back to the Duesenberg and drove out of sight. Then she pulled over on the shoulder of the road, her hands shaking too much to drive. She curled up on the seat and went over her plan, over what she would say and do, over and over everything, trying to stay calm even though she was alone and they were all on that bright porch, laughing and making plans together.

CHAPTER THIRTY-FOUR

BIRDIE PULLED UP OUTSIDE OF THE STANDARD CLUB MIDMORNING THE next day and staked it out. She hadn't slept well, curled up in the back seat of her car on a street near the boarding house, but hopefully Mr. Stevens wouldn't notice the shadows under her eyes. She'd found the hotel easily by asking for directions to Union Station, then retracing her steps. She'd cleaned herself up in one of the station bathrooms and put on one of the best outfits she'd brought from home—a silk scarf tied around her neck, a chevron-patterned light cardigan, a pleated skirt, lipstick, a string of pearls.

She bought herself a coffee from a café and sipped it for over an hour, watching cars and limousines pull up outside the Standard Club, well turned-out families and men in suits coming and going, the doorman holding doors and taking luggage. Finally a black limousine pulled up, the doorman opened the door, and Sinclair Stevens got out.

She fumbled her door open and hurried across the street. "Mr. Stevens!" She waved her hand gaily, trying to look excited, not frantic. "Hello, Mr. Stevens! May I have a word?"

He turned and looked at her, face stern, and when he recognized her his frown deepened. "You may not," he said firmly.

She stepped onto the curb, breathless. "It's Birdie Williams. Remember?"

The doorman watched closely.

"Most definitely not." Sinclair strode through the front door. Birdie tried to follow him, but the doorman firmly blocked her way. She watched, heart sinking, as Sinclair approached the front desk and leaned over it, saying something terse to the woman at the front desk. She handed him a package and then, thank God, he came back out.

She smiled self-assuredly. "Mr. Stevens, I just need a moment of your time!"

He ignored her, mumbling something under his breath and checking his watch as his driver got out and took the package from him.

Might as well jump into it. "I'd like to talk to you about—"

"Look," he interrupted. "I was zozzled. You looked, I swear to God, ten years older at that club. And nothing happened between us. Jesus. Nothing happened, right?" He looked at her hard, and she nodded nervously. "That's what I thought." He watched impatiently as the driver carefully placed the package in the trunk of the car.

She clasped her hands and said urgently, "Sir, I wanted to talk to you about your movie."

Anger flared in his eyes. "I'm not going to talk about the damned *movie*," he said through gritted teeth.

"I *have* to talk to you about it. You see, I'm part of this air show, I work with some wonderful pilots and I'm a wingwalker myself, and we would just be so honored if you would come see our show. It's happening—" When could they get the show together? The driver opened the limousine door for Sinclair. Birdie rushed: "—this Saturday, at three p.m.—"

He waved his hand dismissively. "I'm leaving town Saturday."

"Friday, then!"

He raised his eyebrows. "I'm not going to your *show*, miss."

"You *have* to come see it, because we're just who you need for your next movie, and if you like our show we could come to Hollywood and audition for the stunts, and—"

Sinclair laughed bitterly, but instead of getting in the limo, he turned to her, rubbing his forehead. "Listen, kid. There is no movie."

"I—what?" Birdie froze. "But you said—you're *the* Mr. Stevens, aren't you?"

"I am. Talked your ear off about it the other night, did I? God, I had the whole thing lined up, but guess what I found out at the meeting last night: every one of my investors pulled out. The numbers are looking real bad for my latest flick." He paused and stared off for a moment, then slammed a hand down on the roof of the limo as the driver waited impassively.

"Oh. I—I'm so sorry, Mr. Stevens," She whispered, deflating. Milosh was right. It wasn't just Dad, it wasn't just the circus. Things weren't working out for lots of people right now.

"It's not my fault that that damned upstart put his war movie out a month before mine! How was I supposed to know people wouldn't have the kind of money they had last year, and they'd only go and see one? No matter that it was pure trash!" He hit the car roof again and swore.

"Sorry to waste your time," she said quietly.

Sinclair shook his head. "Look, I'm sure your show is real nice."

It would have been. "It's Peter Pan, only with airplanes. It's got Wendy and Tiger Lily and the crocodile and everything."

"A kid's story, huh." He looked pensive. "That's different. Kids eat that kinda stuff up, don't they?" He drummed his fingers on the limo's roof. "Friday, you said?"

Hope surged through Birdie. "Three p.m. I could leave a flyer at the front desk for you. And maybe if you come and see it— maybe we could inspire you to consider a new script—"

"It's not up to me, kid. It's the investors. If there's no money, there's no movie." Sinclair turned and ducked into the limo. The driver tried to shut the door, but Sinclair stopped him. He rubbed his chin thoughtfully. "I could invite some of them, work your show into a pitch, and see if they go for it."

Birdie's heart started to pound. "Sounds like they might, sir!"

"It's a long shot. But if it worked out, I could definitely be convinced that I owe you a favor, if you know what I'm saying."

Birdie smiled so hard it hurt. "If you bring them, our show will sell it! I promise!"

He laughed shortly. "You got some pluck, you know that? Leave the flyer at the front desk. They'll make sure I get it. But no promises." Sinclair settled into his seat and the driver shut the door.

Birdie couldn't help waving enthusiastically as the car pulled away.

Holy moly. There was still hope!

Friday, 3 p.m. They were all going to kill her when she told them that, but they could make it work.

A strange plane was parked in the field when Birdie pulled up to Henrieta's house. It was painted cream, with TRAVEL AIR stenciled on the tail, which rang a bell somewhere in Birdie's mind. Henrieta's Ford was there as well, and the Studebaker, so Merriwether and Bennie and the twins were probably inside. She wondered if anyone else would be there, or if she'd have to go to the boarding house to track down Hazel and June, and call around to find Oscar.

Birdie's stomach buzzed with nerves as she got out of the car. She'd felt elated leaving the Standard Club, but during the drive she'd had a lot of time to think the plan over. Sinclair Stevens might not show up. He might decide it was too long a shot. And if he *did* come, there was no actual movie anymore, which had been a key part of her plan. Could she really convince everyone to put on the show when there was no film to audition for? Hazel might refuse to work with Oscar. June might reject Birdie's mess of a plan.

A wave of nausea rolled over Birdie as she got close enough to recognize the voices coming through the screen door. She opened it and walked down the hallway to find *everyone* sitting at the big oak table. Merriwether and the boys, Bennie, Colette, and Milosh, all in their little constellations, Henrieta orbiting the table, pouring coffee into cups. June and Hazel sat together, and Oscar stood by the woodstove, hands in his pockets, looking anxious.

They were all there, falling quiet as they looked up at her expectantly.

June stood. "Hazel told me about Mr. Stevens," she said. "That's some plan you got."

Birdie couldn't tell if June was still angry. She looked tense, and breathtakingly beautiful, arms crossed like she only half believed Birdie was serious.

"Did you talk to him?" asked Hazel intently.

Birdie tore her eyes from June. Oscar's hopeful smile. Colette and Milosh's clasped hands, inked stars on their knuckles colliding. Henry and John fidgeting anxiously. Henrieta making herself busy by the stove. Bennie's and Merriwether's steady gazes. Hazel's eyes huge in her pale face.

Birdie nodded mutely.

"What did he say?" asked June.

"He said—" Birdie's voice caught, and she cleared her throat. "Sinclair Stevens said he would come to our show," she said slowly.

John and Henry cheered, and Oscar whooped and cuffed Milosh on the shoulder. Hazel smiled and reached up to squeeze June's elbow.

"Hollywood's a town I could see myself taking a shine to." Bennie grinned at her.

"But?" said Merriwether. "I can tell there's a but coming."

Everyone looked back at Birdie.

"The movie," she said.

"Oh no," said June.

"They've got the stunt pilots they need already," guessed Colette.

"They don't want women pilots after all?" Hazel sounded slightly hysterical.

"No," said Birdie. "None of that. The budget—it's fallen through. He still wants to make a movie, but—"

"He still wants to make a movie!" exclaimed John. "He's coming to our show!"

"Yes, but he doesn't have the money to make it," said Birdie impatiently. "His investors pulled out."

"A man like that can *get* the money," said June. "If he wants it bad enough."

"Not these days," said Bennie. "Not like they used to, anyway."

Birdie blew out a breath. "Yeah, so he said that he might come, and if he did, he would bring his investors and try to pitch another movie to them. But it sounds like it's kind of a long shot." The best she had to offer didn't sound so good. It was quiet for a moment. Maybe she should turn tail and run, before they let her know she'd let them down again.

"I don't care," said Hazel suddenly. "You see that Travel Air out there? I went out to the airfield and convinced them that they should loan me their brand-new model so I can show it off in front of Sinclair Stevens, and dammit I'm going to fly it in the show in front of Sinclair Stevens and get a spot in his damned movie. We're doing this, and we're gonna give it all we got."

Birdie's mouth fell open. Hazel had gone ahead and traded in her Waco for a new plane. Last night she'd been so guarded. Birdie hadn't known she'd get so invested.

"It might not work out." She hated to crush Hazel's enthusiasm.

"We will make it," said Hazel determinedly.

Birdie felt her spirits lift. Maybe Sinclair Stevens wouldn't show up. Maybe the movie wouldn't get made. But they would put on a show, and the circus would be back together. She would have a few days to get Hazel to forgive Oscar—and maybe June would warm up to her, too. "We have a new car, and a new plane, and I'm damned well going to jump off the wing of that plane," she vowed. "We're gonna put on one hell of a show."

Colette smiled ethereally as she rubbed Milosh's back. "See, sweetheart? All that worry for nothing."

"Oh, I told him the show was this Friday," said Birdie. "Three p.m."

"You trying to kill us?" cried Bennie, as everyone howled.

"He's leaving Chicago on Saturday." Birdie raised her voice. "I *had* to tell him that!"

"This is great." June thumped the table. "Three whole days. Print flyers, paper the town, get the show together. We're Merriwether's Flying Circus of the Air! We've done shows on shorter notice!"

"Hooray!" said John.

"We're going to be in a *movie!*" said Henry.

Birdie grinned at June. She hadn't been sure if June thought the whole idea was crazy nonsense. June sounded like she was all in, but she melted Birdie's smile with a hard look. "This is Hazel's dream we're talking about," June said seriously. Birdie's stomach flopped as she read into June's stern expression. *This better work out, or else.*

"It's been our dream for a while," said Oscar, but Hazel didn't look at him.

"I'm sure Sinclair Stevens will be there, and I'm sure that our show will be perfect this time," said Birdie, as confidently as she could. But she wasn't. It wasn't a sure thing at all.

There was nothing else to do but hope, again, impossibly, that things would all work out.

CHAPTER THIRTY-FIVE

BIRDIE PAUSED IN THE DOORWAY OF THE FARMHOUSE. COLETTE SAT JUST in front of her on the porch edge, bent over a bright-green strand of sequins and a dark-green leotard. Milosh sat next to her, soaking rags in kerosene. In the field Bennie hunched next to the propeller of the Moth, tinkering with something. Merriwether had allowed the twins to fly a Jenny over the outskirts of Chicago to drop flyers in the suburbs, in an attempt to get them out of everyone's hair. Oscar was somewhere in the sky as well, out of sight, practicing the Peter Pan choreography. Birdie could hear the distant buzz of the engine grow louder, then fade. Once he landed and refueled, she'd go up with him and begin practicing.

Hazel stood out in the field, her sun-burnished hair in glowing braids down her back. She rubbed her temples next to the new Travel Air as Merriwether gesticulated, and Birdie wondered if the headache Hazel had mentioned at the kitchen table yesterday had come back. Hazel had been up in the air as much as possible that morning, getting the feel of her new plane. June stood by the pirate-ship plane a few yards away. She'd painted stripes to mimic boards of a ship in the brown paint, and now she ran her finger along the body, tapped the white wings, then looked at her fingers to see if the paint was dry. A tricorn hat that Colette had finished gluing together a few minutes ago was perched on her head.

Birdie swallowed the lump that formed in her throat. She'd been avoiding June. What had happened between the two of them was messy, something she didn't have words for. She didn't know what to say beyond sorry, and she knew sorry wasn't enough.

And she'd seen June and Ruth together at the boarding house. She knew something still smoldered between them.

June looked up, right at her, and Birdie's stomach turned anxiously. June jumped onto the wing and struck a pirate pose, hanging from a strut and stabbing the air with an imaginary cutlass. "Ahoy there!"

June's face was shaded by the brim of her hat, but her voice sounded playful. "Ahoy yourself," Birdie called back timidly.

June gestured her closer.

Birdie walked across the field, remembering the first moment she saw June. *Hey there,* that arresting drawl. The smell of cotton candy and funnel cakes in the air, the Coney Island sunset shading June's eyes so dark. "Hey," Birdie said as she approached, kicking the grass.

June hopped off the wing, her expression serious, and Birdie's stomach tightened. June rubbed her fingers across her mouth, then stuffed her hands in her pockets. "Listen, Birdie. How I—the other night—I was kinda hard on you."

Birdie's mouth twisted. "Can't say I didn't deserve it."

June cracked a smile. "I mean, you *did* deserve it." She nudged Birdie's shoulder with her own. "But I can tell that you're trying hard to make it up. I'd have a hard time being that brave, if I was you."

"Thanks." She'd hoped coming back and trying hard would magically make everything better, but she could see how naïve that was. "I wish it was enough."

"What do you mean?"

She turned and looked over the field. On the surface the show was back together, but underneath, everything was still wrong. "So what if I'm sorry? I broke up Oscar and Hazel. I ruined the audition. There's a good chance nothing's going to come of this. After Friday we'll still be in the same fix we were in before: no performance at the NAR, nothing in Hollywood for us. Hazel and Oscar still split up."

The sounds of insects buzzing and birds calling filled the silence between them. A car puttered past on the distant road.

"So what if you don't fix anything." June turned so she faced out toward the field with Birdie, their elbows brushing. "We're all excited and hopeful again. That means something, all by itself." June leaned into her a little. "It means something to me, anyway."

June's skin against hers sent a tingle through Birdie. "I have a question." She answered June's touch with a lean of her own.

"Oh yeah?"

"That flying lesson you mentioned before." Her voice was shaky, and she took a deep breath. "I was wondering if the offer still stood?"

June glanced sideways. Her mouth twitched. "You seemed pretty sure that it wasn't for you."

"I know," said Birdie. "I wasn't ready when you asked me before. I am now."

June smiled. "All right then." She turned to the Jenny and climbed onto the wing. She pulled her leather helmet and goggles out of the rear cockpit.

"Oh, um. I didn't necessarily mean *right* now." The feeling she had last time she'd gone up in a Jenny—off-balance and terrified, cowering on the wing in panic—rushed over her.

June held out the helmet and goggles. "Why not? The paint's dry enough. And I can't risk you changing your mind again." She pulled off her pirate hat and the sun gilded her dark hair a deep, rich gold.

"There's just so much to do before . . ." Birdie trailed off. She had to go back up in the air sometime before the show; might as well be now. She took the helmet and goggles and climbed into the rear cockpit.

"Okay, here's your tach." June hung over the cockpit edge and reached a long arm toward the front panel, pointing to one of the round gauges.

"The tachometer." Birdie tried to calm her mind as she tucked her hair under the helmet. "Tells me how fast the propeller's going."

"You sure you haven't flown before?" asked June.

Birdie smiled nervously.

"Twelve hundred's a good speed, once you get up there, okay?"

"Okay."

"You can basically ignore the rest of these gauges. You know how it's supposed to feel when it's up in the air, right?"

Birdie *did* know how it was supposed to feel. The thought calmed her.

"Throttle," June said, pointing. "Makes it go faster or slower."

"Uh-huh." Dad had given her similar lessons a thousand times before, although she'd never put them to use. Her heart clenched unexpectedly, which just made her mad. He had left *her*—why did she still feel like she was somehow giving up on him?

"The stick makes it go up and down," June continued. "You pull it back, the nose goes up. You push it forward, the nose goes down. Left, it banks left. Right, it banks right."

Birdie made herself focus. "Got it."

"The rudder makes it slew left or right, different from banking with the stick. Watch your feet on the rudder cables." June pointed at Birdie's feet, and Birdie adjusted them.

June walked to the front of the plane. She reached up to the topmost propeller, stood on her tiptoes as she worked her fingers around it—then lunged downward and spun out of the way.

The propeller caught, and the engine sputtered to life.

"You got plenty of time once we're up there." June raised her voice over the idling engine. *Ticktickticktick*, that familiar, electric sewing machine sound. She held on to the wing so the plane wouldn't start rolling forward, but Birdie could feel the plane fighting. It wanted to go. "The tank's almost full, so don't worry about that."

"Okay." Birdie needed this. She needed to get back up in the air and remember how good it could feel.

"These Jennys fly themselves. It's really impossible to mess up. If you dropped dead in the cockpit, the Jenny would keep flying in a straight line till it ran out of gas."

Birdie pinched her lips together. "So, that doesn't really make me feel better."

June laughed as she climbed into the front cockpit and pulled on a pair of goggles. She turned, smiling broadly as the plane began to roll forward. "What are you waiting for?" she yelled. "Go, girl!"

Birdie pulled on her own goggles and looked over the instruments again. She didn't really understand any of them.

Just go. Just feel it.

She pulled the stick into her stomach and gave it some power. The Jenny shuddered, then lurched ahead. She brought the stick forward, then pushed the throttle all the way in. She felt the tail come off the ground as the plane started bumping down the field in earnest, and she pulled the stick back.

The nose rose in front of her, strands of June's hair whipping out beneath her helmet. June's arms went up. Birdie could hear her whooping and hollering, the sound dimmed by the wind and the rattling of the plane as it climbed into the air.

The plane was still vibrating more than she was used to. She glanced down, and the rpms were high. She eased off the throttle, bringing it back down to twelve hundred. Birdie adjusted the stick and leveled out the plane. She wasn't just along for the ride. She wasn't waiting for someone to grab the stick and take her somewhere. June had been right—she knew what it was supposed to feel like.

Her nerves were settling. She climbed out of the rear cockpit. June laughed at her when she appeared on the wing beside the front cockpit. "I should have expected you wouldn't stay where you were supposed to."

"Can you take over for a minute?"

June nodded, and Birdie walked out onto the wing.

However the show went on Saturday, it wouldn't fix every-thing. She might never find Dad. June might not want to kiss her again. She might fall, or get hurt, or end up hurting somebody else. But she wasn't terrified. The chance of failure made it more exciting.

Warm wind. Loud, friendly engine buzz. Upper lip sweat. Thin wires, sturdy struts. Air, air, and more air. She grabbed a strut and leaned out over empty space. She swung out, holding on with both hands, her tiptoes still connected to the wing. She arched back, closed her eyes, and let her head fall back. The sun felt hot on her skin.

She opened her eyes and looked over at June, and began to hum a tune.

June looked back at her.

Birdie took a foot off the wing and swirled it around over empty space.

June shook her head, a smile on her lips.

Birdie took a hand off the strut as well, and used it to blow her a kiss.

CHAPTER THIRTY-SIX

THEY PERFORMED A FULL DRESS REHEARSAL THURSDAY AFTERNOON, AND the whole thing went perfectly. The paint was dry, the costumes sewn. Birdie loved her green tights and sparkly, sequined leotard, hair braided and pinned tight to her head. Colette actually squealed when she saw all of them in full costume: Merriwether and Milosh as pirates, June as Wendy in a well-tailored, light-blue flying suit, and Hazel in her fringed costume. Bennie looked larger-than-life in a crocodile tuxedo, beaming inside the mouth of a giant, paper-mache crocodile head.

Birdie had dropped the flyer off at the front desk of the Standard Club the day before, with instructions to make sure Sinclair Stevens got it.

She'd done everything she could. Everyone would give it their best.

She hoped it was enough.

That night they ate Henrieta's delicious pigs-in-a-blanket, ground pork rolled up in cabbage leaves and cooked until they were silky. Merriwether pulled pies out of the oven—she had made a cobbler out of a bucketful of blackberries that Henrieta had picked by the creek—as everyone trickled outside to enjoy the evening while they cooled.

Birdie watched from the porch as Milosh built a fire and talked John and Henry through his methods. John threw logs onto the fire as Milosh protested. Henry held a handful of sticks and listened. She could tell the difference between the twins instantly now, because it was always John who dove in impatiently, while Henry held back and watched. Henry would do it perfectly the first time, but he would carefully observe Milosh do it over and over again before he tried. John would build a bunch of sloppy fires before he caught on. But both of them would get the hang of it.

Merriwether pushed the screen door open and bellowed over Birdie's head, "Dessert, kids! Come and get it!" Her lips and fingers were tinged purple from the blackberries, a rich, sweet fragrance wafting from inside. Henry carefully set down his sticks while John threw his on the ground and sprinted toward the house. He crashed through the screen door, and Henry followed at a trot, holding the door open as Birdie stood up.

A big bowl of pillowy whipped cream sat in the middle of the kitchen table with a huge spoon sticking out of it. On either side sat pans filled with steaming, golden-brown topping and black, bubbling ooze. John and Henry knocked the piles of bowls over while grabbing for them, and Merri slapped their hands away. John stuck a finger in the whipped cream as Merri served them cobbler and put generous dollops of cream on top. Henry added an extra scoop to his when her back was turned.

The rest of the crew filed into the kitchen, exclaiming over the spread. Oscar took a seat and offered the one next to him to Hazel, but she ignored him and sat at the far end of the table. Merri handed Birdie a bowl. "Butter, flour, salt, and sugar. Oh, and the berries. That's it! I'm not much of a cook, but Henrieta convinced me to give it a shot." Birdie sat next to the boys and took a bite. Tart and tangy and sweet and rich and buttery, the cobbler was heaven after a long day of practice. Birdie almost beat the boys, finishing her bowl. When she looked up, everyone was around the table in a homey, boisterous tableau, except for June.

Birdie grabbed a bowl, filled it with cobbler and cream, and went out on the porch. June sat next to the fire, poking it with a stick.

"You coming to relieve me?" June called. "I'm starting to regret volunteering to tend this damned fire while everyone eats my share of the pie."

Birdie lifted up the bowl to show her, and June applauded as Birdie came down the steps.

"My savior!" she exclaimed as Birdie handed her the bowl. "Lord, this looks amazing." She took a bite, rolling her eyes in ecstasy. "You feeling good about the show?" she mumbled as she took another.

"If Sinclair Stevens appears tomorrow, we're gonna give him a really good show. But no luck getting Hazel and Oscar back together." There was a slight chill in the air. She picked up a blanket and pulled it around her shoulders. "You should see them in there. It's pitiful."

"Oh, don't beat yourself up too much," said June around another mouthful. She was finishing the cobbler in record time. "He was quite the ladies' man before he met Hazel. Hasn't always been in the right in these sorts of situations, but I'm thinking she'll come around."

The fire popped. Birdie's stomach fluttered. She wasn't sure where to sit—next to June? On the other side of the fire? Suddenly she felt shy. "You heading back to the boarding house soon?"

"Yeah." June scraped out the sides of the bowl and licked the spoon. "Yum."

"You and Hazel have a room there together?"

"Yeah, we do." June set the bowl down and picked up her tobacco pouch. She opened it and fished out a paper.

"And Ruth's still staying there, right?"

June flattened the paper against her thigh, sprinkling a thin line of tobacco on top of it. She picked it up delicately and start to roll it between her fingers, back and forth. "Umm, yeah. She is."

Birdie swallowed. "She was so mad at you—at the club, but then when I saw you—later—it seemed like she forgave you." She knew something had shifted, watching them lean into each other under the porch light.

"She did," said June.

"That's great. I'm glad—that kiss—didn't mess things up. You two make quite a pair."

"We mighta made quite a pair," said June, not looking up, "if she hadn't ruined all the chances I gave her."

June's tone was neutral, but her words took Birdie by surprise. "Oh?"

"She's been hot and cold with me ever since we met. Every time she comes on strong, swearing it'll be different. And every time I buy it."

Birdie tried to read into the tense curve of June's shoulders. "Buy what?"

"That she's all in." A note of bitterness crept into her voice. "And I'm over the moon, only to find the next week she's on to someone else, and didn't have the decency to tell me."

Birdie tried to imagine how June must have felt when she walked in on Birdie kissing Oscar. Had it hurt in the same way? "I'm so sorry."

"It's fine," said June. "Sometimes you're never going to make it work, no matter how hard you pretend that everything's okay. Sometimes you gotta give up." She looked up at Birdie. "It's not always a bad thing," she finished softly.

Birdie walked around the fire and sat down next to June. The log was rough against the back of her thighs, and the crickets were loud. June dropped her eyes to the cigarette she was rolling between her fingers.

Birdie stared at the flames, which were going strong now without any tending. "I was in love with my best friend," she whispered. She never thought she was going to say that out loud, ever. In her old life, she wouldn't have dared. "We kissed once. After that, every time I saw her with someone else, I felt like my heart was going to collapse. Every time I was with someone else, I could only think about her." It felt like the first true thing she'd ever said, and it made her sick and scared and relieved all at once.

June glanced at her. She brought the cigarette to her mouth and ran her tongue over the paper to moisten it, then carefully sealed the edge, holding her gaze. Birdie started to tremble, but she kept going. "Until I kissed you." The second true thing, this time a hundred times more terrifying. "Now every time I'm with someone else, I think about you." Birdie was intensely aware of the space between them. How her arm brushed June's, how her knee touched June's knee.

June set the cigarette down deliberately. She turned to face Birdie. Her eyes held Birdie's, flickering dark and warm in the firelight.

"It was a really hot kiss," Birdie said breathlessly.

June's arm slid around Birdie's waist and pulled her in.

Lips met and fingers tangled in a rush of breath and a flurry of motion—Birdie wasn't sure of how they got to every inch of their bodies pressed together so quickly, the kiss urgent and sugar-sweet. June's tongue brushed her lips and Birdie slid her hands around June's arms, shoulders, neck, tangling her hands into the silkiness of June's hair. June tugged at the fabric tucked at Birdie's waist, then impatiently lifted her onto her lap and Birdie pressed against her, heat rushing beneath her skin. She'd wanted this since she'd seen June rolling that cigarette at Coney Island. She'd wanted more when they'd kissed at the club. "June—" she whispered against her lips.

June pulled away. She stared at Birdie's mouth, her hands tightening against her waist. "Yeah?" The hoarseness of her voice flooded Birdie with longing.

"I'm sorry. What happened with Oscar. I just—I *wanted* it to be him, you know? But it wasn't."

The corner of June's mouth lifted. "I remember that feeling. Thinking, if I don't fight this with everything I've got, it'll ruin my life. I thought I was the only one in the world."

Birdie touched June's jaw and brushed her lips softly with a fingertip, feeling her intake of breath. The blanket that had been around her shoulders had slid off onto the ground and the air felt perfect, just barely cool, the smoldering fire warm against her skin. June's hands brushed her skin along the edge of her skirt. Birdie pressed her hands against June's chest and arched against her as she leaned in for another kiss.

The screen door banged, miles away. The sound of voices as someone came outside.

June groaned and put her forehead against Birdie's shoulder. Birdie's cheeks were flaming. She laughed giddily as she looked to the porch, where Milosh and one of the twins were silhouetted in the door.

"Dang," said June. "Guess we better pretend like nothing's happening?" She looked like that was the last thing she wanted to do. Birdie's heart was racing. She couldn't imagine acting normal in front of the others when all she wanted to do was touch June's smooth, warm skin. She picked up the crumpled blanket and grabbed June's hand, tugging her up. June followed her into the cool dark that lay outside the fire's ring of light.

Birdie felt the same aching from the night June had woken her, held her hand, and led her inside. That same sensation, as the dark closed around her, that she could be dreaming. June's warm hand in hers, her own breath and skin damp with longing. But this time she led, this time she knew what she ached for.

She dropped the blanket, pushed the corners out, and pulled June down. Though it was dark, she could feel June's smile as it met hers. She didn't miss the fire's warmth. Her skin burned so hot, she must be glowing. If she took off in that moment, she'd be a light in the sky. She'd blend right in with the stars.

CHAPTER THIRTY-SEVEN

BIRDIE CAME OUT OF HER ROOM, BLEARY-EYED, IN HER NIGHTDRESS TO find that everyone had woken up before her and was full throttle preparing for the show. Henrieta bustled down the hallway and shoved a steaming cup of coffee into Birdie's hands. "Chance of rain today," Henrieta yelled over her shoulder. "That's what the papers say." Birdie heard Merriwether grunt from the kitchen.

"I know, I know," said Henrieta. "A small chance. But still." She squeezed Birdie's shoulder. "How are you, love?" She patted her cheek before she went back to the kitchen. Through the screen door, Birdie saw Bennie pointing at something on the Jenny's engine while Henry listened, already dressed in his Lost Boy outfit. Hazel stood in the hallway with her hair pulled up and her Tiger Lily flight suit on, letting Colette mend a spot where the fringe on one sleeve had come loose. "Morning," Colette called cheerfully.

Hazel put a hand to her forehead. "I have that damned headache again," she said. "And my stomach is in knots. I took the plane out to practice early this morning, one last time, but I had to land. I felt so sick."

"Here's an aspirin," tutted Henrieta, scurrying back with a pill and a glass of water. "Plenty of time for that to kick in before the show. Let me know if you need another."

Hazel smiled gratefully. "Thanks. I don't know what's wrong with me."

Oscar came thundering down the stairs, stopped halfway, swore, and clattered back up them. He reappeared a moment later with his shoes in his hand and a cigarette between his lips.

"Anyone seen June?" Birdie tried to sound nonchalant.

Oscar winked, and she felt herself turning red. "She's around here somewhere. I'll tell her you're looking for her."

Birdie nodded and fled back to her room. She took a sip of coffee and set the mug down on the washstand, heading out to get some water to bathe with, but Henrieta had read her mind and handed her a full pitcher. Birdie closed the door, set the pitcher down, and untied the neck of her nightdress. She flushed as she unknotted the strings, remembering June's hands on the nape of her neck, their legs tangling as June pressed her back against the ground, kisses long enough to get lost in and not close to long enough—

The door opened and Birdie whirled as June shut it behind her. June strode across the room intently and the bed met the back of Birdie's knees. She lost her balance and sat as June leaned in and kissed her hard, hands on the mattress on either side. The room shifted as Birdie clung to June's waist, breathlessly happy.

June pulled away. "I heard you were looking for me?" she said hoarsely, smiling. Her blue flight suit was open to the waist, white shirt underneath revealing collarbones and lean chest. Her hair was pulled back in a low, short ponytail.

"I was," Birdie said, disoriented. She stared at the tan smoothness where June's shirt met her skin.

"You need a hand getting into costume?" June's fingers grazed the open tie at the back of Birdie's neck, sending shivers down her skin. "I could help if you want."

Birdie tried to pull her in but June backed away. "Hey, bank's closed!" she said cheekily, swatting her hands away. "You're way behind schedule, young lady."

Birdie bit her lip. "Guess I *could* use some help." She stood, turned, and pulled her hair over her shoulder, waiting. She could feel June shift behind her. She held her breath as June grazed her shoulders and parted the nightdress—then paused. "What's this?" June's fingers traced the outline of her tattoo.

"Oh, it's—Colette gave that to me." Birdie didn't know what to say. *Just another one of my many mistakes.*

"When I met you, I thought you were just some pretty girl." She could hear June's smile. "Then you said you wanted to wing-walk. Then you did it for the *first time* in your *life* in front of a huge crowd. Then you invented a stunt and planned a whole show around it. Then you went to Sinclair Stevens and convinced him to come see our show."

"*Maybe* convinced him."

"And now this." June's fingers moved against her skin. "You keep surprising me."

"Not always in good ways," Birdie reminded her. "You forgot to mention all the bad surprises."

"Well this is a good one." June's lips brushed Birdie's shoulder. "Makes me wonder what else you've got for me."

June gently pushed the nightdress over Birdie's shoulders. Birdie clutched it to her chest as longing surged through her. "I wish we had nothing to do today," she whispered.

June turned her around to face her, palms hot against Birdie's bare skin, eyes intense—

"Hey!" Merriwether called, sounding like she was right outside the door. "Can I get everyone in the kitchen for a minute?"

Birdie blushed and pulled away. "Get outta here. You stay, and I'll never be ready."

June grabbed her hand. "I got nothing on my schedule tomorrow," she said, smiling. "Maybe we could do nothing then?"

Somehow Birdie managed to steer June to the door in between kisses and push her out. She shut it and pressed her forehead against the wood, flustered and giddy and trying to catch her breath.

She heard June humming that song again as she headed down the hall—*five foot two, eyes of blue. But oh! What those five foot could do . . .*

Birdie walked out to the field, wiping sweating palms on her sequins. She wore basketball shoes with her bright-green leotard and tights, her hair braided and pinned tightly to her head. Cars lined the dirt road that passed beside Henrieta's house, parked in ditches and the field across the street. Children with their parents, other pilots, and young couples and teenagers dotted the field, quickly accumulating into a crowd. The turnout was bigger than Birdie had expected. It was unbelievably humid, but it didn't seem like it was going to rain after all, thank God. It felt like the rouge was melting off her cheeks.

Bennie and Oscar had cordoned off space for their planes to take off and land, and a low wooden fence marked off one edge of the area. People crowded around all four sides. Colette stood with her megaphone on a small makeshift stage on one side of the field.

It was almost 3 p.m. Almost time for the show.

Birdie stopped beside Hazel. "You feeling better?"

Hazel nodded determinedly, though she still looked very pale. "Better enough. I'm going to knock Sinclair Stevens's socks off. How are you feeling?"

Ruth and a group of her girls caught Birdie's eye, laughing and leaning on the fence, looking awfully keen and carefree. "Ready to prove something."

Hazel smiled. "That's what I like to hear." Her expression fell, and Birdie followed her gaze to Oscar coming out of the house in his green flight suit. Hazel turned and headed out to the field. All the planes were parked in a neat row. Bennie wandered between them, patting and checking them all compulsively. An unfamiliar plane, painted all black, was parked next to the pirate Jenny. Birdie frowned at it, her heart lurching when she saw Sinclair

Stevens standing next to it. He was talking to Merriwether, who looked splendid in her pirate coat.

Birdie hurried over, pasting a breezy smile on her face.

"Miss Williams!" Mr. Stevens was all professional charm— waxed mustache, crisp suit, pomaded hair. "I have to tell you, I was captured by the idea of your show—and then I had this wonderful idea, to film your production from the air! I think it would be very arresting to see something like this in the theatre, even better than watching a live performance because you miss so much from the ground. I had a friend of mine loan me some equipment to capture some footage, in case it's something I can use to convince investors to invest in a similar project."

"You'll be *flying* with us during the show?"

"I told him it was all right," said Merriwether.

"That's why it's black!" said Sinclair. "So it won't distract the audience."

Birdie found that hard to believe.

"The crowd will love it," assured Merriwether. "Colette will tell them Hollywood is here to film the show, and they'll all just go nuts over it."

Birdie jumped as the loudspeaker crackled on.

"Ladies and gentlemen, welcome to the first truly aerial performance of *Peter Pan!*" Colette's voice was strong and confident. "You think you've seen stunt-flying before? Our pilots and wingwalkers and fire-breathers will have you gasping in terror, screaming in surprise, and cheering with relief! And believe it or not, a HOLLYWOOD FILM CREW is here to capture the show on film! Who knows! You might be able to say you were there when it comes to a theater near you!"

The crowd, which was swelling by the minute, erupted into cheers.

"What did I tell you?" Merriwether grinned and slapped Birdie on the back. "Break a leg, pretty bird!"

Birdie ran for the green Jenny. Oscar was already inside the rear cockpit. She hopped onto the wing and settled into the front cockpit.

John reached for the propeller of the plane. She turned around and Oscar gave her the thumbs-up and a big grin.

"Contact!" she yelled at John.

"Contact!" he responded, and sent the propeller spinning.

The crowd let out a huge cheer as John got the propeller going. He gave Birdie a solemn nod as he let go of the plane. She swallowed her own nerves and gave him a reassuring smile. This was going to be great. Sinclair Stevens would be wowed.

She smiled at Mr. Stevens extra big as she rattled past the black plane on her way to takeoff. She waved cheekily and winked. He waved back and pulled a leather helmet on.

And just behind him in the crowd, leaning against the wooden fence—she saw recognition light up Dad's face when he saw her.

Birdie saw Dad's smile grow wide and his hand lift to wave, and everything inside of her knotted up in shock—then the plane surged up and Birdie lost sight of him. She struggled up to the edge of the cockpit and peered down, but Oscar was banking away from the stands and she couldn't see anything.

It couldn't be.

Birdie's mind reeled as the plane circled upward.

It *could* be. Chicago was the last place anyone had seen him, and not that long ago. John and Henry had dropped flyers all over town. She was on the flyer. And even if Dad hadn't recognized her picture, he would come and see an air show if he had the chance—

She peered over the cockpit again but they were too far away now to make out individuals in the crowd. She knew exactly where he was standing. She thought she could see a man about the right height, with a mustache.

She could have mistaken a stranger for Dad. Already her memory confused her. Did the man she'd just seen really look exactly like Dad?

What if he disappeared before she landed, and she didn't get a chance to speak with him? What if he was still there after she landed, and they *did* get to talk? Either scenario was terrifying. She wanted to stand in her seat and scream at Oscar to land the plane, and she never wanted to land again.

Dad was here. He had come to find her.

How *dare* he show up, after all he'd put her through.

She heard yelling, deadened by the wind. She turned and saw Oscar motioning frantically. *Nuts!* She was so shocked she'd forgotten what she was doing. She took a couple of deep breaths, trying to recall the sense of calm she'd felt on the wing with June.

The air cooled her cheeks, and her senses cleared. She climbed out onto the wing. Oscar flew low, and Birdie waved and crowed as loud as she could. She posed and flirted with the audience as Colette narrated. This wasn't the time for stunts, just showing off her outfit and introducing her character. Sinclair's film plane swooped close, a huge camera lens extending from the front cockpit. She waved and blew kisses at the camera. June's Wendy plane took off and Birdie climbed back into her seat. The two planes rolled and dove and wove in and out. "Second star to the right, and straight on till morning," Colette called. June and Oscar executed barrel rolls, loop-de-loops, and spiral dives, and Birdie squealed as the plane flipped and swooped.

Then Hazel took off. The designs on her plane looked magnificent, bold and detailed. Merriwether took off right after her as Hook, a big black wig tacked onto her helmet, curls streaming behind. Milosh stood out on the wing, blowing fire as the crowd roared.

Hazel and Merriwether battled as Oscar and June slowly looped around the field, and Birdie's pride swelled as she watched the two planes chase each other. The show was amazing. It was everything she'd hoped it would be.

But something about Hazel's stunts began to catch her eye. Something was off. She wasn't responding to Merriwether's attacks like she should, dipping out of rolls and dives early, flying in the wrong direction, overcorrecting. Birdie could tell Oscar had noticed when he looped the plane in closer.

"Hook captures Tiger Lily!" cried Colette, a desperate edge to her voice, as Hazel neared the end of the field—which wasn't supposed to be happening. She was supposed to be climbing steeply as the pirate plane pursued her, so she could drop into an impressive spiral to the ground. "Who will save her?"

They waited for Hazel to turn the plane and climb for her Immelman spiral, but she didn't. Birdie stood up in her cockpit to watch Hazel's plane as it kept flying straight, right past the end of the field, disappearing beyond the trees.

Birdie shrieked, thrown down into her seat, as Oscar took off after Hazel.

CHAPTER THIRTY-EIGHT

"WHAT THE HELL IS GOING ON?" BIRDIE YELLED AT OSCAR, HANGING over the rear edge of her cockpit.

"I don't know." Oscar's voice was tight. They were catching up to Hazel's plane. Oscar nosed the Jenny up, and the Travel Air disappeared from view as they ascended. "Something's really off. I need you to look down and see what you can see."

Birdie scrambled out of the cockpit, despair filling her mind. *The show.* They were leaving all hope of success far behind them, but Hazel would have never ruined the performance. Something was terribly wrong. Birdie lay down on the wing and pulled her face past the edge.

The tail of Hazel's plane slowly came directly under her, then the cockpit. Hazel was slumped to one side, hands gripping the controls.

"Hazel!" Birdie screamed into the wind. "Hazel!"

Hazel didn't move.

Birdie jumped up and stumbled over the wires to get to Oscar. "I think she's passed out," she panted. "She's not moving, I tried to get her attention but it didn't work—"

Oscar swore a stream, his voice rising in panic. "She didn't feel good, she shouldn't have gone up today, that damned headache, should have known something was wrong—"

"We could follow her until she wakes up?"

"What if she doesn't?" His voice cracked. She'd never seen him look so scared.

Birdie pressed her forehead against a strut and tried to think. They could nudge Hazel's plane gently with the Jenny's wing—but what if it didn't wake her up, and sent the plane careening off course? At least she was flying relatively level right now, over flat terrain. They couldn't jeopardize that.

They were so close to Hazel, but there was no way to get to her. The few feet between their planes was an impossible distance when they were flying through the air.

The memory of Merriwether dangling from the rope above the speeding Studebaker flashed in her thoughts, and her mind started to race. She didn't have a rope ladder to climb down—but what if she climbed *up* instead?

"I have an idea," Birdie said. "I'll climb on top of the upper wing, and I think you can get close enough so that I can grab onto the landing gear and pull myself up."

Wind roared between them.

"That's insane," said Oscar.

"You have another idea?"

"I can't let you do that."

Birdie ignored him. "Get into position, and I'll make sure we can get close enough before I try it." She hung onto the struts as Oscar slowed and let Hazel's plane pull ahead. He dropped a few yards down, aimed slightly to the left, then sped up again. She peered upward as they caught up to Hazel's plane. The wheels were attached to the Travel Air by two straight bars, with two additional bars crisscrossing between them, meeting in an X shape in the middle. She would have to grab onto one of the crossing bars, then get herself up into one of the triangular spaces between the straight bar and the crossing bar. From there she could lean out and get onto the wing using the guy wires and struts.

But the distance between the wing and the landing gear was still too great for her to reach.

"Slow down. You're right under her. Nose up a few feet," she instructed.

When she looked back up, she imagined that if she were on top of the upper wing, she would be able to reach the landing gear.

She looked down. Below the propeller, a neighborhood of houses dotted the landscape. She might be dead before she hit the ground, or she might feel the thud of impact—the slope of a roof, the hard-packed dirt of a road, the sharp stubble of a lawn.

"You need to slow down the tiniest bit," she reported to Oscar. "Barely at all."

He grabbed her hand. "If you get out there and can't do it—I'll understand."

"Shut up, Oscar." She squeezed his hand and let it go. "I'll holler if you need to adjust your position any further. Otherwise don't budge from your course, but keep an eye out. I don't know how my weight will affect the direction of the Travel Air. Be ready to get out of the way."

Birdie shinnied up a strut and reached over the upper wing. She felt around until her hand caught something, and pictured the short strut that held guy wires leading to the fuselage. It should hold her weight. She lunged upward, trusting it to hold her, and threw a knee up onto the wing. It held, and she climbed up.

She stood up shakily, holding onto the strut. She was on top of the upper wing.

This was the place she should have been dancing all along. It was wide open, hardly any wires to trip her. Hardly any wires to grab for, either, if she lost her balance. The slipstream was a constant pressure, less deflected than it was below. She spun in a slow circle, catching her breath at the unobstructed view—and saw a black shape like a crow gaining on them. Her stomach dropped. Sinclair Stevens had followed them, was gaining on them. She couldn't let it distract her. Birdie walked carefully out to the tip of the right wing and looked up. She was directly under the landing gear of the Travel Air, but she wouldn't be able to grab hold without jumping. She couldn't tell Oscar to pull any closer, or they'd risk the Travel Air's propeller slicing the wing.

Merriwether had insisted—never let go of one firm handhold before you had another. *That's how people die.* But what if someone would die if you didn't?

The black plane leveled out on the other side of the Travel Air, the lens trained on her.

She looked up again and tried to block everything else out. Blood pounded in her ears, louder than the wind. She had to jump and trust that she could do it. She trained her eyes on the landing gear, inhaled deeply, and breathed out slowly. She stretched her hands out—almost there, just a few inches.

She crouched, focused—and jumped.

Both hands caught the crossed bars. She almost laughed with relief, but then felt the wing beneath her feet again, pushing up fast. Birdie ducked, got her feet on the crossed bars and tucked herself tightly as the landing gear crunched into the wing below, stopping just short of crushing her. She looked down and saw Oscar peering up from the Jenny's rear cockpit with a look of horror on his face.

The aileron of the right wing was caught in the landing gear.

Her weight must have thrown the trajectory of the Travel Air, or maybe it had been a rogue updraft. The planes had crashed in midair, and now they were stuck together. Neither plane could maneuver like this. It was a miracle they were still headed on a reasonably straight trajectory, and not spiraling toward the ground.

The film crew dipped in closer.

Birdie kicked at the aileron, trying not to panic. Nothing. She let out a frustrated shout and kicked again, harder, and a piece of the aileron snapped. Oscar's plane surged away as the aileron ripped free, the Travel Air leaning into a slight nosedive. There was yelling and scrambling from the film crew's plane as their plane swooped away.

She had to move fast. She dug her toes into the landing gear and leaned out toward the left, but as she reached for the lower wing she looked down. Nothing but hard earth growing closer. She fumbled for the landing gear again, clinging desperately as she took gasping breaths. She wasn't sure if she could clear the distance between the landing gear and the lower wing.

She made eye contact with the film crew's lens as it trained on her again.

Focus. Focus. She reached as far as she could with shaking fingers but couldn't get a good grip. She'd never pull herself up, and that impassive eye would record her failure so that it could be replayed on news reels across the country.

She glimpsed another plane tailing them, sunlight glinting off of a glossy red. June—her eyes dark in a smoky, crowded room, sparkling by a warm fire, brilliant green in the sun—was watching as well, believing she had what it took. And there was Oscar's plane, beside her again! He'd righted his course, limping along as his broken aileron spun in the slipstream. She knew he was watching closely, praying she could see this through.

It was about weight and her center of gravity, about tension and release. It was a dance. Bennie's tune hummed in her head, because she needed music: *dun, dun-a-dun*—and suddenly she could feel the distance and the energy it would take to cross it, feel the rhythm she needed to follow, see the sequence of the movements.

She set her jaw and leaned out again. She stretched with everything she had and barely grazed the wing's edge, but then she breathed, and stretched, and breathed again, and found the extra length inside herself. Her fingers closed around the strut connecting the lower wing to the fuselage. Another deep stretch and extension, the plane as her partner. It would lift her effortlessly if she could gain a little momentum and meet it with confidence, prepare and then UP!

Just like that, she swung her leg up in a *grand battement*, her heel caught on the wing, and she levered herself up and rolled onto the wing.

She gasped with relief and fumbled one hand onto a wire, then the other. Something she could hold tight to and the familiar shape of a wing beneath her was such a relief. She wanted to collapse in a heap, curl up until the trembling stopped—but there was no time.

She stood up and stumbled over to the cockpit. "Hazel!"

Hazel's hands twitched, her head rolling to one side. "Hmmm . . ."

The cockpit was tiny, but Birdie was small. Quickly, she pulled herself onto the fuselage, put a hand on either side of the cockpit, and lowered herself onto Hazel's lap. Then she adjusted their hips so they sat side by side. Hazel's eyes fluttered open, then closed again. "Hazel," Birdie whispered, tears springing to her eyes. Hazel was so pale she looked gray, sweat beading on her skin.

"I'm going to fly the plane now, okay?" She moved Hazel's hands from the stick, and took in the controls.

The controls were much more complicated than in the Jenny, but she could identify the important things—stick, tachometer, throttle. She raised the Travel Air out of its dive and slowly banked the plane around. The show might be ruined, but they would make it back to Henrieta's. Birdie prayed they would get Hazel the help she needed in time.

CHAPTER THIRTY-NINE

THE VIEW FROM THE TRAVEL AIR COCKPIT WAS STUNNING. IT WAS SO open Birdie could watch the ground slip by beneath them without having to even crane her neck. It was also tiny, hot, deafeningly noisy, dirty, and unbearably uncomfortable with Hazel sweating and moaning next to her. Thank God Oscar and June were flying ahead of her, because Birdie hadn't the faintest idea how to get back to the field. The compass said they were flying southeast but that meant nothing to her.

Birdie's head was starting to hurt, and she couldn't wait to land. *Land.* Her skin turned to ice. She had never landed a plane.

Why hadn't she landed the plane when June gave her the flying lesson? She'd let June do it while she danced around on the wing.

Think, Birdie. It was hard to think in such a tight space. She looked over the controls again. She needed to slow down, and she needed to drop in elevation. She could guess how to do it, but what if she was wrong? She'd read about plenty of crash landings in the papers, and plenty of pilots who didn't survive them.

Birdie peeled a clenched hand off the stick and nudged Hazel. "Hazel, I need you to land the plane."

Hazel's head lolled. "What? Birdie?" Her voice was faint and confused. "Where's Oscar?"

Birdie's heart sank. "Listen to me, Hazel. I need you to at least talk me through landing this thing."

"My head," Hazel mumbled. "I think I'm going to be sick."

Birdie swallowed, stomach turning. "It's okay if you're sick. Just tell me how to land the plane."

"When you're close to the ground, pull the power." Hazel's voice was a whisper.

"Pull the power?"

Hazel didn't respond.

Okay. "Pull the power" probably meant pulling back on the throttle pretty quick. Simple enough. She tried to recall the feeling she had when June gave her the lesson. *You know how it's supposed to feel. Just feel it.*

It was hard to *feel it*. It was so stuffy in the cockpit, even though it was open. Birdie leaned her head into the slipstream and took gasps of air, but it didn't help.

Birdie followed Oscar in close to the field, nosing down when he nosed down, letting the RPMs drop. She could see the crowd milling around, watching as she got closer and closer. The number of spectators seemed to have grown exponentially since she'd left the ground.

She hoped she didn't embarrass herself. She hoped she didn't kill anyone. She hoped she didn't die.

The ground was only a few yards below them, the field rapidly approaching. Oscar touched down just ahead of her, and she aimed to hit the field in the same spot. The plane hit the ground and bounced, hit the ground, bounced again. And again. Birdie panicked, but the jouncing roused Hazel. Hazel fumbled for the stick and pulled it back, which killed off the remaining speed. The plane rattled jarringly down the field but stopped bouncing, then flung into a loop as it slowed dramatically.

They came to a halt.

Birdie stood up, then folded over the side. She heard shouting, but it seemed far away. Roaring in her ears—or maybe it was the crowd? Hands touched her. She had to get out. She forced her legs over the side.

The lower wing rushed up to meet her as darkness flooded her vision. Someone caught her, lowered her into a sitting position on the grass.

"Jesus, Birdie." June's voice. "Tell me you're okay."

"I'm okay," Birdie mumbled. "Just need some air."

As Birdie's vision cleared, she saw Oscar and Merriwether pull Hazel from the cockpit. A man crouched down beside Hazel as they laid her on the ground. He took her pulse, looked at her eyes, then turned to Birdie.

"How are you feeling?" he asked.

"I feel really faint," Birdie said shakily. "I don't know what happened."

A cameraman rushed up, pushing the lens in Birdie's face, then hovered over Hazel. Oscar shoved the camera, knelt beside Hazel, and took her hand.

"And this woman has been flying this plane all day?" the man asked.

"Yes," said Oscar.

"And pretty much all day yesterday," June added.

"Carbon monoxide poisoning." He nodded at Birdie. "You're going to be fine. This one—" He looked back at Hazel, his expression grave. "She's obviously had extended exposure. We're not going to lose her, but hopefully there's no permanent damage."

Birdie's chest constricted as tears slipped down Oscar's face. "No no no no." He cupped Hazel's face and put his cheek to hers, saying something under his breath.

The man touched his shoulder. "Help me carry her, quick, and I'll take both of you to the hospital. We'll get a better idea of what the damage is, if any."

Hazel's eyes fluttered open as Oscar pulled away, and Birdie could breathe again.

"Oh my God," Oscar choked out. "There you are."

"I didn't know where you were," she said weakly. "I was worried."

"You were worried about *me?*" He smiled through his tears.

Her eyes welled. "I feel so sick."

"Here, we're gonna take care of you." He and the doctor helped Hazel sit up, then lifted her to standing with the doctor supporting Hazel on one side, Oscar on the other. Oscar kissed Hazel's hand before he put her arm over his shoulder. As they walked away, Hazel laid her head on Oscar's shoulder.

Birdie's head was starting to clear. June's arm was wrapped around her. The crowd buzzed. The camerman gestured excitedly alongside Sinclair Stevens. Merriwether talked tensely with Colette and John. John was nodding, looking grave. Milosh was juggling fire in front of the crowd, trying to cover while they pulled the show back together.

The show.

Merriwether came over with John. "We can do the rest of the show without Tiger Lily. Colette's changing the script slightly. She can handle the storytelling part."

"But Oscar." Birdie had no one to fly her Jenny.

"John knows the show," said Merri steadily. "The major stunt flying is out of the way. He'll fly in big loops during the fight scene, and June will follow his lead. You're gonna to do your stunts, and then I'm gonna to do mine."

Birdie slid out from under June's arm and stood. She gave John's shoulder a squeeze. "This is perfect," she said. "You're gonna do great." He nodded solemnly, his usual exuberance focused and serious.

Bennie ran up at a jog. "Henry's helped me fix the aileron with a bit of hay wire." He was a bit short of breath. "Pretty sure it'll do the trick, so long as John doesn't try anything fancy. You hear me, kid? Nothing fancy!"

John nodded vigorously.

Bennie patted Merri's shoulder. "He's gonna be just fine, don't you worry. He's a smart kid."

Merriwether sniffed hard, nodded, and pulled John in for a hug, kissing the top of his head.

"Ladies and gentlemen!" Colette announced. The crowd went almost silent, everyone eager to be under the storyteller's thrall again. "Hook almost destroyed the brave Tiger Lily, but Peter Pan went above and beyond when it seemed like there was no hope. Tiger Lily will survive thanks to his heroic efforts, but she is gravely injured. It is time for Peter Pan to exact his revenge!"

The silence erupted into cheers.

Birdie smiled at John. "Let's do this."

"Wahoo!" John crowed, his solemnity breaking as he leaped into the green Jenny's rear cockpit.

Things happened that were beyond their control. Planes broke, banks closed, money disappeared, people disappointed.

You could still put on one hell of a performance.

CHAPTER FORTY

The rest of the show went off without a hitch.

Milosh lit the fuses. *BOOM! BOOM! BOOM!* Fireworks mimicking cannon fire combusted in the air beyond the pirate ship and Peter Pan's plane. Birdie dropped down in her harness, swinging by her wire, and brandished her sword at Merriwether and the audience. The crowd went wild as John made a few low passes and everyone saw her hanging by the slender wire. Birdie flipped herself back up. She waved cheekily at Merriwether, then reached up over the wing above her head and hoisted herself up onto the upper surface. The wind was warm and strong. To her delight, Merri hauled herself up on the upper wing of the other Jenny as well.

They did their sword-fighting. Birdie hooked her hands under a guy wire and stood on her head with her sword in her teeth. Merri grinned crazily when the planes came close, brandishing her foil sword with glee, and gave John a proud thumbs-up when the plane circled away from the crowd.

In the final scene, Birdie made her great thrust at Merriwether, who staggered backward dramatically, climbed down onto the lower wing, then onto the landing gear and dropped the rope. Smoke began to pour out of the pirate ship to symbolize its demise.

The Deusenberg sped across the field as the pirate Jenny flew low above it. Merriwether clambered down the rope, Bennie

253

opening his crocodile mouth wide. Merriwether landed in a heap in the passenger seat of the Duesenberg, her curly-wigged helmet staying on gamely throughout.

John made one last pass in front of the crowd, and Birdie stood with her hands on her hips and crowed.

She could hear the stomping, the wild cheering, long before they hit the ground.

"You did it!" she whooped as the plane rolled to a stop. She leapt out of the cockpit, pulled John's helmet off, and scruffed his hair. "You were wonderful!"

June grabbed her hand, pulled her off the wing, and swept her up in a sweaty hug. "Holy cow! That was incredible!" she yelled.

June set her down, and Birdie stumbled back laughing breathlessly. "We did it!"

"And what happened with Hazel . . ." June shook her head. "I can't believe these people in the audience didn't see what I saw. Just wait until that movie crew develops their film. You'll be on the front page of all the papers. You'll be a celebrity!"

Birdie rolled her eyes.

"I'm serious. That was the bravest thing I've ever seen, and I've seen some crazy brave stuff."

Birdie felt herself pinking. "I just—thank you."

"Birdie Williams!"

She turned—and there was Sinclair Stevens, a smile twitching beneath his mustache.

"Mr. Stevens!" Birdie exclaimed. "Did you enjoy your front-row seat?"

"Young lady, that was unbelievable! The crew tells me the footage they recorded is stunning. I can't wait to watch it. I'm thinking that we can do something similar, but have a story line outside of the Peter Pan show, and script the whole rescue. I think this footage might be the ticket to my next film!"

He looked at June and stuck out his hand, and June shook it. "You were amazing up there, young lady. I told the fellas I came with—bet you didn't think girls could fly like that!"

"I'm glad you knew better," said June drily.

"I'm heading back to California early tomorrow." He handed her a card, then gave Birdie one, too. "Tell you what. You get a group to come out there. I'll review the footage, do some editing, and send it out to my investors. If they like it, then we can talk. Nothing these days is a sure thing, but I've got my fingers crossed. What do you say?"

"Oh my gosh!" Birdie tried not to squeal with glee. "Yes, sir! Thank you so much!"

"Thank *you*, Miss Williams." He took her hand and bent over it before he walked away.

June nudged her. "What do you think? Should we go call on Hollywood? You think anything he said was for real?"

"I think it's worth a shot," said Birdie. "I can't *wait* to tell Hazel."

"I hope she's okay," said June. "She looked like she was going to be all right, didn't she?"

"Gosh. I hope so." Birdie looked out over the crowd, and suddenly it came back to her—seeing *Dad*. She'd seen Dad, hadn't she?

She'd forgotten, in all the excitement.

She couldn't *believe* she'd forgotten. At the beginning of the summer she would have jumped right out of that plane to find him. Her eyes scanned the crowd. She wondered what he'd thought of his Jenny painted green. His Duesenberg used in circus stunts. His daughter hanging from the wing of a plane.

If it was him, he would come and find her.

If it was him, and he *didn't* come find her—he didn't deserve for her to look for him anymore.

She looked around. It was easy to find Merriwether, squeezing John and Henry around their shoulders, laughing at something

Henrieta said. Colette held hands with Milosh and listened to a top-hatted, mustachioed man who gestured enthusiastically at Bennie's crocodile suit. Bennie caught her eye, beamed at her, and gave her a thumbs-up. Hazel and Oscar were missing, but they would go find them in the hospital, and do everything they could to make sure Hazel was okay.

And June—June was gazing at her with deep, sunlit hazel eyes, catching her hand with long fingers. "Hey."

"Yeah?" said Birdie.

"Come here." June took her hand, and led her around behind the Jenny's wing. She pressed Birdie against the fuselage in the shadow of the wing, out of sight of the crowd, and when June kissed her, Birdie tasted salt and sun-warmed skin.

June pulled away and touched Birdie's face. "You okay?" she asked. "You seemed a little sad there, for a moment."

Birdie hadn't told June anything about Dad, but she was finding her pretty easy to talk to. "I'm okay," said Birdie. "I just—I thought I saw my dad in the crowd. At the beginning of the show."

"Do tell," said June, raising her brows.

Birdie wanted to tell her everything. How much Dad had disappointed her. How much she still loved him. How he'd been a great father, even though he might not always be a great man, and how confusing it was that both of those things could be true. But who knew, Dad might be right there when she walked around the corner of the wing.

"How about I tell you all about it tomorrow?" Birdie tugged June's hips close, unbuttoned the front of her flight suit, and slipped her hands inside.

"Why tomorrow?" June's fingers toyed with the straps of Birdie's costume. Her breath caught as Birdie lifted the edge of her shirt and brushed the bare skin of her stomach. Then she caught on, and a smile played on her lips. "Oh yeah, since there's nothing else on the schedule . . ." Her voice trailed off as she leaned in for another kiss.

"Let's keep it like that," Birdie whispered, reveling in the perfect texture of June's skin, the lean shape of her curves. "I love how it feels like anything could happen."

ACKNOWLEDGMENTS

Thank you to the amazing people who helped with my research for Birdie's story: Jim Tyson, who works on antique planes and has flown them since 1948 and gave me wonderful feedback on the story, and to Ted McIrvine for connecting us; Carol Pilon, Canadian wingwalker extraordinaire, who emailed back and forth with me answering all sorts of questions, and to Sharyn November who suggested I reach out to her; and to my dad, for taking that field trip to the National Air and Space Museum with me to see the original Curtiss JN-4 up close and personal.

Thank you to Linda Washington, for giving me immeasurable feedback on my story and characters. Thank you to Nora Carpenter, Rachel Hylton, Liz Booker, Val Howlett, Nicole Valentine, and Amy Rose Capetta, for your support and readings and feedback and cheerleading all along the way, and to all of my Secret Gardeners and VCFA peeps and Pneuma Creatives and ECLA buddies who have rooted so hard for me and this story! And a shout-out to all my friends and family and non-writing community who have done the same.

Thank you to Sarah Aronson and everyone involved in the Writing Novels for Young People Retreats at VCFA, especially David Gill, whose approach to story structure broke this one wide open and fundamentally changed how I approach my writing. Thank you to Elizabeth Lutyens and my classmates in her Great Smokies Writing Program course that workshopped Birdie's story.

Thank you to Linda Epstein, my awesome agent, for always believing in and fighting for my stories. Thank you to Rachel Stark, editor of my heart, for acquiring this novel, and to Nicole Frail for seeing it through so kindly and carefully.